Marked for Mercy

A Ridgeline Mystery

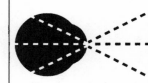

This Large Print Book carries the
Seal of Approval of N.A.V.H.

MARKED
FOR
MERCY

Alton Gansky

Thorndike Press • Waterville, Maine

Middlebury Community
Library

Copyright © 1998 by Alton Gansky.

Unless otherwise noted, all Scripture is from the *New American Standard Bible*, © the Lockman Foundation 1960, 1962, 1963, 1968, 1971, 1972, 1975, 1977. All rights reserved.

All rights reserved.

The characters, organizations, institutions, and events in this book are wholly and purely fictional. Any apparent resemblance to any person or persons, living or dead, any institution, organization, or events is purely coincidental.

Published in 2001 by arrangement with
Cook Communications Ministries.

Thorndike Press Large Print Christian Mystery Series.

The tree indicium is a trademark of Thorndike Press.

The text of this Large Print edition is unabridged.
Other aspects of the book may vary from the original edition.

Set in 16 pt. Plantin by Rick Gundberg.

Printed in the United States on permanent paper.

Library of Congress Cataloging-in-Publication Data

Gansky, Alton.
    Marked for mercy / Alton Gansky.
      p. cm. — (A Ridgeline mystery)
    ISBN 0-7862-3205-6 (lg. print : hc : alk. paper)
    1. Women physicians — Fiction. 2. Assisted suicide — Fiction. 3. Large type books. I. Title.
PS3557.A5195 M3 2001
  813'.54—dc21   00-067741

This book is dedicated to Crystal,
Chaundel, and Aaron.
Three really great kids.

Chapter One

Friday, October 31
4:04 P.M.

"What do you mean, 'No'?"

"No. Two tiny letters that say it all." Gates McClure crossed the exam room to a small desk beneath a wide window, moved aside a chart, a pad of yellow paper, a well-worn Bible and then sat down. The fading fall light filtered its way through the pine trees and the glass pane where it mixed with the harsh fluorescent lights from the fixtures overhead. Outside the window a lazy breeze made the supple branches of a pine swing slowly like a conductor waving his arms before his attentive orchestra. "N–O. No. Nein. Nyet. Out of the question. I'm not interested."

Anne Fitzgerald sighed melodramatically. "I'm not asking you to rob a bank. All I'm asking is that you go to the party with me."

"Halloween is not my favorite day," Gates said firmly. "Besides, I don't much like parties."

"Oh, come on," Anne retorted as she

walked to the desk. "Last year was great fun and you missed it."

"I didn't miss a thing."

"Gates, this is a community event. Everyone of any importance will be there."

"Including bachelors and the like." Gates raised an eyebrow telegraphing her suspicion.

"That's not what I said." Anne paused as if in deep thought, then continued: "I'm sure that a few of the eligible men will be there . . . but that's not my motive for inviting you." She attempted a sincere smile that only betrayed her small conspiracy.

"You're as bad as Mother, and as transparent." Gates rose and walked away from the desk wanting to put some distance between her and her sister. "Every social event is an opportunity to marry me off."

"You're paranoid."

"Mildly," Gates deadpanned. "Paranoia can be a good thing."

"Gates, help me out here," Anne pleaded. "I don't like to go to these things alone."

"Isn't John taking you?"

"No, my hardworking husband is in San Bernardino for some meetings. He won't be back up the hill until eight-thirty or nine tonight. He's coming to the party, but he'll be late. In the meantime, I'll be bouncing around from person to person like a billiard ball, and each one will have some complaint about Ridgeline and the city council."

"That's what you get for being mayor." Gates surrendered a small, sarcastic grin. "With great power comes great responsibility."

"Ridgeline has only 7,000 residents, my job is hardly one of great power. It's not even full time."

"Well my job is full time and I have patients in the lobby waiting for me to finish this conversation with you."

"All you have to do is say that you'll come to the party and keep me company for a while. That's a good sisterly thing to do."

"What costume are you wearing?" Gates asked, hoping to sidestep the issue.

"I'm going as Marie Antoinette." Anne waved her hand and struck a regal pose. "You know, 'Let them eat chocolate.'"

"Cake," Gates corrected. "It's, 'Let them eat cake,' and she didn't really say that. A fictional character did."

"Well, she might have kept her head if she had said chocolate." Anne paused for a moment and then asked: "So you'll come then?"

Letting a sigh slip, Gates turned and faced her sister. The two were close in age with Anne at thirty-eight being three years older. She was shorter than Gates by two inches and wore her chemically aided blond hair stylishly short. Her eyes were an unforgettable blue and were the striking feature of her face. She was thin with pleasantly sharp features, which she softened with expertly applied makeup. Gates always considered her the prettier of the two.

By contrast, Gates wore her fawn hair to the shoulder with only the slightest curl at the end. Like her sister, her eyes were blue, but a shade more pale. Both women were attractive and had more than their share of suitors through high school and college. Anne married John Fitzgerald, a business major at Cal State San Bernardino where she was studying political science.

Gates had never married, but not for lack of offers. She was committed to her medical degree and then to her practice and it was that commitment that compelled her to decline all proposals. That's what she told people. The truth was, she had yet to find that one special person who was . . . comfortable.

"Okay," Gates replied. "But you owe me . . . big time."

"I accept my debt gladly. Now all we need is a costume for you."

"No costume." Gates was resolute. "I'm not dressing up."

Anne was aghast. "But you'll stand out like

a weed in a rose garden."

Wrinkling her brow Gates replied, "I think a rose in a weed garden is more like it."

"That's what I meant," Anne said quickly. "But you still need a costume."

"I'll go as a doctor."

"You are a doctor! Everyone knows that. You won't look any different then than you do now."

"That's the idea."

"Don't worry," Anne waved a dismissing hand. "Leave it all to me. I'll come up with something." She made her way to the door.

"Anne, you're not listening to me."

"The party starts at seven, so don't be late. Hmm, maybe Maid Marian . . ."

"Anne . . ."

"Oh, I know! Mother Teresa!" Anne exited the exam room and walked through the lobby still muttering to herself.

"Anne, I told you I'll be there, but I won't be dressed!" Gates called after her, but Anne was through the outer door before she could finish. Standing in the doorway between the exam room and the lobby she became suddenly aware of six pairs of eyes staring quizzically at her. "In a costume, folks. I meant that I won't be dressed in a costume."

Norman Meade was holding his breath.

Slowly, without the slightest noise, he let the air trapped in his lungs escape. He always held his breath when he was nervous and he had been holding his breath a lot these days.

Forcing himself to take regular, measured breaths, Meade looked around the room. Everything looked familiar. The faded flower wallpaper, the oak chair rail that circumscribed the wall, the mullioned window with its dirty panes. Even the frosted glass diffuser on the overhead light brought a sense of intimate recognition. The truth was, Meade had never been in this room before, nor had he ever entered the house or visited the town of Ridgeline. Still, the familiarity was there.

Meade knew it wasn't the room that brought the waves of déjà vu rolling through his consciousness. It wasn't the pine trees outside the window, or the well-used furnishings. It wasn't the bed. It was the smell of fear and dread and anxiety. It was the palpable sense of uncertainty that filled this home, this room, and so many places like it.

Rooms like this were familiar territory to Norman Meade. He had stood in scores of such rooms and they all had a strange similarity to them. The rooms in Michigan were like the ones in Oregon, which were similar to the ones in Arizona. The furnishings were different as was the decor, but they all had the aroma of sickness, of a mildly reluctant and belated death that patiently hovered nearby.

Meade was frightened. Not by the frail figure that lay upon the bed struggling to breathe, fighting with a traitorous body to see or to just move an inch or two one way or another. He was not fearful of the task he was about to perform or its ramifications. What frightened Dr. Norman Meade was how commonplace all this was becoming to him.

By nature Meade was an emotional man, a sensitive person whose feelings were powerful and undeniable. That had been his problem all along. Even as a child he struggled to make his mind and emotions match, but they seldom did. He was a walking contradiction doing what his mind told him he should do and turning a deaf ear to the screaming empathy buried deep within him.

"I think she wants you to come closer." Meade turned and looked at the man who spoke so quietly. Eugene Crews was a hunched broken man in his early seventies who looked a century older. His hair was an even blend of gray and black, cut short in a style that reminded Meade of his own father. Crews was smoking his third cigarette since Meade had arrived ten minutes before.

Slowly Meade stepped to the side of the bed upon which the emaciated body of a woman lay. Her head was propped up slightly on a large foam pillow and she offered a weak smile. Meade knew that the simple smile was a heroic effort.

Quickly, Meade took in the image of the woman. She was painfully thin, the result of a losing battle with amyotrophic lateral sclerosis — ALS. Most people simply called it Lou Gehrig's disease after the famous baseball player who died in 1941. Somehow the term Lou Gehrig's disease gave the disorder a certain nobility. Meade saw no nobility in the affliction. It was a cruel and horrible way to live . . . to die.

Looking at Darlene Crews as she lay immobile on the bed, arms twitching, Meade could visualize the disease and its progress. There was no known reason or single cause for ALS, and tragically, no cure. Only one in five people lived more than five years after diagnosis. Many died within two years.

Darlene weakly raised her gnarled right hand and held it out to Meade. The arm and hand twitched and shook like a fall leaf on an ancient oak tree. Gently, he took her fragile hand and held it.

"Hi, Darlene. I'm Dr. Meade. I believe you asked for my help."

As he held Darlene's hand, Meade could envision the battle that had been waged in her body. ALS caused the nerves in the brain and spine to slowly shrink until they disappeared. Without nerves to carry the brain's commands for action the muscles slowly atrophied from lack of use. The end result was a wasted, wizened body, dried of vigor, drained of life.

Darlene was suffering the same complications that many ALS victims experience: the loss of the ability to swallow. Meade knew that doctors had inserted a tube through her abdomen so that liquid food could be dumped into the stomach for processing, keeping her alive.

Cutting her eyes toward her husband, Darlene communicated an unspoken request. Immediately, Eugene was by her bedside. Slowly, Darlene pulled her frail hand from the gentle grasp of Meade and pointed to the side of the bed.

"Got it," Eugene said as he bent over and pulled a white piece of cardboard from underneath the rented hospital bed. He held the board up resting its lower edge on the washed-out yellow bedspread. The cardboard had the letters of the alphabet crudely printed on its surface with a black marker.

"She can't talk anymore," Eugene said to Meade, "so I made up this board. It works pretty good, but it tires her out some."

Meade had seen such homemade devices before. They were to him a testimony of the ingenuity born of desperation.

Moving slowly, Darlene began to point at letters. Peering over the top of the board, Eugene said each letter out loud. "T – H – A – N – K – Y – O – U – F – O – R – C – O – M – I – N – G."

Meade smiled. "I wish there were another way."

Darlene responded by slowly shaking her head.

"You understand that you have to do this," Meade offered in quiet, measured tones. "I can help by setting things up, but you have to actually — make it happen."

Darlene nodded.

Looking up from the tortured woman, Meade made eye contact with Eugene who had the look of a man crushed by the weight of the universe.

These things are always harder on the family, Meade thought. *For them the pain never ends.*

"This isn't . . . isn't . . . I mean," Eugene was stammering. He put the alphabet board down on the floor.

"Painful?" Meade rescued the thought. "No, not at all. It's simple, painless, flawless. But I must be convinced of Darlene's com-mitment."

"She's committed all right." Eugene inhaled deeply on the cigarette but Meade could tell that it offered no comfort. The man's hands shook, his lower lip trembled, and he blinked constantly. He had all the marks of a man on the verge of a breakdown. "We asked the doctors at the hospital, but they all said no. You are our last hope."

"How do you feel about all of this?" Meade eyed the man closely.

Eugene shrugged. Tears filled his eyes. "I don't like it, but what can I do? I'm not slowly choking to death. I can swallow a bite of food. But not her." He paused and looked at his wife. "We've been married fifty-three years. Can you believe that? Fifty-three years. And as far as I'm concerned, they were all happy ones."

Meade shifted his eyes from Eugene to Darlene. Her face was graced with a slim smile made weak by a dysfunctional nervous system. Her eyes, however, beamed a message that was impossible to misunderstand. This was a woman who loved her husband deeply.

Continuing, Eugene said, "A few weeks back — I dunno, maybe as much as two or three months — she asked me to do the job. I've heard of people doing that. You know their wife or husband or mom or dad beg and beg until the family can't take it no more, so they do it. I read about one who used a plastic bag."

He shook his head, stepped over to an ashtray that was situated on an old and scarred end table, and snuffed out what little remained of the cigarette. He then wiped his eyes with the back of his hand. A moment later he continued, "I don't know, Doc. I just couldn't do it. She even asked me to stop feeding her through that tube, but I just couldn't. Besides, a home nurse comes by every day to check on her and make sure that I'm doing things right." Eugene released a short, halfhearted chortle. "She can't talk with her mouth no more, but she can still get her point across."

He turned to his wife. "I'm sorry, honey, I just couldn't do it. I couldn't live with myself."

"That's when you wrote to me?" Meade inquired softly.

"Yes. It's the only thing I could think of, and Darlene agreed." His eyes brimmed with tears again. "I still don't know."

Darlene raised her right hand slightly and motioned for the alphabet board. Eugene picked it up and situated it close to his wife. She began to point out letters: M – Y – D – E – C – I – S – I – O – N – N – O – T – Y – O – U – R – S.

"I know, baby." Eugene swallowed hard. "I know."

Watching the couple wounded Meade's heart, but it was a wound with which he was familiar. It hurt and would forever hurt, but still the work, the task needed to be done. His eyes burned with shared tears.

"So how does this work?" Eugene asked softly.

Meade sighed heavily. He was tired, so very, very tired. His life had not turned out the way he had planned. Since he was a child he had wanted only one thing — to be a doctor. It was a dream he followed and fought to obtain. He made it through college on scholastic scholarships and sheer determination. Medical school was the same, but while others struggled to master terms and the abstracts of medicine, Meade had excelled. He thrived on the pressure, the late nights, the thousands of pages to read, experiments to conduct, and tests to take. When it was all over he had graduated third in his class.

After that the plan was simple: internship, residency, specialty studies in internal medicine, and then into private practice.

That didn't happen.

Instead, he now stood by a tormented woman whose only hope was a slow death by asphyxiation when her muscles could no longer draw air into her tired lungs.

"I do everything," Meade answered firmly. "Everything but the final act. You, Mrs. Crews must do that, but it will be something you can handle. But before we get to that, there are a few things that I must do."

"Like what?" Eugene made no attempt to conceal his concern.

"First I need to ask your wife some simple questions. I'll set up a video camera so that I can record her answers. You'll need to help by holding the card so she can point at the letters."

"You're gonna tape this? Like some television show?" Eugene was aghast.

Meade shook his head. "No, sir, nothing like that. It's for your protection and mine. There are certain legal considerations involved, and we need to make sure that false blame cannot be laid on either of us."

Eugene looked confused.

"I don't want you to be accused of murder." Meade was blunt, but not harsh. "Nor do I wish to be accused of murder. As it is, Mr. Crews, I may be arrested and detained. Possibly even tried in criminal court, depending on your district attorney. One thing is sure, they'll take away my license to practice in California. That's what they did to Kevorkian."

"But you've been through that before."

"Too many times, Mr. Crews, too many times. The only reason I'm here with you today is because I am a cautious man."

"Then . . . then it happens?"

"Yes, sir." Meade softened his voice and turned to Darlene. "I have a device that is easy to use. It won't take long."

Darlene raised her hand again and began pointing at letters. "I – M – R – E – A – D – Y."

Gates McClure closed the door behind her and then wearily leaned against it. She took a deep breath and let it out noisily while simultaneously rubbing her temples. Her head hurt, her back ached, and her feet throbbed.

It had been a grueling, taxing day. Seven-year-old Robert Atler had come into the office presenting all the signs of bronchitis. The affliction was not dangerous if treated properly, but from little Robert's point of view the cure was hellish. Gates had wanted to administer a simple antibiotic, but when Robert caught his first look at the syringe he put aside all efforts to be "Mommy's big boy" and began to scream with the intensity of a car alarm. This in itself would have been manageable had it not been for his high flying elbows, thrashing feet, and multiple attempts to escape the small exam room.

When the battle was over, Robert had received his injection (to which he added, "Hey, that wasn't so bad.") and Gates had received several bruises. The whole situation might have been more tolerable had little Robby's mother not thrown in her unsolicited opinion: "You really should learn how to handle children, Doctor."

Robby's rebellion had only been part of the arduous day. Mrs. Peatone had come in without an appointment and demanded to see the doctor "on matters of great importance." Mr. Peatone had tried to poison Mrs. Peatone again. Just like he had done last week and the week before that and all the weeks before that for the last five years. Gates had sat patiently listening as the thin elderly woman unburdened her heart. Tears flowed unceasingly as she recounted the same story that Gates had heard scores of times before. Unfortunately there was no medicine to deal with Mrs. Peatone's insecurity, but a well-timed hug always seemed to do the trick.

The rest of the day was occupied with an unending train of runny noses, hacking coughs, diarrhea, earaches, and fevers. Cold and flu season had arrived in Ridgeline right on time.

All that was behind her now. She was home, right where she wanted to be.

A quick glance around the small living room brought a wave of comfortable emotions rolling through Gates. She loved her little house. Doctors "down the hill" in the cities that surrounded the foothills of the San Bernardino Mountains might live in bigger and grander homes, but none were surrounded by such beauty, and none loved their homes more than she loved hers.

There was nothing palatial about the house. It was just two bedrooms — one which she used as an office — a living room, an open kitchen, and a small dining nook. The exterior was wood siding painted an unobtrusive yellow and a steeply pitched roof with cedar shingles. There were hundreds of such homes in Ridgeline. Small, quaint, and endearing.

In the summer, she liked to unwind by sitting on her front porch watching the squirrels chase each other through her yard. Blue jays haunted the air and shared the trees with woodpeckers. Occasionally, a roving bear would meander through town upending trash bins in hope of finding something to eat that didn't need to be caught and killed first.

Stepping away from the door and removing her coat, Gates yielded a shiver. The fall air had turned cool. It wouldn't be long before the ever-present green of trees would be high-lighted with draperies of gleaming snow. During those months, Gates would be fixing as many sprained ankles and broken bones as colds.

Being a town doctor wasn't as glamorous as working in some specialized branch of medicine, but Gates wasn't attracted to glamor. She was a doctor who was truly dedicated to helping others. Small town practice was ideal for her and she for it. Nothing could persuade her to leave the verdant mountain community for the bustle of a city hospital. No, Gates was right where she wanted to be, treating the people she knew and cared for — even elbow-flinging little boys.

The great joy about a hard day, Gates reasoned to herself, *is reaching its end. There's nothing left to do now but take a long hot bath, pop in a TV dinner, settle in on the sofa, and read a good mystery.* It was then that she saw the small flashing red light on her answering machine.

Walking to the device she stared at the rhythmic pulse of the light. The message indicator listed only one incoming call. Gates knew immediately what it was. It wasn't a medical emergency. It was something far worse.

She pushed the play button. The machine

quickly rewound the tiny cassette tape and then released its captured message.

"Hi, Gates, this is Anne. I just wanted you to know that I found a *wonderful* costume for you. You're going to love it. Now remember, the party starts at seven . . ."

"Seven," Gates said in unison with the message.

". . . and I'll be there to pick you up at ten till. Thanks again. This will be fun."

Gates listened as the machine rewound the tape and set itself for the next incoming message and wished her duty could be done that quickly.

The pain in Gates' head increased a level.

It was over.

Everything had gone perfectly. The equipment set up easily and operated as designed. There hadn't been a hint of difficulty.

So why don't I feel better? Norman Meade asked himself. But he already knew the answer: He never felt better and he never would.

Before him lay the unmoving body of Darlene Crews, the yellow bedspread shrouding her insubstantial form. Her life had left, aided in its exodus by a machine designed by Meade. Darlene's skin slowly paled as the blood in her body, no longer moved by a beating heart, pooled in her body. Her eyes no longer sparkled with life but gazed unseeingly through lenses shrouded by half-closed lids. Her mouth hung limply open.

Death was ugly. It was always ugly and so . . . so . . . unnatural.

"She's at peace now," Eugene offered as he stood by his dead wife. His voice was choked, fractured by the emotion he attempted to hold at bay. He was holding her lifeless hand. Tears streaked his craggy cheeks and meandered slowly through the thick gray forest of stubble on his face.

Peace. Meade had many times steeled himself for the work he did and comforted himself when the work was over with that word, that concept. Peace. Had he helped her find peace, or did he just stop the pain by helping her stop her life? To some it was a subtle distinction, but not to Meade. With every physician-assisted suicide he participated in, he became a little less certain that he was the bearer of peace. Perhaps he never really gave anything, he just removed the unrelenting pain.

As a physician he had many times diagnosed a disease, prescribed a course of treatment, medication, or surgery and thereby not only removed the offensive pain but also gave good health.

Was that what he was doing here? Meade was no longer sure and was too spent to care. Looking at Eugene Crews, the now-hollow man who so lovingly and dutifully caressed a hand that could no longer feel the embrace, Meade knew that more than Darlene had died — a large portion of Eugene's soul had been sucked away.

"Now what?" Eugene asked plainly, never taking his eyes from his wife.

"I need to make a few phone calls."

"Calls?"

"Yes," Meade answered. "First I call the local police and report a death. Then I call the coroner."

"Police?" Eugene turned to face Meade. "Ain't the police the last people you want to call?"

Meade shook his head. "No. I make it a practice to be aboveboard about everything. It helps keep me out of jail. The coroner will take your wife's remains . . ." Meade paused. He hated the term. "He'll need to establish a cause of death."

"Will there be an autopsy?"

Looking at Eugene, Meade shook his head. They had covered all this on the phone before it was agreed that Meade would come. It was also in the letter that Meade had sent to the Crewses. Still, such questions were not unusual. Eugene was sorting through the heavy emotions he felt. Talking — talking about anything — was a form of personal therapy. So Meade would repeat the answers given days before.

"That's up to the coroner, but I'll explain what I did here and what the cause of death was. It will be easy for the coroner to verify. That plus your wife's advanced disease would make an autopsy unnecessary. Still, it's not my call."

Eugene nodded. Then he nodded again. A moment later his shoulders shook and his body convulsed. The dam that held his emotions in check had crumbled. Tears rolled from his eyes in a steady stream, dropping on the limp arm of his wife.

Slowly Meade took in a deep, ragged breath, approached Eugene and put his arm around him.

The phone calls would have to wait.

"Are you Eugene Crews?" the young officer asked. His khaki uniform was sharp and drawn snugly over the bulletproof vest he wore. The vest made the officer look stockier than he was. His gold badge glistened weakly in the fading light. Parked in the long shadows of pine trees was his white patrol car with gold lettering that read: "Ridgeline Police Department." On his chest was a nameplate that read: "Dan Wells."

"No, Officer," Meade answered. "I'm Dr. Norman Meade. I made the call."

The officer gazed at Meade for a moment, his professional detachment betrayed by an involuntary frown. It was clear to Meade that Officer Wells had heard of him.

"Where's the body?"

"In the house," Meade responded evenly. "Do you want to wait for the coroner?"

"The coroner won't come until we call. It's our job to investigate first."

As if to prove the officer wrong a black van pulled curbside in front of the house. Meade could see people peering out their windows from their houses across the street. The sight of the coroner's van solicited another frown from Wells. Two people, a man and a woman, exited the van and walked toward the house.

"This is Dr. Norman Meade," Wells said to the two. They too frowned. "Dr. Meade, this is Mark Toma and Jane Upton."

"Since you know each other, I assume you've worked together before." Meade wanted to offer his hand but it didn't seem appropriate.

"It's a big county, Doc, but a relatively small staff." Wells started toward the door.

"Let's go inside and see what we've got."

Eugene Crews hadn't moved from his wife's side. His weeping had been replaced by a distant, hollow look.

"Mr. Crews." Meade spoke softly, reverently. "Mr. Crews, the police are here, and so is the coroner's office. They need to do their work now."

Eugene didn't move. A few moments later, he lowered his wife's arm and took a step back. Then he stepped forward one more time, bent over the bed, and tenderly kissed Darlene's pale lips. Only then did he turn and walk from the room.

"I'll be in the living room when you need me," Eugene said.

"So what happened?" Wells asked sharply.

"Darlene Crews suffered from ALS. I was called to help end her suffering." Meade walked to an old dresser and picked up a black videocassette tape and handed it to Wells. "This will show exactly what happened."

"You videotaped it?" Wells exclaimed. "That's a little macabre, isn't it?"

"I don't record these things for my entertainment, Officer, I do so to help people in your position know what has occurred. I make it a point not to hide anything."

"You know that helping someone commit

suicide is illegal, don't you?" Wells' voice was firm, pointed.

"Technically, that's true, but how many people do you know that have been convicted of that crime? Especially doctors?"

"Still, I could arrest you."

"Yes, you could, and my attorney would have me out in no time. Besides, your district attorney would be hard-pressed to build a case against me."

Wells' frown deepened. "Did you move the body?"

"No," Meade responded immediately. He knew that Wells was looking for some other cause to detain him. Moving the body could be construed as tampering with evidence should Darlene's suicide be considered a crime. "I have also left all my equipment in place. Nothing has been moved or altered. The tape you have will verify that."

Wells stood silently staring at the body of Darlene. He seemed puzzled, at a loss for what to do next. Meade came to his rescue.

"You probably don't want any suggestions from me," Meade offered, "but let me make a couple anyway. Call your field supervisor and tell him what's going on. He'll come over, take a look around, watch the video, release the body to the coroner, take my statement and that of Mr. Crews, tell me to stay around for a while, then leave."

"You've got it all figured out, don't you, Doc?"

"I leave nothing to chance. I didn't kill Darlene Crews and neither did her husband. Darlene chose to end a very agonizing life. The decision was hers. I merely gave her the means to act on her heartfelt desires."

"Unless, of course, she wishes to back out at the last moment."

"You're mistaken, Officer Wells. Mrs. Crews could have stopped at any time. Simply doing nothing would have been sufficient to stop the process. My device requires that people like Mrs. Crews commit several separate and distinct acts, otherwise nothing happens. You'll see what I mean when you watch the tape."

Again Wells hesitated before acting. Raising his portable radio to his mouth he called for his field supervisor, then said to the others, "All right, let's all go into the living room and wait. Maybe Mr. Crews has a VCR."

Forty-five minutes later the coroner's van drove away with Darlene Crews strapped to a stretcher. A moment later Wells and his supervisor returned to their duties. Sergeant Weissman had proved to be more sympathetic than Wells. He had reviewed the scene, watched the video, and then had given his approval for the removal of the body. Wells was clearly upset that he couldn't arrest Meade.

"It's over now," Meade said to Eugene as they stood on his porch and watched as the vehicles drove away. "Darlene is free from pain."

"It's over for me, Doc, but I ain't so sure it's over for you. It's never over for you, is it, Doc?"

Meade slowly shook his head and carried the IV stand and other equipment to his rental car where he placed them in the trunk. Eugene was right. It wasn't over now, nor would it ever be. He couldn't just close his mind like he was closing the trunk of his car. The night's fresh darkness poured into Meade's heart. "No, Eugene, it's never over for me."

Chapter Two

Friday, October 31
6:50 P.M.

Gates felt ridiculous. How had she allowed herself to get talked into this? Crinoline petticoats, hair in curls, bows, but no corset — she had drawn the line at wearing a girdle.

"You're certain to win best costume," Anne said, beaming over her creation. "I've already had half a dozen people tell me how lovely you are. They think you're adorable."

"Then let them wear this thing," Gates answered crisply. "Scarlett O'Hara? You had to pick Scarlett O'Hara? I feel like I'm wearing an army tent and not a dress. It's a wonder womankind made it through the Civil War."

"Oh, come on. It's not that bad. Besides, if you hadn't waited till the last moment, I would have had more choices. It was this or a Lady Godiva costume."

"Lady Godiva? How can they have a Lady Godiva costume?"

"The hair, dear. Think hair."

"Where do you find these places?"

"I'm not without my sources." Anne's voice took on a conspiratorial tone. "As mayor it's important that I know these things."

"Costume shops are requisite knowledge for politicians?"

"Sure," Anne replied glibly. "One never knows when one may need a disguise."

"I don't think you could get very far out of town with what you're wearing."

"So you like it?" Anne struck a regal pose. With a towering powdered wig and ornate dress she looked every bit like Marie Antoinette.

"It's you, Anne," Gates quipped. Looking around the room she commented, "Not many here tonight."

"Oh, it's early. There will be more folks soon. The band is not even playing yet."

Gates glanced over at the small group that was setting up on the stage of the Community Center. The band, four adolescent boys with dreams of platinum records in their heads, was tuning electric guitars and testing the microphones.

"They're from the high school," Anne offered. "I understand they've been practicing all week."

Just then one of the boys, a tall, lanky lad with dishwater brown hair, viciously dragged

35

his plastic pick across the strings of his guitar. A loud noise — something akin to tires squealing on sandy pavement — reverberated in the hall. Gates was no musician but she estimated that at least two of the six strings of the instrument were out of tune. Such was the tuning process, or so she thought. She felt her heart shudder and her eardrums cower as the boy nodded approvingly at the sound. His partners affirmed his work with nods of their own reinforced by the word, "Cool."

Gates looked at Anne with an expression that said more than words could communicate. This was going to be a long night. Anne answered with raised eyebrows and a shrug.

Shortly after seven a steady stream of people trickled in, each dressed up in some fashion meant to draw attention. Some costumes were clearly homemade, while others were rented. There were two Lone Rangers, a go-go dancer, one nun, a large quantity of cowboys and cowgirls, and even someone in a gorilla suit.

By seven-thirty the hall was filled with Ridgeline residents and their friends. People, mostly couples, meandered around the room, cups of punch in their hands. Everyone complimented everyone else on their choice of costume, and a constant drone of voices filled the small hall.

The voices were instantly stilled when the

band began to play a loud, hard-driving rock tune. As though rehearsed, the crowd turned in unison to gaze in wonder at the — music. A moment later the gathering returned to their conversations, speaking louder to be heard over the potent efforts of the young men on stage. The room had, in the space of half an hour, gone from near silence to bedlam.

"Quite the party, wouldn't you say, Doctor?" Gates turned to see a pirate standing next to her.

"Oh, hello Ross," Gates offered. "You look positively buccaneerish. Does this mean that my subscription is going to go up?"

"Not if I can find sufficient treasure here," Ross replied. Ross Sassmon was the owner and editor of the local paper.

"I don't think you'll find anything buried here," Gates said. "This is nothing but your usual mass of locals."

"True, but maybe there's a story here. At the very least, I can write an article about the party and maybe get a quote from your sister. Where is she anyway?"

"Shaking hands and asking for votes probably." Gates glanced around the room trying to spot Anne. "She's dressed like Marie Antoinette, so she shouldn't be too hard to spot." Not seeing Anne, she shrugged. "You'll have to find her on your own. So why are you covering the party? I would have thought that you would have had Bill Gregory assigned to do that."

"Normally I would, but I sent him out on something else. Besides, money being tight like it is, I'm having to cut back a little." Ross raised his plastic cup of punch to his lips. "Can I get you some punch?"

"Thanks, no," Gates replied. "So what important story is Bill chasing down?"

"The police were called over to Spruce Street. Someone died."

Gates frowned. "Who?"

"I don't think she was one of your patients, Doc. They kept pretty much to themselves."

"Now how would you know who my patients are, Ross? Even I forget some of their names."

"Okay, don't get snippy with me or I'll write a scathing article about your party-side manner." Ross took another purposeful sip of punch. "It was a woman by the name of Darlene Crews. We heard about it over the police scanner. Both the police and the coroner were called out. Do you . . . did you know her?"

Shaking her head, Gates replied, "No. I met her husband once. He came into the office with a pretty deep splinter in his thumb. He said he got it while chopping wood for the fireplace. He and his wife are with a big HMO down the hill, but he didn't want to drive off the mountain just for a splinter."

"Was his wife with him?"

"I have no idea. That was over a month ago."

"How old a man is he?"

"Look Ross, if you want a story, then you're going to have to wait for Bill to get back, because I don't know any more than that."

Ross smiled. "You don't know how old he was?"

"In his seventies, I would guess," Gates said firmly.

"Okay, okay," Ross held up his hands. "Sorry. Nosiness is a genetic trait in journalists."

"I bet it cuts down on your dinner invitations."

"A little . . ." Ross stopped short. "Now there's a creative costume," he said sarcastically, nodding toward the door.

Gates turned to see a tall man with short black hair enter the room. He was wearing dark slacks, a dress shirt open at the collar, and a light brown sports jacket with patches at the elbows.

"Maybe he dressed up like a college professor or something," Ross offered with a grin.

"This can't be," Gates uttered quietly. She

squinted as she stared at the man.

"You know that guy?" Ross asked.

"It's been a long time, but I think that's him."

"Who?"

"You mean to tell me that you don't recognize him?" Gates looked seriously at Ross.

It was Ross' turn to squint. "Well, he does look a little familiar. He's a good-looking guy. Is he an actor or something?"

Gates shook her head.

"Come on, Gates, at least give me a hint."

"He's no actor, but you know him."

The man with the dark hair was searching the room with his eyes. Gates remained frozen in place. A few moments later, he caught sight of her and beamed a smile across the room.

"Is he a politician?" Ross was becoming exasperated.

"He's headed this way," Gates offered. "I'll introduce you. Then you'll have a bigger story than you thought possible."

Despite her cool affectation there was a struggle going on within Gates McClure: her stomach tightened, her heart beat faster, and her thoughts sped in circles like race cars on a track. A portion of her was glad to see an old acquaintance; another part wished she could disappear before he made his way through the crowd.

"I was hoping to find you here," the tall man said. His voice was soft and smooth; his words delivered effortlessly. "I wasn't sure you would be, but here you are. How have you been, Gates?"

"Fine, Norman," she replied uncomfortably. "I've been fine. What about you?"

"I've been well," Norman replied with a modest smile. "Considering everything, I mean."

Ross cleared his throat.

"Oh, I'm sorry," Gates said. "Ross, this is Dr. Norman Meade. Norman, this is Ross Sassmon, editor of our weekly paper."

Thrusting his hand out, Ross said, "Pleased to meet you, Dr. Meade . . ." He stopped abruptly. "Norman Meade? *The* Norman Meade?"

"Yes, I'm who you think I am." Meade never let his smile slip.

"You're the one they call . . ." Ross cut himself short.

"Dr. Death," Meade said filling in the unfinished sentence. "At least that's what some of the irresponsible press call me."

"I'm . . . I'm . . . sorry," Ross stammered. "You just caught me off guard."

"I tend to do that," Meade replied gracefully. "I know that I'm a bit controversial."

"A bit?" Ross exclaimed. "The *Los Angeles Times* just did a page one story on you. Let's see, that had to be about three weeks ago."

"Four," Ross answered, "but who's counting?"

"And you know Gates?"

Meade nodded.

"We went to UCLA medical school together," Gates said, struggling to keep her mixed emotions out of her voice. "We met in a study group. We graduated the same year. I interned in Riverside, while . . ."

"I went back to New Mexico for internship and additional training," Meade interjected.

Gates studied Norman Meade for a moment. She had not seen him in over a decade. He had aged well and still possessed those simple good looks that had made him so popular in medical school. He had gained some weight, probably the result of genetics and middle age, but was still trim. He stood three inches taller than Gates which meant he was about six-foot-one. His black hair lay limply on his head. Just a few strands of gray were visible. Tiny creases of crow's feet were etched around his dark brown eyes. His smile was still radiant.

There was, however, something else that Gates noted: there was a heaviness about him. Not a physical weight, but . . . she struggled to define it . . . a heaviness of heart and soul.

"I would like to ask you some questions," Ross said eagerly. "Perhaps we could step over here away from the crowd and . . ."

Meade silenced him with an upraised hand and a simple smile. "Mr. Sassmon . . . It is Sassmon, isn't it?" Ross nodded. "Mr. Sassmon, I came here to speak to Gates, but I promise that I will give you an interview."

"But . . ." Ross protested.

"I believe Gates said that your paper is a weekly, is that true?"

"Yes, but . . ."

"When is your next deadline?" Norman was still smiling pleasantly.

"Not for a few days, but I would like very much . . ."

"I plan to hang around for a few days. I'm staying at the Ridgeline Bed and Breakfast. Why don't you give me a call tomorrow morning and we'll set up a time when we can get together. Agreed?" Meade pushed his hand out to Ross who took it. "Great."

"Well," Ross said. "I imagine you two have some recollecting to do, so I'll give you a little space."

An unsettled silence filled the vacuum left by Ross Sassmon's exit. Gates felt awkward and slightly perplexed. Norman Meade was a famous man, or an infamous man at least. There were those who touted him as a medical Robin Hood, doing for the needy what the rich medical industry would not. Others despised him as an evil man who found some perverse pleasure and enormous monetary benefit from killing people.

Unlike so many others, Gates was uncertain what her feelings were about the man. She knew that she loathed what he did, but a part of her was still attracted to this one who had been so serious in medical school.

"Thank you," Meade said quietly.

"For what? For introducing you to Ross?"

"No," Meade said with a chortle. "The news media can usually find me all by themselves. No, I'm thanking you for not turning on your heels and walking away. I get that a lot these days."

"I can imagine," Gates said as she wondered why she hadn't done just that.

"I'm afraid my life has become a little complex since we last had coffee together."

"I would think that complex is an understatement."

"Well, it is, but I'm trying not to be overly dramatic."

Uncomfortable silence returned. Eye contact was broken.

"This is a bit of a surprise," Gates offered a few uneasy moments later.

"I should have packed a costume." Meade looked around the room. "I feel a little conspicuous."

"Only at a Halloween party can one dress normally and feel conspicuous."

"You look lovely," Norman offered easily. "Perhaps the layered hoop skirt look will make a comeback."

"Let's hope not. This thing is killing me. Give me a pantsuit any day."

Silence returned. Meade looked down at his shoes; Gates nervously looked around the room. She caught Ross looking her way and talking to Carl Berner, the town's police chief. The conversation looked serious.

"Why are you here?" Gates blurted out. There was no viciousness in her tone, but the words were serious enough.

"Still direct, I see."

"I think it's a good quality, but my mother and sister think it's a fault."

"It's a good quality." Norman smiled, revealing stunningly white teeth and sparkles in his eyes. Gates had found that smile captivating in medical school; now was no different.

"Do you mean here at the party or here in Ridgeline?"

"Both, actually."

"I'm at the party because I thought you might be here and I wanted to see you again. It's been a long time, you know. I'm in Ridgeline because I was asked to be."

"Asked?"

"Yes, invited. And before you ask, let me make it easier. Yes, I came to Ridgeline to help with a physician-assisted suicide."

There was a churning in Gates' stomach; a mixing of anger, fear, repulsion, and curiosity. Both medical school and years of medical practice had taught her not to be reactive and to view everything in an unemotional, open, nonjudgmental fashion. At times such detachment was difficult — at the moment it was nearly impossible.

"Here? In Ridgeline?"

Norman nodded.

"When?"

A heavy sigh escaped Meade's lips. It was clear to Gates that he had been through such things before. She hadn't noticed at first, blinded as she was by the surprise visit of an old friend, but he looked weary, drawn, perhaps even near exhaustion.

"Today. Earlier."

Thoughts buzzed in her mind. Seconds later she had put two and two together. "Darlene Crews?"

Meade nodded again. "How did you know?"

"Ross was just saying that the police had been called to their house. He sent a reporter over there."

"Not unusual. She wasn't a patient of yours, was she? I didn't see your name in our family research."

"No. I met the husband once."

A blanket of uneasiness fell on the two. Gates struggled with what she was hearing and what she was doing. Here she was standing next to a man who was nationally known as Dr. Death and who, in the course of casual conversation, just admitted to helping someone end her life. The situation was now more than awkward, it was upsetting.

"Look," Meade began, "I'm not here to recruit you to our cause or even to attempt to persuade you that what I do is good and right. I'm here just to say hello to an old friend."

"I'm not sure what to do or say," Gates said. "I don't wish to be inhospitable or rude, but our views are very different. No, that's the wrong word. Not views, but beliefs. I don't understand how you can help someone commit suicide then stroll over to the local community building to attend a Halloween party and pick up an old friendship."

"It's not that easy, Gates," Meade said firmly. "This is not a hobby with me."

"I didn't say it was," Gates retorted strongly.

"I thought you were different," Meade said wearily. There was a hint of anger in his voice. "I thought that maybe we could have some coffee and conversation like the old days."

"These aren't the old days, Norman. Those days are gone and will never return. We can't leave the present and pretend we're in the past."

"I know," Norman rubbed his eyes and then looked around the room at all the gaily dressed people. The band was playing a tune that was close to being recognizable, a few people danced, but most stood in small clusters and talked. A few people stared in Gates and Meade's direction. "It looks like word is spreading that I'm here. This is why I don't go out in public very often."

Gates wanted to feel sorry for her old friend, but her abhorrence of his actions made it difficult. In medical school he had always been gentlemanly and kind. He made friends easily and always seemed to have a joke at the ready. He studied hard, always finishing in the top 10 percent of the class. Now as Gates studied the man next to her, she realized that all those things were still in place, but they were masked by actions that could not be ignored.

"I'm sorry if I seem aloof," Gates said softly. "I'm uncertain how to act."

"Perhaps it was a mistake for me to come." Meade continued looking around the room. "They all stare at me," he said, nodding at the gathering, "but statistics show that as many as half of them would call on me for help if they ever found themselves in Darlene Crews' situation."

"What was her situation?"

"End stage ALS," Meade said matter-of-factly.

Gates nodded in understanding. She had seen several such patients and knew how difficult and tragic ALS was.

"Her husband had called me. My assistants did the necessary research on their situation and . . ." Meade stopped abruptly and fixed his gaze on a man who was pushing his way through the crowd.

Gates turned to see what had seized Meade's attention. A tall, balding man in an expensive dark suit was approaching Meade with strong purposeful strides. His fists were clinched and his jaw set tight. It appeared to Gates that the man didn't blink.

"Oh, great," Meade said wearily. "Just what I don't need today."

"Who's that?" Gates asked, but before Meade could answer, the bald man stepped

Middlebury Community Library

within three feet of Meade. The tension between the two was palpable.

"I found you again, Meade," the man spat his words. "And I bet you've been up to your old tricks."

"Let's be civil, Dr. Warren," Meade offered calmly. "There's no need to disrupt the party. I'd like you to meet . . ." Meade began to motion toward Gates.

"I don't want to meet any of your cronies, Meade." Warren's words were venomous. "Just the sight of you makes me sick. Knowing that there are others like you is more than my stomach can tolerate."

Gates stiffened and started to speak but Meade was faster.

"Look, Warren, no one invited you to come here, no one is holding you here now, and no one is forcing you to hire private detectives to follow me around. Why don't you shut that constantly running mouth of yours and leave before you prove to all the people what an idiot you are."

"Idiot? At least I didn't kill anyone today, Meade." Warren's words were loud and echoed through the room. Even the band stopped playing to watch the confrontation. "How many does that make this week, Meade? How many more do you plan to murder next week, Meade?"

"I haven't murdered anyone . . ." Meade started.

"Oh that's right, you call it physician-assisted suicide. Well it's still murder to right-thinking, decent people."

Meade laughed loudly. "How would you know what was decent?"

Warren took a step closer. Gates stepped between them.

"Just a minute!" she said firmly. "This isn't the time or place . . ."

"Get out of the way," Warren shouted as he grabbed her shoulders and wildly pushed her to the side. Gates fell in a heap to the floor, her dress cascading around her. When she hit the concrete floor she released a small cry of pain and reached for her hip.

Meade lost control. Without hesitation he seized Warren's neck with his left hand and brought a crashing right fist down squarely on Warren's nose. The punch had Meade's full weight behind it. Warren screamed in pain, staggered back several steps, and dropped to his knees. Slowly he pulled his hands away from his face — they were streaked with bright-red blood.

Swearing loudly, Warren leapt to his feet and charged Meade. He was stopped mid-stride by a strong hand that seized the back of his shirt.

"That's enough." It was Carl Berner, police chief. He was dressed like a 1920's gangster, wearing a broad pinstriped suit and a black fedora. Carl was an imposing man, no less than six-feet-four in height with broad muscular shoulders. His face was smooth with strong features that could reveal the joy he felt or cloud over with a fierceness that had more than once frightened angry men into submission.

Feeling Carl's large hand on his collar caused Warren to spin around. "Don't mess with me you . . ."

"Watch it!" Carl shouted in the man's face. "I may not look it right now, but I'm a police officer and one more word out of you could land you in big trouble."

Warren shook with anger but said nothing.

"Are you all right?" Carl asked Gates as she struggled to her feet. "Do you want me to call an ambulance?"

"No, no," Gates said straightening her dress. "I'm fine."

"I want you to arrest this man," Warren voiced loudly, pointing at Meade. "He hit me. That's assault and battery. You saw it. You all saw it. He hit me and I want to press charges."

"What I saw," Carl said evenly, still holding Warren by the collar, "was you attack our town doctor. Now that's assault and battery."

"But you saw . . ." Warren stammered.

Carl turned his attention to Gates. "You wanna press charges, Doc? You've got the right, you know."

Gates looked at the man. She was furious enough to demand that he be lynched right there, but she held her tongue. "Tempting as that is," she replied, "I think I would be happy just to have him tossed out of here."

"You hear that, fella?" Carl said to Warren. "She's willing to let you go. Of course, if you open your mouth one more time, I'll arrest you for disturbing the peace. So what's it going to be, partner? You gonna stroll out of here nicely, or do I call for a patrol car?"

"I'll leave," Warren said weakly. Then he turned his attention to Meade. "This isn't over, you murderer."

"It needs to be over," Meade said angrily. "And if I end it, you won't like it."

Carl released Warren, who stared at Meade for a moment then turned to Carl. "You should be arresting him, officer. He murdered someone today. He murdered Darlene Crews."

A few people in the gathering crowd gasped.

"That's right," Warren said loudly, "you have a murderer at your party tonight. Dr.

Death has come to town. Watch yourselves. Watch your families."

"You had better leave." Carl's words were an order, not a suggestion.

After Warren had left, the band began to play again and people gathered in small groups to discuss what they had just witnessed. Gates, Meade, Carl, and Ross stood together. A moment later, Anne joined them.

"Are you all right?" she asked breathlessly. "I was clear across the room when it all happened and . . ."

Gates reached over and hugged her sister. "I'm fine. Don't worry. At least I have a reason to leave and get out of this dress."

"Gates, I'm sorry about what happened. Ed Warren is a real hothead. He's been following me for six months now trying to make my life miserable. He hates me and what I do, but he shouldn't have pushed you."

"Well, I suppose I should thank you for coming to my defense," Gates said cautiously.

"No thanks is necessary. If I hadn't shown up in the first place none of this would have happened." Turning to Carl Berner, he continued, "Look, officer, I'm sorry about all of this. Maybe I should explain who I am . . ."

"I know who you are, Dr. Meade," Carl said firmly. "I read the papers. I also know about Darlene Crews. I think you should stay around for a while. I have some questions. In the meantime, stay away from that other fellow or I'll put both of you in jail. Got it?"

"Got it," was all Norman Meade said.

Chapter Three

Friday, October 31
10:20 P.M.

Home felt good. It was quiet, warm, and most of all empty. No people dressed in costumes, no surprise visitors from the past, and no ranting and raving doctors.

The night had been a miserable experience for Gates. Merely showing up was an act of guilt-driven discipline. Gates had always been a private person who avoided crowds. It wasn't that she didn't like people, in fact she loved people, she just felt uncomfortable in large gatherings.

Being the center of attention was something Gates avoided. But once she had been knocked down by Ed Warren, and after Norman Meade had hastily left, she immediately became the focus of nearly everyone in the hall. Her pastor, Paul Chapman, began the long stream of questions about her condition. Are you hurt? Can I get you something? Do you want to talk about it? And he was just the first. Soon scores of people were asking after her health and mental state, and, of course, seeking information about the scuffle.

New questions had followed. Was that really Dr. Death? What was he doing here? Is he a friend of yours? What is he up to? Did he really kill Darlene Crews?

Gates had done her best to be polite and give what information she could, but it had become too much to endure. Fortunately, Anne came to her rescue by escorting her to the ladies room. It was there that Anne performed her own inquisition.

"Are you all right?" Anne had asked, her powdered wig bouncing slightly with each movement of her head.

"I'm fine, but I want to go home."

"No, stay awhile. You'll feel better." Anne put a hand on Gates' shoulder. "So how long have you known Dr. Death?"

"His name is Norman Meade, and we met in medical school. We used to study together."

"Were you an . . . item?" Anne inquired, eyes widening at the thought that her sister may have been romantically involved with the notorious Dr. Meade.

"No, not really." Gates rubbed her hip. The fall to the floor was going to leave a substantial bruise. "We occasionally had coffee, but nothing beyond that. We may have gone out a couple of times."

"*May* have gone out a couple of times?"

"All right, we *did* date a little, but nothing worth talking about," Gates conceded.

"Do you think he wants to renew the relationship?"

"I don't know what he wants," Gates snapped, "but I do know what I want. I want to go home."

"But if you do, people will think you're hurt and worry about you."

"I don't care. My evening is shot."

"Please stay a little longer," Anne pleaded. "I mean you went through a lot of trouble to get dressed up and all. And you do look wonderful. Have some punch, eat snacks, you'll feel better. Besides, you haven't talked to anyone all night."

"I spoke to two doctors and got knocked on my fanny for it."

"You know what I mean." Anne displayed her best sad and pleading face.

Gates had acquiesced. She visited with people. She talked. She ate snacks. At nine-thirty Anne's husband John arrived, much to Gates' delight. With him to keep Anne company Gates made good her escape.

Now, surrounded by the comfortable confines of her home, Gates finally felt the tension of the day begin to melt away. All she wanted now was a cup of hot chocolate and to go to bed. But the first thing she had to do was to get out of the Scarlett O'Hara dress.

Walking toward the bedroom she saw the blinking light of her answering machine. Her first impulse was to ignore it until morning, but professional discipline won out.

She punched the "Play Messages" button. A moment later the voice of Norman Meade filled the room.

"Uh, hi . . . Uh, this is Norman and I'm calling to apologize about tonight. I really didn't plan for anything like this to happen. I mean, Warren is crazy and I don't know how to handle him. He's a stalker and I wish there was some way to make him drop off the face of the earth . . . I'm sorry, I'm ranting again. Anyway, I apologize and hope that you will forgive me. I would like to buy you breakfast tomorrow to make amends for tonight. I promise nothing exciting will happen. I'll make sure of it. So how about it? It will be like old times except without the anatomy books. I will be at the Tree Top Café at eight tomorrow if you want to join me, and I hope you do. Thanks for understanding."

Gates groaned. What to do now? A part of her, a large part, wanted to see him again, yet another stronger element of her wished that he would just go away. Still, a decision had to be made. She thought for a moment, then made up her mind. First, however, she was getting out of that dress.

Chapter Four

Saturday, November 1
8:10 A.M.

The Tree Top Café was in its usual weekend frenzy. Three waitresses, each dressed in a white skirt and pink apron, dashed back and forth from the kitchen to the tables, carrying coffee and plates loaded with eggs, bacon, and rolls.

The customers were the usual mix of locals and tourists from the cities at the base of the mountain. As a rule, the visitors were more demanding and more likely to complain. The locals were happy as long as their coffee cups didn't run dry.

Gates, dressed in a loose fitting white T-shirt, blue jeans, and white sneakers, took in the scene around her. It was only the first day of November and no snow was on the ground, yet the crowded restaurant was evidence that a tide of humans would descend on Ridgeline immediately following first snow.

Ridgeline itself was not a ski community, but the High Peak ski resort was only twenty miles farther up the mountain. Snow-bunnies, as Ridgeline residents were prone to call the tourists, often stopped in town for food, shopping, or to sit in one of the town's three bars and talk about their exploits on the slopes.

When snow did fall, the Tree Top Café would be standing room only, with a line of hungry skiers snaking from the tiny lobby and out into the parking lot. During those days, Gates, like many of her neighbors, stayed home for breakfast.

Beth Hinkle, owner of the establishment, loved to see a crowd. The bigger the group, the more money in the till. Beth was a tall, middle-aged, painfully thin woman with straight black hair tightly pulled back into a ponytail. She was a stern person, quick with her opinion and impatient with the views of others. That sternness was reflected in her drawn face. This was her restaurant and she ruled it firmly, dispensing orders to her employees in curt, clipped sentences like a drill sergeant. Gates had wondered how anyone could work with her. Even now, from her perch behind the cash register, she kept a close eye on the waitresses as they scampered along the aging linoleum floor.

"More coffee, Doctor?" one of the waitresses asked.

"Thanks," Gates replied with a meager smile.

The woman poured the dark fluid into the stained white cup situated in front of Gates. "Care to order now, or do you still wanna wait?"

"I think I'll wait a few more minutes," Gates answered, looking at her watch. It was ten minutes past eight. Norman Meade was late.

"Okay," the waitress replied, and then dashed off to the adjoining table.

Gates sighed and looked out the window. A gray squirrel scampered down a yellow pine, along the black pavement of the parking lot, and between two parked cars.

"You don't think he's going to stand you up, do you?"

Gates turned to see Beth Hinkle standing by the table.

"Oh, hi Beth," Gates said, offering a smile of courtesy. "Who are you talking about?"

"Why, that doctor fellow, of course," Beth answered quickly. "That was quite a ruckus last night, wasn't it?"

"It was that, Beth, it was that."

"Did you get hurt bad? That fall looked pretty nasty."

Had the question come from anyone other than Beth, Gates would have been flattered by the concern; but knowing Beth the way she did, she knew that Beth's real interest was some bit of information to pass on in the form of gossip.

"Not bad," Gates said, shaking her head. "I got a decent-size bruise on my hip. The concrete was very unforgiving."

"Speaking of unforgiving, I hope you're not planning on forgiving that . . . man."

"Dr. Meade?" Gates didn't like the direction the conversation was taking.

"He never should have been here in the first place. Men like him are nothing but trouble. I mean, look what happened to you."

"Dr. Meade didn't knock me down, Beth, Ed Warren did."

Beth folded her arms. "Still, it wouldn't have happened if Dr. Death hadn't come here. You know why he came, don't you?"

"Yes, I do," Gates replied firmly. She could feel her neck tense. She was good at many things, but tolerating impertinent people wasn't one of them. "And his name is Dr. Meade."

"I don't care what his name is," Beth spat. "He's a killer, and he came here to kill someone, and did. If you ask me, he should be in jail right now."

Slowly Gates closed her eyes and then opened them. She could understand Beth's concern, but she couldn't endure her arrogance.

Beth continued: "Ain't nobody got the right to take someone else's life, if you ask me. Nobody."

"The way I see it," Gates began, "no one asked you. At least no one at this table."

Gates watched unflinchingly as Beth's face clouded over. "I don't have to listen to this."

"Beth, I don't think you've listened to anything yet."

Beth pursed her lips tightly, wrinkled her brow, then spun on her heels and stormed away.

Great, Gates thought, *now she'll probably poison my food.*

Several emotions collided in Gates' psyche. First was a sense of embarrassment over the tone she had taken with Beth. As a rule, Gates tried to avoid confrontation as much as possible, but it was an effort that failed as often as it succeeded. Her mother attributed it to the undiluted Irish blood that coursed through her veins, but Gates knew that was nothing more than myth. Besides, both her mother and sister were far more even tempered.

Second, Gates was awash in confusion. She had just come to the defense of a man she had not seen in over a decade, and a man with whom she had strong ideological differences. As much as it galled her, Beth had been right. No one had the right to take the life of another. Technically, of course, Meade didn't take anyone's life, he simply arranged for them to take their own. Still the distinction was blurry in Gates' mind and the end result was the same.

Those emotions, coupled with her ill-defined feelings about Meade's unexpected resurfacing, left Gates confused. And when she was confused, she became irritable.

One other matter bothered her: he was late. Looking at her watch, she realized that she had now been waiting nearly twenty minutes. That might not be so bad if the bed and breakfast wasn't just two blocks down the street. She would give him ten minutes more and then she would leave.

"Dr. McClure," a deep voice said behind her. She turned and saw Carl Berner standing tall in his khaki uniform.

"Hello, Carl," Gates said as he stepped to her booth. "What brings you here?"

"Actually, I was looking for you."

"Me?"

"Yes, may I sit down?"

Gates nodded. "Of course."

Carl dropped his large frame onto the booth's vinyl seat. The leather from his holster and Sam Brown belt rubbed noisily against the material. It sounded to Gates like Carl was attempting to squeeze his massive bulk into a balloon. He motioned to a waitress for coffee.

"I was supposed to meet someone here," Gates offered, "but I think I'm being stood up."

"I'm afraid I may be the cause of that." The waitress brought the coffee. Carl grabbed the sugar dispenser and poured a long stream of the granules into his cup.

"How so?"

"I know that you're waiting for Norman Meade," Carl answered. "He told me so only a few moments ago — right after I arrested him."

Gates felt her eyes widen. "You arrested him?"

"You seem surprised."

"Well, I would have thought that you would have done that last night at the party or at Darlene Crews' place."

"Why?" Carl inquired, point blank.

"Because of Darlene and the physician-assisted suicide."

"I didn't arrest him because of what he did at Darlene's."

"You didn't?" Gates asked, puzzled.

"No, I didn't," Carl took a long sip of

coffee. "I arrested him for the murder of Ed Warren."

Startled, Gates sat back. "Doctor Ed Warren? The guy from last night? The man that . . ."

"That knocked you to the ground," Carl interjected. "We found him dead in his room at the Cliffside Motel. Apparently he checked in last night after his confrontation with Meade. Sometime last night or early this morning he was killed."

"How? I mean what makes you think it was Norman Meade?"

"The usual," Carl said easily, as if talking about a recent car problem. "Meade has motive, we saw that at the party, and he had opportunity. He was in town, after all."

"But still . . ."

"That's not all. He made threats in the presence of others. You heard what he said to Warren. He has no alibi. Besides, we found certain evidence that points us right at Meade."

"Like what?" Gates asked.

"Can't give you details yet," Carl answered. "But I thought you should know. You being his friend and all. He is your friend isn't he?"

It was a good question. Would Meade consider Gates his friend? "I haven't spoken with him in over ten years, Carl. Not until last night, I mean. We were friends in medical school, but that was a long time ago. I know very little about the man now."

"Do you think he could kill Warren? I mean he does kill people for a living."

"I don't know. If this were a decade ago, my answer would be no. Back then he was as kind as he was smart. But like I said, that was a long time ago."

"Did he have any other contact with you since the party?"

Gates shook her head. "No. Well . . . he left a message on my answering machine asking me to meet him here this morning."

"Did he, now?" Carl's eyebrows went up. "Would you still have that message?"

"I think so," Gates replied. "Unless someone has left another message over it. That sometimes happens."

"Then we'd better get over there pretty quick." Carl exited the booth and stood. "I'll follow you over to your place."

"So then what happened?" Anne was seated on the sofa in Gates' home, leaning forward in rapt attention. Gates was situated opposite her in a rocking chair that had belonged to her grandmother. She rocked slowly.

"Not much, really," Gates answered. "Carl came in and listened to the message on the answering machine. I hadn't listened that closely at first so I missed it, but Carl picked up on it right away."

"So your Dr. Meade did make a threat?"

"He's not *my* Dr. Meade," Gates retorted, "and I suppose what he said could be construed as a threat of sorts, but it wasn't very specific. He just sounded embarrassed and frustrated to me."

"I wish I could hear it," Anne offered.

"Well, you can't. Carl confiscated the tape as possible evidence."

"So what are you going to do now? Are you going to see him? In jail, I mean."

"Carl says he's been asking for me, but I don't know. I'm not sure what to do. You know more about these things than I do, Anne. What do you suppose will happen next?"

"I'm no attorney, but I guess it all depends on the evidence they have. A judge will have to rule about things like bail, or even whether there's enough evidence to hold him beyond seventy-two hours. Of course, that can't happen until Monday at the earliest, and probably won't happen until Tuesday or Wednesday. The courts aren't open on weekends."

"If Norman is being held for murder, can he get bail?"

"It happens all the time. Bail is going to be pretty stiff, I would imagine." Anne leaned back on the sofa and crossed her legs. "You haven't answered my question: Are you going to see him?"

"He was a good friend in school. I suppose I should, but I'm uncomfortable with the idea."

Anne nodded, then asked, "If he weren't Dr. Death would you go see him? I mean, if he were some other friend from school. Would you go see him then?"

"I don't know." Gates shifted in her seat and rocked some more. "I've never been in this situation before. And I have strong feelings about what Norman does. I don't think it's right. I *know* it's not right."

Anne didn't respond.

"He's doing the opposite of what a doctor is supposed to do. It's wrong. It's immoral. It's unethical."

Anne remained quiet.

Gates looked at her sister who sat uncharacteristically silent on the sofa. "What's going on in that head of yours, Anne? You don't think what he did to Darlene was wrong?"

"I'm not so sure."

"Oh, come on, Anne. Surely you can't take

71

his side in this. Helping people commit suicide is as wrong as it gets. And that goes double for doctors."

"From what you told me about Darlene's disease, she must have been suffering greatly. Isn't ALS a horrible affliction?"

"Yes, but . . ."

"Gates," Anne interrupted. "I'm not saying that Norman Meade is right. I'm just saying that if it had been me in Darlene's place, then . . . well, I can understand her decision."

"Oh, Anne, I don't believe this."

"What if it were me, Gates?" Anne's tone was serious. "What if it were me lying on that bed slowly dying, with no hope for a cure. If I were really suffering, really in agony, would it be so wrong to wish for death?"

"Anne, there's more to this than you realize. It's just not that simple."

"I know that I'm no doctor, but you don't have to be a doctor to recognize pain and suffering."

"That's true, but wrong is still wrong."

"Is it?"

"Yes!" Gates got up and crossed the living room to the window. The day was bright, the sky a light blue and sprinkled with small milky clouds. It was hard to believe that suffering could occur in such splendor. "There are absolutes in the world and the sanctity of life is one of them."

"Well, I suppose I agree with you," Anne said softly. "But then again, I'm not the one stewing in pain."

There was silence. The two women were lost in their thoughts.

"I knew I shouldn't have gone to that party," Gates said, breaking the hush.

"Go see him," Anne advised. "Go see him today."

"Why?"

"Because he asked to see you. Because he was your friend. Because the whole truth is not yet known. Because, if it were me alone in a strange town, I would want to see someone I know."

"He won't change my mind," Gates declared.

"That's not really the point, is it?"

Gates thought for a moment. "No, I guess it isn't."

The mélange of emotions swelled in Gates again.

Gates had never been inside a jail before, not even the small four-cell lockup situated at the back of the Ridgeline Police station. She was surprised at how light and open the structure was. Long, thin windows were situated just below the ceiling in each cell. The windows were fixed glass, and too narrow to allow any enterprising prisoner the opportunity to slip out. The walls were constructed of concrete block painted a bright white. Fluorescent lights, each protected by a heavy wire mesh, were suspended above the short hall. There were no lights in the cells themselves.

"He's in the last cell on the left," Carl said, pointing down the hall. "Since he's the only one here, you should have all the privacy you want. I'll wait in my office. This door will lock behind me, so when you're ready to leave just press this button," he indicated a small beige plastic doorbell-like button mounted next to the door.

"Okay," Gates said. "How long do I have?"

"As long as you like," Carl replied. "Since he's our only prisoner at the moment, we can be a little flexible."

"Thanks."

Gates heard the door shut behind her as she walked down the narrow hall formed by the bars on her left and right. As she approached, she could see hands on the bars and a face pressed against the door as Norman struggled to peer down the corridor. It was a pathetic picture.

A few steps later she was standing at Meade's cell. He was dressed in the same clothes he had been wearing the night before. His face was wan and covered with dark stubble. His eyes were red and his short black hair mussed. He looked horrible, tortured, fearful.

"Thanks for coming," Meade said. "I had hoped to see you again, but under different circumstances."

"Did you do it?" Gates asked sternly.

"Like I said last night, you like to get right to the point."

"Actually, you said I was direct, and that doesn't answer my question."

Meade offered a meager smile. "No, Gates, I didn't kill Ed Warren. I'm not capable of such violence."

Gates cocked her head but said nothing.

"Oh, I know what you're thinking," Meade said, as he stepped away from the bars. "You're thinking that I didn't get the name Dr. Death for nothing. Well, I've never killed anyone, Gates. Do you hear me? Never. All I do is help suffering people end their suffering, but they make the final act. Never once have I done anything that directly resulted in the death of another. Despite what you and the others may think, I am not a monster."

"I never said you were a monster, Norman. Don't put words in my mouth."

"I'm sorry. This thing has me on edge."

Gates nodded sympathetically. "Being

charged with murder would do that."

Meade gave a little chortle. "There's a chair there if you want to sit down."

Looking to the rear wall of the corridor, Gates saw a metal folding chair. She took it and sat down.

"You look nice," Meade offered.

It was Gates' turn to chortle. Unconsciously she looked down at her attire: jeans with a wide leather belt and a loose-fitting white T-shirt. "Jail has done something to your eyes, Norman."

He smiled. "Perhaps. I've been in jail several times before, but this is different. Before, I was arrested for aiding a suicide, but nothing like this." He paused for a moment. "Of course, there was Florida."

"What happened in Florida?"

"Helping a person commit suicide in Florida is considered second-degree manslaughter — a felony. The law, which is almost 130 years old, defines suicide as 'self-murder'."

"You helped someone die in Florida?" Gates asked.

"Three years ago. That was the first time I was ever in jail. Fortunately, my people were able to get the charges dismissed."

"And who are your people?"

"Contrary to what some have said, I don't

get paid for what I do. I make no charges and accept no payment. I'm part of an organization that is funded by gifts from people who believe that we all have a right to end our own suffering and to do so with a measure of dignity."

Gates felt herself stiffen. Meade must have noticed. He lowered his voice and approached the bars. "I have spent some time in jail, Gates. Not much, usually just a few days until my attorney gets a hearing. So far every case has been dropped. But all those dealt with medical suicides. This is different. This is first-degree murder."

"Have you called your attorney?" Gates inquired.

"Of course. It was the first thing that I did. Then I called for you." He frowned. "Your Gestapo police chief would only allow one call to my attorney."

"Carl is an honest man who takes his work seriously. He's far from being Gestapo. So why did you call for me?" Gates' question was asked in even, unemotional tones. The kind of question doctors asked of patients.

"Because . . . well, because I need a friend, and because it is very important for you to know that I did not kill Ed Warren."

"But you hated Warren, didn't you? I know he hated you."

"That's a fair assessment, Gates. But hating someone isn't the same as killing him. It's not in my nature."

"You did explode at the party, Norman. You probably broke Warren's nose."

"I was protecting you, Gates. You know, you're starting to sound like the police."

"I'm just trying to figure things out, Norman. I'm not trying to be judgmental. But this is all rather confusing. First, you pop up out of nowhere, and then you land in jail. This is a little hard to take in all at once." Gates watched as Norman began to pace his cell. "By the way, just how did you find me here in Ridgeline?"

"Oh, that was easy. I called the alumni association at UCLA. They had your address. I could have gotten it through the state medical board too. Practicing physicians are easy to find. Besides, in school you were always talking about how much you loved Ridgeline and how you planned to return here."

"So what happens now?"

"I assume that they will hold me, interview me, and set an arraignment date. Your police chief said that the county will send up some homicide investigators to gather evidence."

Gates nodded. "Ridgeline is too small to have a full-fledged police department. Anything beyond the usual police work requires that we get outside help. Carl's good, but he doesn't have the resources that large departments have. Most of the time he deals with drunk drivers, the occasional bar fight, and traffic violations."

"He sure seems efficient."

"He is that. He worked for the Los Angeles Police Department for twelve or so years before coming here. I guess he had had enough of LA."

Meade stopped pacing and turned to face Gates. He was calm, but she could see that his self-assurance was eroding.

"Gates," he said softly, "I know a lot of years have passed without so much as a phone call. I also know that you feel strongly about what I do, but I need your help. This goes way beyond just me. It's the whole movement. Whether I like it or not, I have come to represent the right-to-die movement. There have been others that have done what I do and have received a great deal of press coverage, but they have done more harm to the cause than good. That's why I've been so careful in what I do and how I do it. Being arrested for the murder of Ed Warren could end all that."

"Would that be so bad?"

"Yes!" Meade shouted. "Yes it would. You may not approve of the suffering taking steps to end their agony, but your approval isn't necessary. These people have real needs and they have rights."

Gates scowled at Meade. She didn't like being lectured and liked even less being yelled at.

Raising his hands, Meade signaled his apology. "I shouldn't have yelled. I'm just on edge. Jail does that."

"I don't see how I can be of any help," Gates said evenly.

"Let me ask you something. What did you feel when I first walked into the party last night? Was it revulsion? Was it fear? Was it terror?"

"No."

"What did you feel?"

"I'm not sure."

"Not sure you know, or not sure you want to say?" Meade prompted.

"At first I felt surprise, and then . . ." Gates' words trailed off. "And then I felt happiness at seeing you."

"As I did when I saw you. I know we only dated a few times, but I felt like we had a bond. Something special that goes beyond friendship. You didn't love me, I know that. But so what? Didn't we have something special, even if we didn't have romance?"

"We did have a special friendship," Gates conceded. "But that was another time and another place. We're not the same people."

"Sure we are. We're older and more experienced in life, but we are still the same ideological, starry-eyed medical students who were going to change the world."

"I'm just a doctor with a general practice in a mountain community."

"Don't belittle yourself. You do a good and noble work here. It's something to be proud of. You care and you work where people live. And it's that caring spirit that I need now."

"I still don't see what I can do to help."

"First, ask your sister if she could pull a few strings for me."

"What strings?"

"Your sister is mayor, right?"

"Yes. How did you know that?" Gates asked.

"Chief Berner mentioned it when he was taking my statement. He asked how it was I knew you and such things. He also asked if I knew your sister. Anyway, they will only hold me here for a short time, then they'll move me to a county detention center. I don't want to go there. I want to stay here. Your sister might be able to pull that off."

Gates nodded. She had heard that the bigger jails could be unpleasant and even dangerous. It seemed like a fair request. "I'll talk to her, but she makes up her own mind. And being mayor doesn't mean that she gets everything she wants."

"She'll pull it off," Meade said confidently. "The next thing I need is from you. I can't keep track of what's going on in the outside world. I need to know how the investigation is going and things like that. You could keep me informed."

"Isn't that your attorney's job?"

"He'll be busy building my case, and people tend to clam up around lawyers — especially my lawyers. Besides, he doesn't understand the community like you do."

"So you want me to keep you informed?"

"It would mean a lot to me, Gates — more than you can know. I need a friend now, even a friend who hates what I do."

Gates lowered her head in thought. He wasn't asking all that much and if she were in his shoes, she would appreciate having someone to talk to.

"Okay," she said. "I'll do what I can."

"Thank you, Gates. You are a lifesaver."

"No. I'm just a confused woman caught up in something she doesn't understand."

"Oh, you're a whole lot more than that," Meade said beaming. "A whole lot more."

The conversation lulled into silence for a few moments, then Gates asked: "Is there anything I can get for you? Anything special that you need? Books? Magazines?"

"Just your trust, Gates. Just your belief and trust."

"I need to ask a favor, Carl," Gates said as she took a seat in the office of the Chief of Police. She had left the lockup and Carl was preparing to escort her to the front door when Gates asked for a moment of his time.

"A favor is it?" Carl stated as he sat down behind his desk, an old gun-metal gray piece of furniture. "Well, let's hear it."

"Actually, it's a couple of favors that I need." Gates sat back in the wood chair and crossed her legs. She wanted to appear comfortable, casual, which was the opposite of what she was feeling. Although Norman had asked that Gates intercede on his behalf with Anne, she chose to go directly to Carl Berner herself. It would be a simpler, cleaner approach; besides, she had another motive. "I wonder if you would let Dr. Meade have use of the phone from time to time. I know that he's already called his attorney, but he may need to make a few more calls."

"This is a jail, Gates, not a hotel."

"I'm aware of that, Carl, but it's not like you're full up. Besides, he's been arrested on the suspicion of murder. He hasn't been convicted yet."

"It sounds like you think he's innocent." Carl leaned forward and rested his elbows on the desk, his chair squeaked in protest. "He may be guilty."

"Perhaps, but that's for the courts to decide and not us. Come on, Carl, I'm not trying to interfere, but what could a few phone calls matter?"

"Before I commit to anything, I think I'd better hear what else it is that you want."

"Two things more. One, let him stay in jail here in Ridgeline until his arraignment instead of transferring him to the county jail."

"That means that I would have to assign a deputy to transport him to the courthouse. That'll take an officer off the streets."

"How was he going to get down there in the first place? I don't think UPS takes prisoners as packages. I bet one of your deputies would be transporting him anyway. The only thing I'm asking is that you wait until it's absolutely necessary before you move him."

Carl scratched his square chin. "Is there more?"

"I would like to see the crime scene."

"Oh, is that all," Carl said with exasperation. "You haven't been reading those mystery books again have you? Are you wanting to do a little private-eye work on the side?"

"No, of course not, Carl."

"Then what? Why do you want to see the crime scene?"

"I'm not certain, but I feel like I need to see it."

"Let's see now," Carl said as he took a piece of paper and a pen from his desk and began to write on it with exaggerated motion. "Just a few favors. Unlimited use of the phone by the prisoner, ignore procedures and keep a prisoner in our jail at the city's expense, and allow a civilian to peruse a felony crime scene. Well, that doesn't seem like too much to ask."

"Cut the sarcasm, Carl. I'm not asking you to let the man go, I'm just asking for your help."

"These kinds of favors could cost me my job, especially if I was still in LA."

"You're not going to lose your job, Carl," Gates said firmly. "You're helping me, not Dr. Meade. Besides, my sister is the mayor and I'll make her life unbearable if she terminates your employment."

Carl smiled broadly. "Why is it I think that you would be good at making her life miserable?"

"Good police instinct," Gates returned the smile.

"May I ask why you want all these things? Is there something between you two that I should know about?"

Gates shook her head. "Nothing like that, Carl. Nothing like that. It's just . . . it's just that I owe him a debt."

"A debt?"

"Yes, and I'm not real keen on talking about it, so don't ask. I will tell you this: he saved my life."

Carl furrowed his brow. "He saved your life?"

Gates only nodded.

Putting the pen down, Carl began to rub his temples. He sighed noisily. "I respect you a great deal, Gates. I don't know if you knew that, but I do. Okay, if you're alive because of something Meade did, then I guess I can bend the rules some. But you will tell me the whole story someday."

"Okay, but not now."

"The investigators are at the crime scene now doing their work, so we'd better not go over there yet. They should be done by early evening. I'll give you a call and let you know when we can go."

"Great. Then I can drive . . ."

"Oh, no you don't. I'll pick you up, escort you there, and follow you closer than your own shadow. You will touch nothing, take nothing, and move nothing. You can look, and that's it. Got it?"

"Got it," Gates answered as she stood to

her feet. "I appreciate this, Carl. I really do."

"Yeah. Well, you had better. And I had better not get a scathing phone call from your sister or anyone on the council. I just hope you understand who it is that you're helping."

"Me too, Carl. Me too."

Chapter Five

Saturday, November 1
5:00 P.M.

From her front window, Gates watched as Carl Berner pulled his patrol car onto the concrete drive in front of her home at precisely 5:00 P.M., just as promised. Carl was always punctual; always meticulous. It was one of the things that Gates appreciated about him; that and his quick wit and dedication.

Gates had come to know Carl when he and his wife Sharee had brought his youngest son, a skinny boy of ten, into the medical office to have a cut on his hand treated. They had been impressed with the way Gates had taken time to talk to the boy and make him feel comfortable. Even the required tetanus shot went without tears, an unusual situation for a lad who had always been terrified of hypodermics.

Over the months Gates and Sharee had developed a friendship, getting together two or three times a month for shopping excursions to the malls down the hill. It wasn't the shopping that mattered, it was the time away. Sharee needed "adult time" away from her three children, and Gates needed "escape time" away from the office. Had this relationship not been there, Gates would never have asked the favors she had of Carl.

Not waiting for Carl to come to the door, Gates donned a short leather jacket to fight back the fall chill and walked briskly to the car. Carl was just stepping out when he saw her.

"Afraid people will talk if I came to the door?" he asked lightly.

"People will talk no matter what you do," Gates answered. "Ridgeline has an excellent grapevine."

"Truer words were never spoken. Get in. I'd like to get there before it gets dark."

Seating herself in the front seat, Gates quickly shut the door and fastened her seatbelt. "I hope it's all right to ride in front. It's not good business for people to see their doctor driven around in the back seat of a cop car."

"Oh, I don't know," Carl rebutted. "They might show up at the office just to find out what was happening. You could charge them for an office visit."

"Tempting as that is, I think I'll stay up here."

"Have it your way."

Gates changed the subject. "Are the detectives still at the motel room?"

"Nah. They left about half an hour ago. They said there wasn't much physical evidence, but they found the usual fibers and hairs and the like. Of course, it is a motel room, so it's hard to tell who might have left what."

"There's an unsettling thought," Gates added. "How's Norman?"

"Your friend is fine. Unhappy as can be, but fine. One of my officers will bring him something to eat from the Tree Top."

"Don't let Beth Hinkle know. She already has him tried and convicted and ready to be hung in the town square — and that was before anyone knew about Warren's death."

"Well she may not be far from wrong," Carl said seriously.

"Why are you so dead set against him, Carl?" Gates asked as Carl steered the car down a narrow, tree-lined side road.

"I don't like him," Carl proclaimed. "He came into my town and helped someone commit suicide, then he has the audacity to call us and the coroner like nothing has happened. Then there's the videotape."

"What videotape?"

"He videotaped the whole thing," Carl said

angrily motioning with one hand while gripping the wheel with his other. "From start to finish he videotapes the whole thing. It's too weird."

"Wait a minute," Gates interjected. "You mean to say that there is an actual videotape of the suicide?"

"Yup. I've got it in my office."

Gates thought for a second then asked, "Can I see it?"

"Why would you want to see that? It's like watching a snuff film, only without the gross violence."

"Snuff film?"

"Yeah," Carl explained. "People, usually outside the country, make a movie with actors and actresses — except when it comes to the murder scene they really kill the person. They were popular in the '70s and '80s."

"That's repulsive," Gates said with disgust. "What's this world coming to?"

"Nothing good, that's for sure."

"I would still like to see the video. It might help me understand what Norman's been doing."

"I'll think about it," Carl said reluctantly.

It took less than ten minutes for Carl to steer his way through the residential streets and onto State Highway 22 that served as the main road through town. Five minutes after that, they pulled into the small parking lot of the Cliffside Motel.

The motel was a small, cheap-looking bungalow-style building that had been constructed in the early 1950s. Several such motels were spaced along the main road that led to the ski resort a few miles up the mountain. The rooms were small and filled with outdated furniture, but the skiers never seemed to mind.

Of the twenty-two rooms that made up the U-shaped structure, one stood out. It was a corner room on the west wing and was made noticeable by the yellow band of ribbon that cordoned off an area about twenty by twenty feet in front of the entrance. The ribbon bore the words "Crime Scene. Do Not Cross." The words were repeated along its length.

Seeing the room in which Ed Warren had been murdered made Gates' stomach tighten. She didn't know Warren beyond her brief and uncomfortable encounter the night before, but that was enough to make her dislike him. Yet, the thought of him being killed in that room less than a day before made her feel sorry for the man.

"There's Dan Wells." Carl nodded in the direction of a white police cruiser parked two spaces down from the motel room. "Looks like he was just leaving."

Wells was standing by the open door of his patrol car. When he saw his boss pull in and park, he closed the car door and ambled over to greet him.

"Hello, Chief," Wells said wearily. "I was just getting ready to head back to the station and then call it a day."

"I don't blame you," Carl said as he and Gates exited the car. "You've been stuck here all day."

"Just part of the job," Wells replied, then to Gates he said: "Hello, Doctor."

"Hi, Dan. How's that wife of yours?"

"Still pregnant, and still eager to have that kid."

"She has another month to go, doesn't she?" Gates asked.

"Three and a half weeks." Wells beamed. This was their first child and he had made no secret about how eager he was to be a father. "Six weeks from now the kid will be playing baseball."

Gates laughed. "That's a little soon, don't you think?"

"Maybe. But then again he is a Wells, you know."

"How do you know it's going to be a 'he'?" Carl asked.

"Sonogram, Chief," Wells answered. "This is the age of high-tech. There are no secrets

93

anymore. Judy had a sonogram done some time back and the doctor told us it was going to be a boy."

"I bet that broke your heart," Carl gibed.

"Not a bit, Chief, not a bit."

"Well, I'll let you get home to Momma, but first I need to get into the room. You still have the key?"

"Sure." Wells reached into his pocket and extracted a large bronze-colored key. He then turned, ducked under the tape barricade and unlocked the door, which he swung open. "The homicide guys said they were through, so it's safe to move around."

"Did they say if they found anything?" Carl asked as he held up the tape for Gates to pass under.

"Not really. They took samples of things, and dusted for prints, but there wasn't much left behind."

"Not even fingerprints?" Gates asked.

"Oh there were fingerprints all right, Doc," Wells answered. "Lots of fingerprints. That's the problem. This room has had someone different in it almost every night for the last month and the people who stayed here left plenty of prints. The maids don't wipe down the walls and door jambs unless they look dirty. Those homicide boys will be cross-checking prints for weeks."

"And if the killer wore gloves," Carl added, "it will all be a waste of time."

"True," said Wells. "Can I leave the key with you, Chief? I need to get home, if it's all right."

"Sure. Give my best to Judy."

Gates and Carl walked into the room. The walls were covered in a blue, flower-patterned wallpaper that had been faded by years of exposure to sunlight. Black smears were everywhere on the walls, around door jambs, and on the smooth oak headboard of the bed.

The covers on the bed were rumpled but still in place, as if someone had gone to sleep without taking the trouble to pull the bedspread back.

It seemed odd, almost macabre to be standing in a room where such a final act of violence had taken place. As if to provide a counterpoint to the brutality, a small basket of fresh fruit sat on the inexpensive and scarred dresser.

"We found him on the bed," Carl said. "Still dressed. Shoes still on."

"There's not much to see," Gates admitted.

"The detectives took the devices with them."

"What devices?"

"We found an IV stand with an empty IV

bag hanging from it. It had one of those electronic devices on it. I don't know what you call them."

"An IV pump?" Gates asked. "A box with a digital read-out on it?"

"Yeah, one of those. When we found Warren he was hooked up to the thing."

"Someone gave him an IV? Right here next to the bed?"

"That's what it looks like. We're having the contents of the bag analyzed and the coroner will tell us what was in Warren's blood."

"Did the bag have any markings on it?"

"It was marked 'Saline.' "

Gates shrugged. "That's harmless. Saline is given to patients all the time. It's used to prevent dehydration."

"I know that."

"How do we know that Warren wasn't giving himself an IV? He was a medical doctor, wasn't he?"

"Yes. But why would he give himself an IV?"

"I don't know. Maybe he had a medical problem. Or maybe he had the flu and was loading up on fluids to keep the nausea down."

"I doubt it," Carl said, shaking his head. "The equipment belongs to your friend Norman Meade."

"How do you know that?" Gates asked, nonplussed. "Almost anyone can get an IV stand."

"Remember the video I told you about? Well, the things we found here are identical to the ones Meade used when he killed . . . helped Darlene Crews die."

"Maybe that's just coincidence."

"Possible, but not likely. We asked Meade where he kept his equipment. He told us that he had stored it in the trunk of his car. We checked. His trunk was empty."

There was silence.

"You know," Carl said firmly, "you're probably defending a killer here."

"I'm not defending him, Carl, I'm just asking questions."

"Well, ask all the questions you want, but Norman Meade killed Ed Warren as sure as I'm standing here in this room."

Gates didn't respond. Instead, she walked over to the small closet that was opposite the bathroom. "There are no clothes here."

"They've been removed and stored down at the station. The next of kin will want them."

"Does he have next of kin?"

"We're checking on that. We should know soon. I can tell you that he traveled light. Just a couple of shirts and an extra pair of pants."

Turning, Gates walked over to the bathroom. It, like the room, had seen better days. Glancing around, she saw the same black smudges on the walls, toilet, and freestanding sink. There were no personal items. Those too must have been taken along with the clothes.

"Satisfied?" Carl asked.

"No," Gates replied. "There's something wrong."

"Like what?"

"I don't know. At the moment it's just a feeling."

"I didn't know you were a psychic, Doc."

Gates cut him a harsh look. "That stuff is nonsense. I just feel like something is being overlooked."

"Come on, Gates. We're all professionals. Those homicide detectives from down the hill are some of the best. They know what they're doing, and so do I."

"Was he restrained?"

"Who? Warren?"

"Yes, Warren. Was he bound? Gagged? Handcuffed? Signs of a struggle?"

"No. But I don't see what that has to do with anything."

Instead of speaking, Gates turned and faced Carl.

"Oh," Carl said. "I see what you're getting at."

"Would you let an attacker hook an IV up to you?"

"If he had a gun, I might."

Gates shook her head. "You can't put in an IV with one hand, Carl. It's definitely a two-hand operation. I know, I've done hundreds of them. And we've both seen that Warren has the ability to become physical, even violent. I've got the bruise to prove it."

"Well, maybe there was another person involved, and that person held the gun."

"In that case, you have another killer on the loose, don't you?"

Carl frowned, "Okay, so what's the answer?"

"I have no idea, Carl. Absolutely no idea." Gates exited the bathroom. "I think we need to look at that video of Darlene."

Lea Ballew held the flame from her Bic lighter to the end of the cigarette, inhaled deeply, and then blew a long stream of blue smoke into the cramped confines of the van.

"I hate it when you do that," Jeff Penna said with disgust as he waved his hand in the air. "At least crack a window or something, will ya'?"

"Stop being a baby," Lea snapped as she rolled down the passenger-side window.

"Secondhand smoke is a killer too. You

should know, you just did a report on it last week."

"That was last week, this is now." She ran her hand through her long, dark-brown hair, then shook her head. Her hair fell unerringly in place, lightly touching her shoulders. "And take it easy on the corners, I'm getting carsick."

"Well, that cigarette ought to fix you right up," Jeff said sarcastically. "I know it's making me feel better."

"Just drive the van, will you? There's a drop-off on my side of the road that looks like it descends a couple of thousand feet."

"What did you expect from a mountain road?"

"I shouldn't even be on this road. I should be an anchor by now."

Jeff groaned. "Oh, not this again. You're a great reporter, why would you want to be stuck behind a desk? Look at the scenery. There's nothing like this in Los Angeles."

"Why? I'll give you two reasons why: money and recognition. That's why." She inhaled deeply again. The lit end of the cigarette glowed bright red. She held the smoke in her lungs for a moment before allowing it to escape through her nostrils.

"There's more to life than that, Lea. A whole lot more."

Lea stared at her driver. Jeff Penna was the best news cameraman in the business; sharp, focused, and possessing an eye for gripping video. He was solidly built, worked out regularly, ate only health food, and kept himself immaculately groomed. His dark hair and Hispanic olive skin made him a prize catch for any woman, but he was happily married with two children. He, at least to Lea, was naïve and possessed of a debilitating optimism about life.

"Television is my life, Jeff. There's nothing more."

"You're not serious, are you?"

"I'm not in the mood to talk about me, or you, for that matter, so let's just concentrate on the story at hand. How long before we arrive in Ridgeline?"

"We're about halfway up the mountain now," Jeff said, thinking. "I put us there in twenty minutes."

"Okay," Lea said. "First things first. We'll set up in front of the motel for the first part of the report. Maybe we can get a spokesperson from the police department there. We'll do a thirty-second opener, then we'll do voice-over for the other footage. After that, I'll close with fifteen seconds on camera."

"Sounds good."

"Then we'll find a place to stay so we don't

have to drive the two-and-a-half hours back to LA. Besides, we might be able to do another story tomorrow."

"It's a good thing you have an admirer in the coroner's office. This was a good tip. I doubt any of the other media know about it."

"I hope not. But even if they don't, they will after tonight's broadcast, and then Ridgeline will be swarming with reporters."

"But we will have broadcast the story first."

"Exactly." Lea took another drag on the cigarette. She hated the things, but she was addicted like so many others, and when she tried to quit she became unbearable to work with. Maybe later. Maybe after she had made her mark in the business, then she would feel confident enough to quit.

"I can't believe it: Dr. Death in jail for killing a rival doctor. Now that's news."

"Believe it Jeffy-boy. It's news all right and it's our news."

Chapter Six

Saturday, November 1
6:10 P.M.

The muscles in Gates' neck tightened like wet leather and her stomach churned as it slowly filled itself with acid. She felt warm, on her way to hot. Her breathing was shallow.

Before her was a nineteen-inch RCA color television that faithfully displayed the images being fed it by an aging Sony video player. The images were sharp and clear; the voices crisp. Gates wished it weren't so.

Gates McClure was not a squeamish woman, having developed a strong constitution during the many hours of dissecting cadavers in Gross Anatomy class. During the following years of her training and practice as a physician, she had seen just about everything. So it wasn't the images themselves that made her uncomfortable, it was what the pictures represented.

Norman Meade was standing over an elderly woman whose body was atrophied and corpse-like. The only thing resembling life in the woman were her eyes, which darted back and forth from Meade to a scruffy elderly man who stood by her bed holding a cardboard sign with letters of the alphabet printed on it.

Gates had listened carefully as Meade had asked question after question of the woman. At the end of each question Darlene would point at the sign and spell out her simple one-word answers.

"Darlene," Meade had asked in gentle, soothing tones, "do you know who I am?"

Darlene nodded and spelled the word "yes."

"Did I come here uninvited?" Meade asked.

"N-O."

"Did you invite me here?"

"Y-E-S."

"Now that I am here, do you want me to go away?"

"N-O."

"What do you want me to do for you, Darlene?" The question was asked softly, but the words were clearly recorded on the videotape.

Slowly, and with a painstakingly heroic effort, Darlene began to spell out a sentence: "I-W-A-N-T-TO-D-I-E."

Meade repeated the sentence aloud, giving voice to a woman incapable of speaking. "You want to die?"

"Y-E-S."

"And you want me to help you die, is that right?"

"Y-E-S."

"Do you want to die because of your disease?"

"Y-E-S."

Meade nodded. His shoulders were slumped, his head bowed, and he rocked almost imperceptibly from side to side. Gates recognized the body language of sadness and depression.

"Darlene, do you understand that I cannot end your life, but that I can make it possible for you to do so?"

"Y-E-S."

"Do you understand that you will be the one who actually ends your life? That you will be committing suicide?"

"Y-E-S."

Meade turned his attention to the elderly man holding the sign.

"Mr. Crews, you are Darlene's husband?"

"Yes, I am. For fifty-three wonderful years." Tears were streaming down the old man's face.

"Mr. Crews, does Darlene now, or has she

ever had psychological problems?"

"No, none."

"Has she ever been treated for depression, schizophrenia, or any other mental or emotional problems?"

"Never."

"Do you think that she is depressed now?"

"I know she wants to die."

"But is she depressed? Enough to be suicidal?"

"Not that I can tell."

Meade nodded. "Mr. Crews, do you feel that Darlene is making this request on her own and without any pressure from friends or family?"

"It was her idea. I didn't like it at first, but she is suffering so much."

"This is a hard question, I know, but do you feel that Darlene should be allowed to end her own life?"

Eugene Crews nodded his head and then wiped away the tears on his face with the back of his hand. "It's what she wants."

Meade returned his attention to the frail Darlene. "Darlene, is it true that you want to end your own life, and that this choice is your own?"

"Y-E-S."

"Are you ready to begin?" Meade asked gently.

"Y-E-S."

Situated near the bed was a chrome IV stand from which hung a single plastic IV bag bulging with clear fluid. Meade pulled the stand closer to the bed.

"Darlene, I'm going to give you an IV. It's just simple saline solution — salt water, and it won't hurt you."

Meade bent over a small black doctor's bag and extracted a small item from it. Gates immediately recognized it as an IV needle still encased in its protective plastic bag. He set the unopened package on the edge of the bed. Once again he reached into the black bag and removed a cotton ball and a small bottle. Opening the bottle, he removed the lid, placed the cotton ball over the mouth of the bottle, and then tipped it. A second later he replaced the lid and returned the bottle.

Alcohol. Gates thought it ironic that he should be concerned about infection. It was hard to deny one's training.

Meade then rubbed the saturated cotton ball on Darlene's arm, near the crook of her elbow. Picking up the IV needle, he bent over her and palpated the skin gently.

Looking for a vein, Gates reasoned. *Not an easy task in an arm that atrophied.*

"This is the worst part, Darlene, I promise. You may feel a little stick." Meade had expertly positioned the camera so that Gates could see the needle pierce the skin. Darlene made no noise and committed no movement. Apparently, having a large-bore needle pierce her skin was a small matter when compared to the suffering she had endured.

The simple operation went off without a hitch. The IV was in place and Meade had taken a moment to turn the small plastic stopcock to the setting that would allow a consistent flow of fluid into the electronic IV pump mounted to the stand.

As Meade was punching in numbers on the small numeric keypad that was on the front of the pump Gates noticed another device mounted to the stand — a device she didn't recognize. It was a black plastic box about a foot long and six inches wide.

"Now, Darlene, here's the tricky part," Meade said as he took hold of the black plastic box. "This is a trigger of sorts, but not like the trigger of a gun. This trigger requires that you enter five numbers that I will give you in a moment. Darlene, for this to work you must enter those five numbers in just the right order, and you must do it all by yourself. Do you understand?"

Darlene began pointing at the sign. "Y-E-S."

"Now there is something else I want you to know," Meade continued slowly. "Do you see this big red button here?"

Darlene nodded slightly.

"I'm sorry, Darlene, but you need to spell it out for me."

"Y-E-S."

"Okay. Thank you. This big red button is the stop button. If you push that button at any time, then everything will stop." Meade turned slightly and turned the trigger toward the camera. Gates could see the red button, which was larger than the other ten buttons on the keypad. It was clear to Gates that Meade was making sure everything was being recorded.

"If you press the five numbers that I give you, then some medicine will be added to your IV line. Do you see how the IV line passes right through this box that I'm holding?"

"Y-E-S."

"Well, inside this black box is a mixture of medicines, valium and morphine. They will make you very sleepy. After you sleep, the medicine will continue to work. You will die in your sleep. It is painless. You won't even know it's happening. Do you understand everything I've just said?"

"Y-E-S-D-O-C-T-O-R."

Gates was moved by Darlene's extra effort to spell out doctor. It was clear that she was growing weary. Meade had noticed this too.

"I know you're tired, Darlene. Would you like to rest?"

"N-O. N-O-W."

"Just one last thing, Darlene," Meade offered quietly. "I know this seems awfully complex, but it's important for everyone to know that you have enough mental capacity to make this kind of decision and to act on your own behalf. Are you ready?"

"Y-E-S." Gates watched as Darlene moved her head slightly to better see her husband who was still holding the spelling sign. "I-L-O-V-E-Y-O-U-S-O-M-U-C-H-T-H-A-N-K-Y-O-U."

Eugene Crews' face was awash in tears. The sign he held shook as he struggled to contain uncontainable emotion. "I love you too," he said, his voice choked and broken. "I'll see you soon."

"S-O-O-N."

She turned her attention back to Meade. Gates could see a tear run down his cheek too. "O-K."

Meade nodded and then held the trigger box so that Darlene could reach the buttons. "Please listen carefully, Darlene: 5-2-1-0-6."

There was no hesitation in Darlene's action. She raised her enfeebled hand and began touching buttons. A soft beep was emitted as each electronic key was pressed.

She entered the numbers flawlessly and then let her arm drop to the bed. She would never again spell out a word.

Slowly she turned to face her husband. Gates felt tears well up in her own eyes as Darlene Crews made a valiant effort to do what everyone else did without thought. She smiled.

Meade reattached the trigger box to the IV stand. Then leaned over Darlene and kissed her forehead. He then took a step back. The video camera was fixed on Darlene.

Gates watched as Darlene slowly closed her eyes, opened them, blinked, then closed them one last time. Her husband had set the sign down behind the bed and gently held one of Darlene's hands with one of his own, and soothingly stroked her thin gray hair.

No one spoke.

The tape continued to play, unveiling the saddest scene that Gates had ever witnessed. The tape faithfully, accurately, and emotionlessly recounted the events of hours before. She was deluged with sorrow so deep that she thought she would drown in the dark waves of grief. She felt swelling anger too, but was uncertain how to direct it.

As she watched, Meade stepped forward and touched Darlene on the neck feeling for a pulse in the carotid. As if he doubted his own fingers, Meade moved his fingers from her neck to her wrist.

"It's over," Meade said with finality. Quickly he brushed a tear away.

Eugene Crews, now a widower, could contain his emotions no longer. The dam that held back the fear, the anxiety, the hopelessness, could not retain the sorrow. He dropped to his knees, sobbing loudly, uncontrollably.

Meade walked around the bed, lifted Eugene Crews to his feet and then took him in his arms. He offered no words. Gates knew that most people would encourage a cessation of the weeping saying, "It's all right. Everything is going to be fine." But it wasn't all right, and things weren't going to be fine. Eugene had just watched his wife die and there was no bringing her back. Nothing would ever be the same again.

"Had enough?" Carl asked gently.

"More than enough," Gates replied softly. "Thanks for letting me see the tape."

"I'm not sure I did you any favors, Doc. That's a pretty hard thing to watch."

"I'm okay," Gates said, feeling like she had just lied. She didn't feel okay at all. "Does the tape go on much longer?"

"Quite awhile actually," Carl answered. "He let it run until just before Officer Wells showed up. Wells watched the video at the house." Gates sat still as her mind replayed the images she had just seen. She had witnessed many surgeries and difficult treatments as a doctor, but never had she seen someone end her own life. The thought pummeled her emotions and insulted her ethics. "Come on, Gates, you need to go home. I'll take you. Maybe a good night's sleep would help."

Gates wondered if she would sleep at all that night.

Carl had just pulled off the main road and was about to wind his way through the serpentine streets to Gates' home when the radio in his patrol car crackled to life: "P-10 are you available for 415 domestic on Spruce Street?" It was Terri Stringman the senior dispatcher.

Unlike big city police departments which prided themselves on tight radio protocol and formality, the small Ridgeline police force, which was comprised of ten officers and three civilian office workers, operated under much more relaxed conditions.

"415?" Gates asked. She was seated in the front seat of the patrol car.

"Domestic disturbance," Carl answered as he picked up the radio's microphone. "My 10-20 is Highway 22 and Butte Way. I have

113

a passenger in route to Chumash Street. Where's Jacob?"

"He's made a traffic stop about five miles out of town."

"Okay, I'll take the 415."

"Proceed to 2040 Spruce Street. Neighbors called and said there's a lot of shouting. They think the owner may be in trouble."

Carl furrowed his brow. "2040 Spruce? Isn't that where the Crews' live?"

"10-4, P10."

"Okay, I'm on my way. As soon as Jacob is free have him back me up."

"10-4."

"There's a domestic disturbance at the Crews' house?" Gates asked. "What's going on?"

"That's what I intend to find out as soon as I drop you off at your place."

"Don't be silly. You can do that later," Gates said firmly.

"No can do, Doc. This is official police business. It might not be safe."

"Don't be melodramatic. I'm going with you."

"You're a civilian, Gates. I can't take you on a call," Carl said firmly.

"Don't you allow citizens to go on a ride-along so they can see their police depart-ment at work? That's one of your public relations programs, isn't it?"

"Yes, but . . ."

"And if I was on one of those ride-along programs right now wouldn't you still take the call?"

"Yes, unless the call is unusually dangerous, like a shooting or something."

"Which this isn't. Carl, just pretend I'm one of those ride-along people."

"But they sign releases of liability and . . ."

"I'll sign a release later, Carl," Gates responded. "If this were someone other than Eugene Crews, I wouldn't argue with you, but this could be important. Stop wasting time and let's go."

"Do you talk to your patients this way, Doc?"

"When they're as stubborn as you, yes."

Carl laughed. "You're a handful, Gates, a real handful."

Even with the windows rolled up to keep the cool evening air out, Gates could hear the shouting. Carl had wasted no time in driving to the Crews' house on Spruce Street. He made the ten-minute drive in half the time.

Finding the home proved no problem for two reasons. First, Carl was already familiar with the address because of Darlene Crews' suicide. Second, a large and very loud woman was standing on the front porch screaming viciously at an elderly man cowering, slump-shouldered next to the wood porch rail.

"How do you deal with this kind of stuff?" Gates asked, taken back by the uncomfortable scene before her.

"Carefully and forcefully," Carl answered as he parked the patrol car next to the curb. "More cops get injured and even killed answering calls like this one than anything else."

"Be careful," Gates said.

"I plan to. You stay out of the way." Carl grabbed the microphone of his radio. "P10, show me 10-8 at 2040 Spruce."

"P10, 10-8 at 2040 Spruce," the radio voice repeated.

Carl pulled his large body out of the car and slowly walked toward the porch. Gates noticed that Carl moved cautiously, the thumbs of his hands tucked under his Sam Brown belt, placing them just inches from the gun that was on his right hip and the nightstick that hung on his left. This gave the impression that he was casually strolling toward the two, but Gates could see that he was ready for action.

Gates opened the car door. The woman, whom Gates judged to her be in her mid-forties, was still screaming, spewing forth an avalanche of wicked emotions and hot words.

The woman was rotund with oily blond hair that was pulled back into a tight bun on the back of her head. Even from the street, Gates could tell that the woman was perspiring from the physical exertion of lambasting old man Crews.

Crews, for his part, said nothing, did nothing. He looked pained, frightened, and sick all at the same time. He offered no words of defense. Instead, he stood stone-still, his shoulders slouched in resignation, his head bowed in defeat.

"You stupid old man," the woman spat loudly. "You stupid, selfish, old man. Did you think I wouldn't find out? Did you think that I would never know?" Droplets of spit were ejected from her mouth as she screamed in her high nasal voice.

"Excuse me," Carl said firmly as he reached the stairs that led up to the porch.

"You worthless trash," the woman continued. "You don't deserve to live. You don't deserve to exist."

Suddenly, the woman raised her right hand above her head and brought it crashing down on Eugene Crews' cheek. The open-face slap had the woman's full and substantial weight behind it. Crews staggered back against the rail; blood poured from his mouth.

"I ought to kill you myself," she spewed.

Again she raised her hand, but Carl was already on the move. Taking the steps in a single bound, he launched himself onto the porch, seizing the woman's upraised hand. In a fluid motion, Carl spun her around, yanked her arm down and behind her back in a hammer lock.

"That's enough," Carl commanded as he pushed her against the exterior wall and leaned his own weight against her, pinning her body to the wall. Carl reached for his handcuffs with his free hand.

"This doesn't concern you, pig," the woman shouted. "This is none of your business."

"It is now, lady," Carl said as he snapped one of the cuffs on her wrist.

"No it's not," she screamed. With her free hand she pushed with Amazonian strength against the wall. Gates watched as the motion caught Carl off guard. He took a step back. The woman started to turn, but she never completed the act. Carl still had a hand on the cuffs and he quickly twisted the cuff on her arm. The cold, hard metal dug into her flesh and pressed against the distal ends of her forearm. The pain proved too much for her and she dropped to her knees. Still twisting the cuff, Carl forced the woman to the deck, face down.

"You're breaking my arm," she shouted.

Without a word, Carl put a knee in her back, grabbed her free arm and pulled it behind her, then he attached the other cuff.

"I'll sue," she shrieked, swearing vehemently. "I'll have your badge for this."

"Lady," Carl replied with forced calmness. "If the likes of you can have my badge, then I don't want it. As it stands now, I still have my badge, and that lets me put you in custody. Now I'm going to offer you a word of advice . . . shut up."

Gates charged up the stairs and to the side of Eugene. He had dropped to his knees. His mouth was bleeding profusely, his skin was pale and clammy, and his breathing labored.

"I don't like the looks of this," Gates said as she placed two fingers to Eugene's neck.

"Is he all right?" Carl asked.

"I can't breathe," Eugene said. "It feels like there's an elephant on my chest."

"Serves you right," the woman spat.

"Shut up," Carl shot back.

"Carl, I think you need to get her out of here, and I think you had better call an ambulance."

Without a wasted word or motion, Carl had the woman on her feet and marching to the patrol car. From her position on the porch, Gates could see Carl holding the microphone of his portable to his mouth; he was calling for help.

"I'm going to take care of you," Gates said to Eugene. He nodded in response. Slowly she helped him from a kneeling position to a seated one, letting him lean back against the rail.

He was pale, his skin was moist, and his breathing labored. Gates was certain that the man was having a heart attack.

"Are you on any medications?" Gates asked.

"No," Eugene whispered breathlessly.

"Have you ever had trouble with your heart?"

He nodded slightly. "I've been having some pain . . . ever since my Darlene . . . I thought it was stress. Am I having a heart attack? Am I dying?" Pain was etched deeply into his face.

"Try to relax. Nobody dies on my shift," Gates said. "It's bad for business." Eugene smiled. "The ambulance will be here momentarily. Then we can get you taken care of."

"Sorry to be a bother." Eugene winced in pain. "I don't care if I die, but my daughter, I don't want her punished."

"Your daughter?" Gates said. Then the reality struck. "The woman who hit you, she's your daughter?"

Eugene nodded. "I haven't seen her in

years. No calls. No letters. She just showed up and took to bellowin' like some crazy person."

Gates turned to see Carl walking up the steps. He knelt beside the stricken man. "The ambulance is on its way," he said. "How's he doing?"

Gates shrugged. "I wish I had a med bag here. As it is, I can't do anything but wait."

"That's his daughter in the car," Carl said.

"I know. Mr. Crews just told me." Gates looked at Carl's face, which was enough to know how he felt about a daughter who would attack her own father so viciously.

"May I ask a few questions?" Carl began.

"No," Gates answered. "Mr. Crews is going to rest. You can ask your questions later."

"Gates, please don't interfere with my work," Carl stated flatly.

"*My* work takes precedence right now, Carl," she responded firmly. "If you want to be helpful, then go into the house and see if you can find some aspirin."

"Aspirin?"

"It'll help, trust me."

Carl did as he was instructed and returned a minute later with a clear plastic bottle. Gates took the bottle, quickly popped the top and removed one pill.

"Here," Gates said to Crews, "chew this."

She placed the small white capsule in his mouth. He grimaced at its bitter taste. Simple aspirin had more valuable medicinal powers than the easing of pain, especially with a heart attack.

Crews began to shake his head. "I don't want to press no charges," he said to Carl. "It's my fault."

"That's not what I saw, Mr. Crews," Carl said softly. "She gave you a nasty slap, and look at the trouble it's caused."

Again, Crews shook his head slowly. Bits of chewed aspirin were stuck to his lips and tongue. "Like I told the Doc, I been having pain since my Darlene died."

"Well your daughter hasn't helped," Carl stated.

"Don't matter none. I don't want to press no charges."

"But . . ."

"Let it go," Gates said. "This isn't the time for a debate."

The undulating scream of a siren sailed through the trees and echoed off the mountain. The sound made Crews tense. Gates was becoming more concerned as she watched Crews' labored breathing and frequent seizures of pain. He needed help and needed it immediately.

"Promise me," Crews said breathlessly as if

he had just ran up a long and steep staircase. "Promise you won't throw her in jail."

Carl hesitated. "Mr. Crews . . ."

"Promise me!"

Gates flashed Carl an unmistakable look that demanded that he agree with the ailing man.

"Okay, Mr. Crews, okay," Carl answered reluctantly.

Crews nodded easily and relaxed some.

The ambulance cut its siren as it turned onto Spruce Street, its flashing red lights splattering on trees and houses. Neighbors, alarmed by the presence of the police and the ambulance, oozed out of their houses to watch. This was the second time the police had been called to the Crews' small home in two days.

It had taken less than twenty minutes for Gates and the paramedics to determine that Eugene Crews was fit enough to be transported down the hill to the hospital. The process moved easily and quickly. A portable EKG unit spewed out a ribbon of paper with a jagged line inked on its surface that reflected Crews' heart function. Neither Gates nor the paramedics could see any irregularities. That was the good news. The bad news was that Crews was still having trouble breathing and was in considerable pain.

"So what do you think the problem is?" Carl asked as he and Gates watched the ambulance pull away from the house. They were standing at the foot of the porch stairs.

"Hard to tell without a full exam and tests," Gates answered, assuming a clinical tone. She hated cases like these. There was too little information. "It's possible that he's having a heart attack. I mean the symptoms were all there, but the EKG was clean. He may be having an anxiety attack. That would make sense, considering all he's been through. The ER doctors will be able to tell."

"But it could still be a heart attack?"

"Possibly." Gates turned to face Carl. "What now? Are you going to let his daughter go?"

"I have to, if he's not going to press charges," Carl clenched his jaw. "I hate to cut her loose. I suppose I could arrest her for disturbing the peace, interfering with a police officer in the course of his duty, maybe even resisting arrest."

"But you promised Crews that you'd let her go. Not an easy decision."

The conversation was interrupted by the arrival of Jacob Weissman who had pulled his patrol car in front of Carl's. "I missed everything?" Jacob asked as he approached the two. He was a tall, lanky man, middle-aged with bright eyes and a light step.

"Yeah, Jacob, it's all over," Carl answered.

"Sorry I couldn't take the call, Chief, but I had made a traffic stop and the driver, some seventeen-year-old kid, was acting real jumpy. I got his permission to search the car. That's what I was doing when the call came in."

"Find anything?" Carl asked.

"Yeah. That's him in the back." Jacob nodded toward his car. "He had a Baggie of cocaine. Can you believe it? Seventeen and carrying coke. It's crazy. It looks like I'll be taking him down the hill to Juvenile Hall. Who you got in the backseat?"

"Crews' daughter," Carl said, "but I'm cutting her loose. Hang around a minute in case I need your help. She's got an attitude."

"Sure."

Carl and Jacob walked to the patrol car, Gates followed close behind. Carl opened the back door to the car.

"It's about time," the woman spat. "This backseat is not very comfortable, you know."

"Shut up," Carl snapped.

"You can't talk to me like that," the woman protested.

"Get out of the car," Carl said harshly. The woman complied. Exiting the vehicle was made difficult by her size and the fact that her hands were cuffed behind her. Neither Carl nor Jacob offered to help. Wiggling and grunting the woman labored to extract herself. A moment later she stood outside the patrol car. Carl slammed the door.

"The least you could do was help me . . ."

"Here's how this is going to work," Carl said authoritatively. "I'm in a real bad mood and it's your fault. So I'm going to talk and you're going to listen. I will ask questions and you will answer them. If you don't, I'm going to put you back in the car and then you can spend the rest of the weekend in my jail. Is that clear?"

"I heard you," was all the woman said.

Gates studied the woman. She had a slovenly appearance, with oily, unclean hair. The loose-fitting green dress she wore was threadbare and stained. Her mouth seemed small on her round, rough face and was turned down in a perpetual frown. Her eyes held a fierceness.

"I got my rights. You can't . . ."

Carl reached over and opened the back door to his patrol car again.

"Okay, okay," the woman protested. "No need to be so sensitive."

"Your father insisted that I not arrest you." Carl was staring the woman squarely in the eye. Gates felt a strong sense of gratitude that

126

she was on Carl's side and not in the woman's place. "For his sake, I promised to release you, but I could be persuaded otherwise real quick. Do you understand?"

Opening her small mouth the woman started to speak, but then changed her mind. Instead, she just nodded.

"Good. What's your name?"

"Martha. Martha Crews."

"Where do you live, Ms. Crews?"

"What business is that . . ." Carl cut her off with a raised finger. "I live outside Baker. Down in the desert."

"Do you have an address?"

She shook her head. "I live in a trailer on some people's property. There's no address. All I got is a post-office box." She gave the mailing address. At Carl's insistence she also described the location of her trailer. Carl wrote down the information in a small notebook that he had extracted from his shirt pocket.

"Why were you attacking your father?"

"Why?" She laughed harshly. "He killed my mother, that's why! He should be in jail."

"The matter is under investigation. When was the last time you saw your mother?"

"I don't know. Five, maybe six years. Who keeps track? Anyway, I haven't talked to them in a long time."

"Then how did you find out about your mother?"

She was slow to respond.

"Then how did you find out about your mother?" Carl repeated.

"I've got a friend in town and he lets me know what's going on. He should have told me, you know."

"How could he if he couldn't contact you?"

"I don't know, but the whole thing is wrong. It's just plain wrong."

Carl scratched his head. "Slapping your elderly father is wrong, lady. There's no way around that. Why he doesn't want to press charges is beyond me. I'm tempted to jail you on principle, but I made a promise."

"I guess my temper got the best of me."

"No doubt there. Turn around." Carl unlocked the cuffs. "Okay, this is how it breaks down, Ms. Crews. You're free to go, but I don't want to hear that you're causing any more trouble because I won't be talked out of arresting you again. Got that?"

"Yeah, I got it."

"Do you have any questions for me, Ms. Crews?" Carl asked.

"No. Why would I?"

"I just thought you might be interested in

knowing what hospital your father is being taken to, but I guess I was wrong." Turning to Gates, Carl said, "Come on, Doc, I'll take you home."

Chapter Seven

Saturday, November 1
8:00 P.M.

A heaviness had settled on Gates like the darkness had settled on the mountain, and with it came an aching, gnawing sadness that chewed at her insides. Gates had learned over the years to affect a hard, controlled exterior, but anyone who knew her well understood that she was an emotive, empathetic person. It was such empathy that had led her into the caring science of medicine. Only in medicine was she able to satisfy the enormous appetite of her intellectual curiosity and to appease the compelling need to help others. Generally, this was a satisfying arrangement, but at times it could be agonizing.

Standing over the stove, she mindlessly stirred a small pot of tomato soup and kept watch over a grilled-cheese sandwich heating in a pan. It was her ability to sense the pain of others that made her an exceptional doctor, but with such an ability came an emotional price tag. Viewing the videotape that so clearly portrayed the agonizing condition of a desperate woman, her love for her husband, and the emotional display of Norman Meade as he aided her to conclude her life had savagely ripped at Gates' sensitive soul.

The tape alone was sufficient cause for a mild funk, but the vitriolic display of emotion and violence she had witnessed at the home of the Eugene Crews was pushing Gates over the edge. It was during the silent drive to her house, Carl stewing in his own emotional juices, that she had decided that tonight she was in need of "the elixir" that she was now absentmindedly preparing.

It was her mother's cure for everything: grilled-cheese sandwich and tomato soup. There was something in the combination of the two elements that could almost miraculously ease any human angst. Her mother had fixed it when Gates would have a childhood fight with her friends, or when the boy Gates had so dearly hoped would ask her to the prom asked someone else instead. Red tomato soup made with a touch of milk, and yellow cheddar-cheese sandwiches, grilled in butter until the bread was just lightly scorched. The perfect blend of the two foods could bring peace to the Middle East, stop a labor dispute, and make democrats and republicans love each other. It was, indeed, miracle food.

Gates needed miracle food.

Her discomfort was punctuated by an eruption of confusion. *This whole thing should be so simple,* she kept repeating to herself. The evidence was there in the hotel room: the identical IV stand, the same brand IV pump, the peculiar "trigger" — everything. At least that's what Carl had said. Since the homicide detectives took the apparatus with them, Gates had not actually seen it apart from the video, but Carl wouldn't lie about such things.

It still didn't make sense. The ring of truth wasn't there. Something was wrong, out of place, but Gates couldn't put her finger on it. It felt like those times she had walked into her office and could instantly tell that someone had been there. Her receptionist or nurse had arrived early and moved something — a journal or Gates' coffee cup — and it was enough for her to know that something had changed; that something was different.

Gates felt the same way now. Why would Norman Meade kill Ed Warren? Sure Warren haunted Meade, following him from place to place to make his life miserable, but was that sufficient reason for murder?

Turning the stove off, Gates placed the

sandwich on an old chipped Melmac plate and poured the soup into a large mug. Making her way into the living room she sat on the sofa and gazed out the front window into the clear night. Needle-laden pine branches danced serenely to the gentle minuet of the breeze. The soup was hot and rich, and diaphanous steam hovered hauntingly above the cup. The sandwich oozed yellow cheddar cheese that filled the air with its simple appetizing aroma.

Slowly Gates raised the sandwich to her mouth and bit off a small morsel. Her motions were slow, but her mind raced with thoughts. An outside observer would have thought the pretty woman on the sofa was in a trance. Her eyes were fixed on an unidentifiable point beyond the window. She didn't blink or shift in her seat. Instead her mind did all the work, allowing the body to breathe and eat, but little more.

At first Gates struggled to think things through, to find a reason, a clue as to what she should believe about the enigmatic Norman Meade. He maintained his innocence, but there was sufficient reason to doubt his claim. But could Norman Meade actually murder someone?

Isn't that what he does these days? The cynical part of her personality asked.

Technically, no, the trusting faction of her mind replied. *He helps others commit suicide to end their suffering.*

An artificial distinction, Reason argued. *Killing is killing regardless of the motive.*

Not so, Trust rebutted, *motivation matters. Norman kills no one, they kill themselves.*

It's a short step from one to the other.

Norman is dedicated to life. To saving life. I should know that better than anyone.

The inner debate stopped abruptly. Logic, reason, intellect were being elbowed aside by emotion — hot, furious emotion that turned her stomach, repressed her breathing, clinched her muscles, and made her heart race.

Darkness.

Alone.

Soft noise.

Pause.

Loud noise.

Hands.

Hot breath. Pungent breath.

Pain.

Gates slammed her eyes shut in a vain attempt to seal out what was already in her mind. Sights could be blocked out, screened from view, but memories needed no entrance and no invitation. They could come and go as they pleased. This one came unsolicited, unbidden. It was a fierce memory that had not plagued Gates for several years. Now it had returned with acrimonious intensity, banging, clawing, scratching at the door of her mind. She thought she had exorcised the demon thought, purged the poison memory from her recollection, but she had not. Like a legendary serpent hidden and nearly forgotten at the dark bottom of some Scottish loch, the retrospection surfaced to wave its ugly head in the full and pale moonlight.

Hands, hard and rough.

Breath, stale and putrid.

Words, hushed and harsh; violent and offensive.

Pain, piercing, throbbing.

Helpless, hopeless, lost.

A small cry escaped Gates' lips and she lurched. Her thighs were burning, stinging. Opening her eyes she saw her lap covered in thick red fluid. It pooled and oozed and flowed in tiny red streams down her legs and onto the sofa and carpet. *Blood? Why so much?* Hot. Stinging pain. *Not blood,* Gates reasoned, *tomato soup.* Despite the burning trauma to her skin, Gates felt a palpable sense of relief.

"I don't believe this," she said aloud, looking at the blue jeans and white T-shirt she had put on before leaving for the Tree Top Café this morning. "This stuff will never come out."

Taking the one napkin she had brought into the living room she began to blot up the spilled soup. Each time she touched her legs a stinging sensation raced along the skin. It took only a moment for her to realize that the one napkin was insufficient for the job. Not wanting to spread the mess any further, she quickly undressed, removing her jeans first, then her T-shirt and wadding them up into a ball. Stepping over the small pool of soup at her feet, Gates quickly made her way to the tiny laundry room attached to the back of the house. Running cold water in the washing machine, she dropped in the stained clothes. Returning to the kitchen, she snatched up a roll of paper towels and a spray bottle of carpet spot remover.

Back in the living room, Gates, dressed only in bra and panties, knelt down next to where she had been sitting and began to clean. As she scrubbed, she fumed. "That was a stupid thing to do," she scolded herself. "There was no reason for me to react like that." Her subconscious knew better.

She continued to scrub the carpet and the sofa wishing that she could scrub her stained memory as easily, but there was no stain remover for a spotted and soiled soul. As each moment passed the skin on her now bare legs began to hurt more. She tried to ignore the pain, but it was persistent and would not be dismissed so easily.

Surrendering to the truth that the carpet was going to need professional help, Gates stood and walked into the bathroom. Turning on the ceiling lights as well as the vanity bulbs that ran above her mirror, Gates studied her burned thighs. The skin had been turned from healthy pink to an angry red by the assault of the hot soup. Bending over, Gates peered the best she could at the injury. There were no blisters. A substantial first degree burn, but just a first degree burn and nothing more. The skin would be sensitive for a few days and she would be required to wear material softer than denim, but she would be fine.

"I'll bet the shower will feel good tomorrow morning," she said sarcastically to her mirror image. She stared at the reflection of the woman in the mirror: brown hair slightly disheveled, eyes reddened by pain and frustration, posture slightly stooped from the day's emotional drain. The image reinforced the unpleasant truth: she looked as bad as she felt.

Silently she wished that Norman Meade had never shown up in Ridgeline.

Gates lay on top of the blue-and-white

striped comforter that covered her bed. She would have preferred to snuggle underneath the covers, but her legs protested any contact, even that of cool, soft sheets. Even the clean, damp, white towels that were resting on the burns brought protestations from her sensitive nerves. Yet she knew the moisture would ease the pain and diminish the feeling of heat trapped in the flesh. Next to her lay a tube of antibiotic ointment that she planned to slather on before going to sleep. By morning, she told herself, most of the pain would be gone.

But it wasn't gone now, and while she was far from being in agony, she was still too uncomfortable to fall asleep. To pass the time she watched news programs on the small color television that was situated on her dresser. Gates was not much of a TV person, but she did enjoy educational programs and the occasional witty sitcom.

Time crept by slowly, due in part to her pain and frustration over the day's events. It was 11:00 when she picked up the remote control and changed channels to KGLA channel six out of Los Angeles. Los Angeles was another world, a planet size different from the community of Ridgeline. Where the mountain community was peaceful and serene — most of the time — LA was always filled with human misery. Gates wasn't really interested in drive-by shootings, holdups and big-city politics, but there was nothing else on to hold her interest. She had decided to see what news stories were in the offering and if none of them proved interesting, or if they promised to be too depressing, then she would turn off the set and read.

The lead story caught her eye. No sooner had the flying animation of the station's logo disappeared than the deeply tanned news anchor named Ian Tanner said, "Good evening. Tonight we begin with an exclusive, breaking story from the small mountain town of Ridgeline. Lea Ballew has the story live on location. Lea . . ."

Gates grabbed the remote and pressed the button that would raise the volume.

"Thank you, Ian. I'm standing just outside the small police station here in the beautiful community of Ridgeline in the San Bernardino Mountains. Here among the towering pines death came calling yesterday — twice. Death is no stranger to any of us, but this time death has a name: Dr. Norman Meade. Dr. Meade is also known as Dr. Death, the physician who has championed the right-to-die movement in recent years.

"Sources tell me that Dr. Meade aided in the medical suicide of a Mrs. Darlene Crews.

Crews had been suffering with ALS, also known as Lou Gehrig's disease. Sometime yesterday afternoon, with the help of Dr. Meade, Darlene Crews ended her life.

"But the story does not end there," the reporter went on. "For early this morning, long-time opponent and outspoken critic Dr. Ed Warren was found murdered in his hotel room. Dr. Meade — Dr. Death — has been arrested for the crime."

There was a brief pause before the image of Lea Ballew was replaced by a previously taped report that showed the front of the Crews' home. The scene was dark enough that the cameraman had turned on a bright flood light.

They must have arrived shortly after we left, Gates reasoned.

Lea's voice-over continued the story. "It was here in this small house that Darlene Crews chose to end her life of torment. Such events are no longer rare in our society and Dr. Norman Meade is certainly no stranger to physician-assisted suicide. But what makes this story unique is what happened here." The video image changed from the Crews' house to the Cliffside Motel. The yellow plastic ribbon was still visible and flapping gently in the night breeze. "Shortly after seven this morning, police were called to this room at the quaint Cliffside Motel where they discovered the lifeless body of Dr. Ed Warren. Police say that Dr. Warren confronted Meade at a Halloween party, which Meade was attending shortly after Darlene Crews' death."

Gates, already irritable by the day's events and her burned legs, became all the more peeved by Lea Ballew's unspoken message. Her choice of words was leading tens of thousands of viewers to picture Norman as breezing into town, snuffing out the life of an elderly lady, and then choosing to finish the night off by enjoying a casual party. Watching the video had convinced Gates that as reprehensible as Meade's work was, it was not done lightly or without cost to the man.

"Police are reluctant to reveal any more information," Ballew continued with feigned gravity, "but this reporter has learned that certain devices used by Dr. Meade were found in the motel room next to Warren's body."

The scene switched from video back to the live broadcast. "Dr. Meade is expected to remain in jail here in Ridgeline until he is arraigned on murder charges. Back to you, Ian."

Immediately the image of the newsroom appeared on the screen with Ian Tanner gazing into the camera with a look of wonderment. "Amazing. Thank you, Lea. I'm sure you'll be keeping us posted as new information is revealed. Now on to other news. A new White House scandal has erupted . . ."

Switching off the television, Gates sighed audibly. "Swell," she said to the empty room. "Just what Ridgeline needs." Slowly she removed the damp towels from her legs and smeared a layer of ointment on her tender flesh. Then she switched off the light that was on the nightstand next to the bed. She lay atop the covers and stared into the blackness. The breeze outside had increased and she could hear its low moan as it rounded the corners of the house. It was as if the night had turned suddenly anxious. It was a feeling that Gates could understand.

Chapter Eight

Sunday, November 2
9:55 A.M.

"Gates," Anne called out as she walked to the car that Gates had just parked. Gates felt fortunate to find a space close to the front doors of the church. In deference to her still-tender legs, she didn't want to walk very far. When she awoke this morning, her thighs felt much better and their color had faded from lobster red to cotton-candy pink. When she showered they still protested, even though she washed them gingerly and in water far cooler than she would normally choose. Not wanting to wear pantyhose she chose an eggshell pantsuit and a jade green silk shell top. The linen pants were beginning to irritate the tortured skin.

"Good morning, Anne," Gates said as she slowly extracted herself from the car.

"What's wrong with you?" Anne asked, her face creased with worry.

"Nothing really," Gates replied with a smile. "I spilled a little soup on myself last night and burned my legs."

"Is it serious? I mean, shouldn't you be in a hospital or something?"

"No, it's not that bad. It's more like a sunburn." Gates shut the door to her gray late-model Honda Civic. "These pants are rubbing against the burn more than I thought they would. Not to worry, Anne, I'll live."

"You are not having a good weekend, dear," Anne said with concern. "First being knocked to the ground, and now these burns."

Gates had almost forgotten about the bruise on her hip. She was a walking disaster area. "I've had better days."

"Not to mention the fact that your friend is locked up in jail. Did you see that news report last night?"

"Yes, and can we get inside? The service is going to start soon."

"Oh, of course. I wonder if Pastor Paul is going to say anything about all this?"

"I hope not," Gates said as she led the way to the church.

The sanctuary of Mountain View Community Church was a simple wood and stucco building that had been built in the early '70s. The church itself was founded in the mid-'60s. Gates had been coming to the church since she was a child. She had attended

Sunday School here and had even taken her turn teaching the children's church. It was a place of peace, of comfort, of inspiration. It was a place she deeply loved and a place she deeply needed to be.

As a rule, the people were friendly, the services lively, and the congregation active. Today was typical of most Sunday mornings. Children scampered around the building, teenagers gathered in small groups, talking and giggling, senior citizens made their way into the building to take their places in their favorite seats. A few of the church's six deacons wandered around shaking hands and cracking jokes.

Inside, Pastor Paul Chapman was listening intently to an elderly woman with short gray hair. He nodded gravely from time to time, and then took her hand and gave it a comforting squeeze.

Gates worked her way through the small clumps of people who stood in the center aisle chatting aimlessly, and sat on the back pew. She always sat on the back pew, not because she didn't want to be noticed, but because she enjoyed the service more when she could see the whole congregation. Anne sat next to her.

"Where's John?" Gates asked.

"Oh, you know my husband, always talking

to someone about something," Anne replied. "Last I saw him he was looking at Fred's new truck."

Gates nodded. John was as gregarious as Anne.

"Good morning, Doctor," someone said cheerfully. Gates turned to see her pastor standing nearby. "How are you feeling after your little incident at the Halloween party?"

"Oh, fine, Pastor," Gates said. "No real damage."

"That's good to hear. And how are you doing, Madam Mayor?" Paul Chapman held out his hand, which Anne took.

"Just great, Pastor. Able to sit up and take nourishment — without spilling it."

Gates cut a quick and wicked look at her sister. Pastor Chapman looked confused.

"Inside joke, Pastor," Anne said. "Just teasing my sister."

Pastor Chapman nodded. "When I teased my sister, she always hit me."

"Now there's an idea," Gates said.

"Not here," Chapman retorted, "and not now. The service is about to start, and it's hard for me to maintain the congregation's attention when fists are flying." He smiled. "On a more serious note, how are you holding up? I mean with this Dr. Norman Meade thing and all?"

"I'm doing well, Pastor. There's nothing to worry about."

"That's good to hear," he said. "I can't tell you how many people have been asking me questions about this whole affair. Of course, I don't know anything more than the next guy." He paused. Gates was sure that he was hoping for some new revelation.

"There's not much more that I can tell you, Pastor. I hadn't seen Norman Meade for years. It was a total surprise when he walked into the party."

Chapman nodded. "I imagine it was. It's horrible when a murder occurs so nearby. It affects a lot of people."

Murder? Gates wondered if he was referring to Darlene Crews or Ed Warren. He said murder, not murders. Singular. Did that mean that he didn't view Darlene's suicide as a criminal act on the part of Norman? What would her pastor say about Darlene's situation and death? She started to ask when the piano music began.

"Uh, oh," Chapman said. "I think that's my cue."

"Excuse me, Pastor," a man said as he stepped to an empty place on the pew next to Anne. "I need to sit down before I get in trouble with my wife."

"Hello, John," Chapman said. John was tall

147

and thickly built, with short, dark hair that was quickly receding from his forehead. "I wouldn't want to be responsible for that." Quickly, Chapman turned and walked to the front of the church and took his place in a high-back, white enamel chair just to the right of the pulpit.

The service followed the same pattern of worship it had for the last five years. Paul Chapman had been pastor for a little over three years. He was a better than average preacher who made frequent use of humor in his sermons. Amiable, outgoing, intelligent, he had won over the two-hundred member congregation as had his wife, Sally.

Martin Ranking, the church youth and music leader, stood behind the pulpit and led the congregation in a blend of choruses and hymns. The congregation was responsive and sang enthusiastically. Gates enjoyed the music, although she possessed no musical talent of her own. Her voice, a pleasant alto, joined the others in songs of praise.

When Paul Chapman stood in the pulpit he commanded attention. His six-foot frame was trim, and his gray, pin-striped suit hung sharply, almost with precision. He was a dapper man, with sandy-blond hair that he kept trimmed close to the scalp. But the most endearing thing about the pastor of Mountain

View Community Church was his wisdom and genuine concern. Anne had said several times that Chapman's preaching was secondary to his ability to win people with his humor and insights. "If I had his people skills, I would be in the state senate," Anne had offered more than once.

But he was a good preacher who could capture almost anyone's attention. His sermons were practical and to the point. Many times Gates, Anne, and John had joined her parents for a Sunday lunch only to carry on a discussion of that morning's message.

Gates felt good to be in church. There was a release, a comfort that could be found no place else. Already the tension that had settled in her neck and stomach was released. A new perspective was filtering through the thickly confused emotions that had been clogging her thinking like light through the deeply colored stained-glass window situated high in the back wall. Still, her mind wandered as she struggled to focus on the message.

Questions were circling in her mind like moths fluttering around a porch light; similar every one, but each unique. What should she do now? Should she do anything? She was no detective and murder was far from her field. Still she felt that something was wrong; something out of place like a jigsaw puzzle piece that has been forced into the wrong place by an impatient person. She certainly didn't agree with Norman about doctor-aided suicide. The whole idea was reprehensible. Yet Norman, who had always been a caring person and an even more caring doctor, believed that the suffering had a right to end their own hopelessness and pain.

If only Norman Meade were different; if he were bitter, abusive, acerbic, then she would feel far more comfortable dismissing him as a crank and charlatan. But Norman was kind and sensitive. She had seen that in the way in which he treated Darlene Crews. He hovered over her like a loving family member. He took his time when he spoke to her; he was polite; he was concerned about causing her pain with the IV needle, and even offered to postpone the event so that the weary Darlene could rest. The clincher, however, was the genuine sorrow he displayed when Darlene had died. Clearly, as if she were watching the video in her mind, she could see him wipe tears from his eyes. And when Eugene Crews collapsed in sorrow, Norman had picked him up and embraced him until Eugene reconstructed his shattered composure. These were not the acts of a madman or a calloused, self-absorbed killer.

Regardless of Norman's concern, regardless of their past, and regardless of the deep debt that she owed him, he still committed an unconscionable act with Darlene, and he may have killed Ed Warren. The last thought bothered Gates. Carl Berner might be convinced that the man in his jail was the killer, but Gates was still unconvinced, although she couldn't give concrete reasons why she believed that.

A sentence, a single powerful line, percolated down through Gates' churning thoughts and firmly demanded a hearing. It was from the sermon, and her subconscious had grabbed the passing phrase and reeled it in like a fisherman working a marlin. The pastor was quoting a verse of Scripture. It was a familiar passage: "You shall know the truth, and the truth shall set you free."

The words were powerful, not because they were new, for Gates had known that verse from John chapter eight since she was a child. It was the application that was new, and in that newness was power. It was not an unusual event for Gates to sit in church, her mind preoccupied with the challenges of her work or personal life, only to have a single line from the sermon work its way into her thoughts, and to have that one truth make a huge difference in her life — a difference so significant that had she sat in church hour after hour for the whole day to hear that one line, it would be worth it.

It was happening again. "You shall know the truth, and the truth shall set you free." There was the problem. There was the solution. That simple verse did two things for Gates: It defined her confusion, and it gave her direction. Her problem was that she did not possess the truth of the matter. She had not allowed Norman to tell his side of the story, to unleash his views. She had declared him wrong, a medical anathema, and shut him out. She doubted that he could ever convince her that suicide was right under any circumstance, but she could at least listen, and in the process perhaps convince him that his philosophy was wrong.

But more important than that was the murder. She had felt that something was wrong, and instinctively knew that Norman could not have killed Warren — but that was a feeling, not a fact. She needed the truth, and without the truth she would never be able to put the matter to rest. Freedom would come from the truth, her freedom, and if he was truly innocent, Norman's freedom. The problem was finding and recognizing the truth.

Gates had known from adolescence that truth could be difficult to find. It, like a struggling fish, could easily slip out of the hands of the one attempting to possess it. She must have the truth. She must discover the truth. For not to do so would leave her with one of the many opposites of truth: ignorance — self-imposed, selfish ignorance, and there was no freedom in that.

The truth was out there. The question was: How to find it?

Chapter Nine

Sunday, November 2
2:00 P.M.

The Ridgeline Police Station was a white clapboard T-shaped building set back a dozen yards from Highway 22, which ran through the heart of Ridgeline. A broad macadam parking lot blanketed the ground in front of the structure, and tall ancient pines encompassed the grounds. On a normal day the parking lot would have one or two of the department's five patrol cars sitting idly in their painted stalls, and half a dozen other cars from employees.

Today was different. The normally open expanse of pavement was crowded with large Ford and Dodge vans from half-a-dozen television stations, microwave dishes mounted to their roofs and pointed skyward. Other cars, mostly sedans with the call letters of radio stations or the names of newspapers, occupied the other parking places. A gathering of people further crowded the lot. They were a subdued group that projected a corporate frustration and ennui, like a crowd at a rain-delayed baseball game waiting for the national anthem and first pitch.

It was clear to Gates that she would find no open parking spaces in the lot today, so she pulled into the next lot in front of the hardware store. As expected, Lea Ballew's story that aired the night before had aroused the attention of the other media who had flocked to Ridgeline and positioned themselves outside the police station, a situation that was certain to put Carl Berner in a very foul mood.

Gates had been unable to get that single Bible verse out of her mind: "You shall know the truth, and the truth shall set you free." Even after church as she, Anne, and John joined her parents for lunch at Middy's, an upscale restaurant that was attached to the Blue Sky Motel where wealthier tourists chose to stay, Gates could not stop the perpetual rebounding of that thought. Nor did she want to. Even as Maggie and Thomas McClure recounted their just-ended trip to Kingman, Arizona to visit his brother, Gates' mind churned in high gear. There was freedom in truth. She knew that much. In fact, every time she heard or quoted that verse, her thoughts focused on just the part — "the truth shall set you free." What she had never taken note of was the qualifier that preceded the promise — "you shall know the truth." That clause now flashed neon bright. There was the source of her quandary. She did not know the truth about Norman Meade. She did not know the truth about the murder. She did not know the truth about her own feelings. For the truth to set her free, she must first know — really know — the truth.

But how would she come to this enlightenment? Gates knew only one way: ask questions.

The meal continued, and Gates did her best to participate. She also did her best to endure the jibes of her sister Anne, who was taking great pleasure in teasing her. When Maggie McClure asked Gates why she was so distracted Anne answered for her: "Oh, you know, Mom, Gates never could hold her soup."

This forced a recounting of the previous night's events in all its scalding detail. Maggie was immediately concerned, but Gates assured her that the burns were minor and just a little more irritating than her sister.

After lunch, Gates, motivated by her new commitment to truth, drove directly to the police station. She wasn't sure why, or what she might say, but she wanted to talk to Norman again. Now she stood beside her Honda Civic and looked at the crowd of reporters huddled around the front steps of the police station.

Taking a deep breath, Gates crossed the small planting strip that separated the two parking lots, and began to weave her way through the numerous bodies toward the front door of the station. When she reached the foot of the stairs, she looked up and saw Dan Wells standing by the door, his thick arms crossed in front of his chest and a dour expression shadowing his face.

"Hey, Dan," Gates said as she started up the steps. "You here to keep everyone out?"

"Hi, Doc," Wells replied with a small nod. "You can come in."

"Doc?" a voice called out. "Are you a doctor?"

Gates turned to see who was speaking, but the whole crowd had turned to face her.

"Are you here to see Dr. Meade?" a woman in dark pinstriped skirt and coat shouted.

"Is he sick?" another reporter asked.

"What's your name?" still another called.

Wells quickly stepped forward and raised his hands. "Settle down folks. This is our town doctor and she's here on personal business. Now let her get on with it."

Gates knew that Wells had no idea why she was here, but that he was protecting her from a hailstorm of questions.

"You'd better get inside," Wells said covertly to Gates. "I'd consider it a favor."

Nodding, Gates quickly stepped inside the station, leaving the swelling commotion behind. Her entrance into the small office area was greeted by the upraised faces of Carl Berner and the dispatcher Terri Stringman. A young woman with straight brown hair sat behind a computer, quietly typing. Carl looked grumpy and Terri looked annoyed.

"Quite a gathering you've got out there," Gates said.

"I've never liked the media," Carl growled. "I suppose they're a necessary evil, but I still don't like them. Especially, when they're on my doorstep."

"Amen to that," Terri interjected.

"Why are they just sitting out there?" Gates asked.

"They've been showing up all morning," Carl answered. "Ever since that Ballew woman did that report last night, every reporter within two hundred miles has been pouring in here, and they all want to talk to Meade or his attorney. They grilled me for half an hour. I gave them nothing but one word answers. That drives them crazy."

"Attorney?"

"Yeah." Carl nodded toward the door that led to the lockup. "He's in there now talking with his client."

"Can I go back and see Norman?" Gates asked.

Carl shrugged. "It's all right with me, but his lawyer may object. If he does, then you'll have to leave. He has priority."

"I understand," Gates said. "Anything new turn up since yesterday?"

"No, but I think things will move quickly. The media has made this a national case. I think we may even have the autopsy report by mid-afternoon tomorrow. The arraignment will be soon after that. Have you heard anything about Eugene Crews? Do you know how he's doing?"

"No," Gates said, shaking her head, "but I plan to call the hospital later. I'll let you know what I find out."

"I'd appreciate it. Go on back. If the lawyer kicks you out, then you can come back later."

"Okay." Gates walked through the door that led to the short hall that ran between the four cells. A man was seated in the same folding chair that Gates had used the day before. He was leaning back in the chair and had his legs crossed. He was taking notes in a leather folder. He looked like a lawyer; he was wearing a dark blue suit and black shoes. His hair was gray, combed straight back, and was long enough to curl in the back. Hearing the door close behind Gates, he turned to face her. His eyes were dark, but reflected an innate intelligence.

"Who are you?" he demanded in a resonant baritone.

"I'm Dr. Gates McClure," she replied evenly, irritated at the man's brusqueness.

"Gates!" Norman cried out. Since she was still at the far end of the hall all she could see of Meade was his hands gripping the bars of his cell. "I'm glad you're here." Then to the seated man he said, "Linden, this is the woman I was telling you about."

The lawyer uncrossed his legs and stood to his feet. "Dr. McClure, I'm pleased to meet you." He extended his hand. Gates took the few steps necessary to travel the length of the hall, and shook the man's hand. "I'm Linden Vanderlip of Andrews, Vanderlip and Andrews. I represent Dr. Meade."

"Mr. Vanderlip," Gates said. "I hope I'm not interrupting."

"We were just finishing," Vanderlip replied. "I understand we owe you a word of thanks."

"For what?"

"For talking Chief Berner into allowing Norman to stay here a little longer and having free access to the telephone. That has been helpful."

"Carl is a good man," she said. "It didn't take that much convincing." Gates turned to Norman. He was dressed differently than the last time she had seen him. He was wearing a dark brown polo shirt and tan chinos. His face was shaved and his hair neatly combed. Despite the new clothes that Gates assumed Vanderlip had brought with him, Norman looked tired, stressed. His posture was slightly stooped and his eyes looked red from lack of sleep. This was wearing on him. "How are you doing, Norman?"

"I'm getting by," he answered wearily. "I've been arrested several times before, but this is different."

"You'll be fine," Vanderlip said. "I'm pretty sure that things will go our way. I'm confident that we will have you out on bail after the hearing."

"So Norman will be able to get out on bail?" Gates inquired.

"It happens," Vanderlip said. "We will be able to show that Meade is not a flight risk and that he's always cooperated in his other arrests. It's not a lock, but I'd be surprised if he's still in jail Wednesday."

Gates was surprised at this information, and oddly, a little relieved. "There's a lot of media out there. This is getting quite a bit of press coverage."

"That's not surprising," Vanderlip said. "We expected it."

"Would you like to sit down?" Norman offered, motioning to the chair.

"No thanks, I'm fine," Gates answered. "I went to the crime scene. The detectives were already gone, but Carl filled me in. It doesn't look good. They found your IV stand and pump."

Lowering his head, Meade began to pace his cell. "I can't believe this. I just can't believe this. Who would want to do this to me?"

"Ed Warren might," Vanderlip offered.

"Ed Warren?" Gates said with surprise. "You don't mean to suggest that Warren killed himself to implicate Norman?"

"It's a possibility," the lawyer answered. "Or maybe he was attempting to frame Norman and something went wrong."

"No," Meade said. "Warren hated me, but he loved himself too much to commit suicide. Shoot me in the back, maybe; kill himself, never. As far as a setup goes, well, it just doesn't seem like something Warren would do — certainly not with real drugs in the trigger."

"If you didn't kill Warren," Gates said, "then who did? Who else hates you that much?"

"If I knew that," Norman snapped, "then I

wouldn't be in here."

"Easy, Norman," Vanderlip said. "I think the good doctor is just trying to be helpful."

"I . . . I know she is," he stammered. "I'm sorry, Gates. Being confined makes me edgy. This whole thing seems like something out of a horror novel."

"I understand," Gates said sympathetically.

"What else can you tell us about the crime scene?" Vanderlip asked. "I plan to go there, but I'd be interested in your take on it."

"There's very little to see. It's a standard motel room. Carl said they found the body on the bed with an IV hooked up. There was no sign of a struggle, just Warren on the bed with an IV. Apparently there's no doubt that the IV belongs to Norman. It had that trigger device on it. And that's what bothers me. How does one give an IV to someone who is combative? It can't be done without leaving the victim bruised."

Vanderlip nodded. "That's a very good point."

"Here's something else that puzzles me," Gates added. "When I watched the video I noticed that you gave a series of numbers to Darlene to enter on the keypad."

Norman nodded. "Yes, that's true. I do that to demonstrate that my patient is both

163

coherent and rational enough to carry out the act. If for any reason, they cannot enter the code correctly, the whole system shuts down."

"So if Warren actually hooked himself up to the IV or someone did it for him, then he would need the code to activate the trigger?"

"Yes," Norman answered.

"How is the code set?" Gates asked.

"It's not hard really," Norman replied. "On the back of the box is a series of small switches. They're black like the trigger box itself, so I doubt you'd see it on the video. By setting these switches a code is established. When the code is entered properly, a small electric pump dispenses the meds into the IV line."

"The morphine and valium?"

"Yes," Norman answered.

"So anyone could set those switches. Is that true?"

"If they knew about them and how they worked. The system is not very sophisticated, but it works well."

Looking down at the floor, Gates slowly shook her head as she took in what Norman was saying. The idea that someone — a doctor — could design a device like the one being described boggled her mind. She felt a sadness, like a part of her innocence had been stripped away by this dirty business and her profession sullied. Still, none of it made sense. Everything was too elaborate. Something was missing.

"Is there anything else you can tell us?" Vanderlip asked.

"Norman," Gates said ignoring the question. "I don't think you killed Ed Warren. I loath what you've done, but I don't think you killed Warren."

Norman smiled. "Thank you, Gates. That means a great deal to me."

"I don't want to be misunderstood here, Norman. I still think what you do unconscionable and the very antithesis to what we as doctors swore to do."

"I understand," Meade replied. "No need to belabor the point. I know exactly where you stand."

"This whole setup was planned in great detail," Gates said, "and well in advance of the event. The use of Norman's suicide machine makes that clear. If Norman was going to kill Warren, then using his own equipment would be the most self-incriminating way to do it. It just doesn't make any sense."

They each fell into their silent thoughts. A moment later, Norman said, "Gates, I feel like you have something else on your mind."

Gates wondered if she was that transparent

or if Norman was that insightful. "Eugene Crews is in the hospital."

"What? How?" Norman was aghast.

"His daughter showed up and was furious over her mother's death. She slapped Mr. Crews. Knocked him down. Carl was called to the scene, and since I was in the car I went with him. We saw her slap her father. Carl took charge of the scene and I went to aid Mr. Crews. He presented with shallow labored breathing, complaints of heaviness in his chest . . ."

"Heart?"

"That's what I assumed. The paramedics arrived and took him down the hill to the hospital. His EKG looked normal, so it may have been an anxiety attack, but we couldn't take any chances."

"How is he now?"

"I don't know, but I plan to make a call later."

Norman began to pace like a lion in the zoo. He was shaking his head and rubbing his hands together. "I don't understand. I don't understand. He doesn't have a daughter. We check these things. He has no daughter."

"No daughter that you know about," Gates said bluntly.

"I don't understand," he said again. "No. No daughter. How could we miss that?"

"I don't know, Norman," Gates said firmly, "but that's not my point."

"Then what is your point?"

"I oppose what you do on several levels. This is just another such level. You may have felt that you were helping Darlene and maybe even Eugene, but in the process you may have damaged the lives of others — such as Martha Crews and who knows who else. Everything has a price, Norman, and in euthanasia other people pay it."

"Dr. McClure," Vanderlip cut in. "I appreciate your candor and your help, but I don't think my client needs a guilt trip from you. Certainly not now. He has other things to think about. I have been the legal adviser to Mr. Meade for a number of years and I can tell you that he takes nothing for granted and he takes his work very seriously."

"As do I, Mr. Vanderlip," Gates said strongly. "As do I."

Leaving the jail proved far more challenging than entering. Accompanied by Carl Berner who had signaled Officer Wells to stay put and make sure no one entered the building, Gates exited the front of the building and was suddenly awash with reporters, each holding microphones or tape recorders. Questions came in a steady flow, each overlapping a question asked by another. To Gates, who was surrounded by the reporters, it seemed like pandemonium.

"What's your name?" a woman reporter asked.

"Dr. Gates McClure."

"Are you a medical doctor?" another forcefully inquired.

"Yes."

"Is Meade ill? Did something happen to him?"

"Not that I know of," Gates said, then added: "I'm not his doctor."

Carl spoke up. "Come on everybody, back up. There's nothing here for you."

The crowd was unconvinced. "If he's not ill, then why are you here?"

"Why shouldn't I be here?" Gates replied tersely as she began to press her way down the stairs.

A tall black man that Gates had seen on television called out. "Are you part of the Dignity in Death group? Are you one of his supporters?"

"No," Gates answered. "No, I most definitely am not part of that group. Now if you'll let me get past . . ."

"Are you his girlfriend?" a pretty blond shouted.

"No." Carl stepped in front of Gates and

began to firmly push aside those who stood in their way.

"Did he call for you? Did he ask for your help?"

"I have nothing newsworthy to tell you," Gates answered loudly. "I'm not the story here. I'm just the town doctor."

"Was Ed Warren a friend of yours?"

Realizing that any answer she gave only encouraged the piranha-like behavior, Gates refused to respond any further. Before exiting the building, Carl had warned her that this might happen. "They've been out there all day, and some have spent most of the night in their cars and vans. They're going to be pretty hungry for some news, so watch what you say. In fact, say nothing if you can."

"But won't that make it appear that I'm hiding something?" Gates had wondered aloud.

"Yes, but any answer you give can have the same effect," Carl said before opening the door. "Just refer them to me and Meade's attorney."

Gates nodded.

"By the way," Carl had said as he took hold of the doorknob. "This is why I should have sent Meade down the hill to jail. We're too small a group to handle all this, and there's only one way out of the station. You ready?"

Again, Gates nodded.

Together they had stepped into the fray. Carl had been right about everything. These people were ravenous for some news to send back to their stations or newspapers. Carl did his best to keep the reporters back, but several, most likely pushed from behind by their more zealous counterparts, bumped, tussled, and rubbed against Gates. She winced several times as people accidentally smacked into her tender, burned thighs.

Closely following her Moses as he parted the sea of people, Gates emerged on the other side of the crowd. The few steps from the top of the stairs and through the first twenty feet of parking lot had seemed an endless, arduous journey. In reality it had taken just two or three minutes. Once through the media mob, the questions ended, as though the simple passage through their midst had put her out of their realm.

As Carl escorted Gates to her car, she asked, "How did they know I was there to see Norman?"

A chuckle dribbled out of Carl. "We only have one prisoner, Gates, who else would you be there to see?"

"I could have been there on other business."

"True," Carl nodded. "True enough, but

170

not likely on a Sunday."

When they reached the Honda, Carl opened the door. "What now, Doctor?"

"What do you mean?"

"I hope you're through with this mess," Carl said seriously. "I've been around awhile and I've spent most of my life in police work. I've got a feeling that this is going to get pretty messy."

"Messy?"

"Yeah, messy," Carl said as Gates sat down in the car. "Cases like this that involve a public personality can quickly get out of hand, especially if that person is associated with a controversial cause. People start drawing lines in the sand to see who will cross over. Those who hate Meade will use this to their advantage; those who love him will stand opposite them. Oil and water, Gates. You can't mix 'em."

"There's nothing I can do to change that, Carl. You know that."

"You can keep clear of the whole matter. I know that you want to help and that you feel like you owe this guy something, but I think you ought to steer clear."

"Thanks for the advice, Carl. Will you let me know when the coroner's report is in?"

"You're not listening to me, Gates."

"I've been around awhile myself, Carl. I

think I can handle whatever comes my way."

"That's not the way to think, Gates." Carl's expression turned sour. "In police work that's a danger sign. You start thinking that you're invulnerable and the next thing you know, you're lying in a pool of your own blood."

"I'm a doctor, Carl, not an officer of the law. I have no intention of arresting anyone, or getting in anyone's line of fire. I live in Ridgeline because I like the serene quiet life." Gates shifted in the seat to reach for her seat belt. She winced as the linen fabric of her slacks scraped across her sensitive legs.

"Hey, you okay?" Carl asked.

"Yeah, just a little sore."

"From what?"

"I don't want to get into it, Carl, but I gave myself a slight burn. Nothing to worry about. And, no, I don't want to tell you what happened."

"Yet another secret." Carl feigned hurt. "I'm beginning to think that you don't trust me."

"Another secret? What do you mean another . . ." Gates recalled mentioning the debt she owed Norman. "Oh, it's nothing like that. I'm just too embarrassed to tell you."

"So when are you going to tell me what's between you and Norman Meade? I know you don't support what he does. It seems to me that you would want him locked up."

Gates thought for a moment. What did she want? She asked herself the question, but no answer came. The question just bounced around in her mind, ricocheting from one emotion to the next. "If he killed Ed Warren, then he should be locked up, but I don't think he did it. Don't ask why I think that, because I can't give you a satisfactory answer yet."

"So you're not going to tell me what connects you two beyond medical school?"

Hot breath. Rough hands. Pain. Pushing. Weight. Fear. Terror.

Gates winced again, but this time, for a different reason than her burned legs. "Not now, Carl. Not now."

Carl stood quietly looking at Gates. "Okay, just tell me that it has nothing to do with this case. Can you do that? Can you assure me that it has no bearing on the man in jail back there?"

"It was a long time ago, Carl. A very long time ago. It has nothing to do with all this."

Carl nodded approvingly. "Okay." He paused then added, "Take care of yourself, Gates."

"I will."

"I mean it." The serious tone returned.

"So do I."

Slowly and cautiously, Carl closed the car door for Gates.

"So why did you pull me back when that lady doctor came out?" Jeff Penna asked, making no effort to conceal his pique. "I thought we were here to cover the story."

"Don't be so dramatic," Lea Ballew said, blowing smoke from her cigarette into the air. They were leaning next to the station's van that they had driven last night. "Did you see any of our competitors get anything we don't already have?"

"No."

"Then give it a rest, will you? That woman wasn't going to say anything to us. You could see it in her eyes and in her manner. She's self-possessed. No way was she going to cave in to a bunch of city reporters in her town."

"Do you think she's important?"

"Yeah, I think she's important, but I don't know how yet. Did you hear her name?"

"It's an odd name: Gates McClure."

"*Dr.* Gates McClure. A medical doctor she said." Lea put the cigarette in her mouth and reached into the van. A moment later she had a cell phone in her hand. She dialed a number, removed the cigarette and waited for someone to pick up. Someone did.

"This is Lea," she said brusquely into the

phone. "I want you to have somebody run down some information on a Dr. Gates McClure." She spelled the last name. "She's the town doctor here in Ridgeline. See if you can find some connection between her and Norman Meade."

Lea paused for a moment as the person on the other line spoke. Then she answered: "I don't know. Maybe they went to school together. Maybe they were lovers. It could be anything, just look into it for me. What about that other stuff I asked for?" She paused and listened. "Well, stay on it. There has to be something out there." She switched off the phone.

"No word yet?" Jeff asked.

"Nope, but they'll turn up something."

"So you think this Dr. McClure and Meade are connected?"

"Yeah, I think they're connected. I just don't know how . . . yet."

Lea dropped the smoldering cigarette to the ground and snuffed it out with her shoe. "There is more here than meets the eye. I'm sure of it."

Chapter Ten

Sunday, November 2
7:30 P.M.

"Tomorrow's going to be an ordeal," Anne said as she sipped her apple-cinnamon herb tea. "I stopped by my office. Several of the television stations have called wanting some official response. Fortunately this all happened on a weekend when my office was closed."

"I bet you're glad that I insisted on that unlisted number," her husband, John, said. He was eating hot apple pie with vanilla ice cream on it. "It doesn't take much brains to look up our number in the phone book."

"I thought Anne suggested the private line," Gates said. "At least that's what she told me."

"Are you trying to get me in trouble, Gates?" Anne asked glibly.

"I'm just trying to get even for all those cracks about my legs."

"Ah, the famous soup incident," John said. "How are the legs?"

"Better," Gates replied. "Now they only hurt when I'm conscious." Anne started to speak but Gates cut her off. "Don't go there."

"But it was such a nice opening," Anne replied with wide-eyed innocence.

Gates and Anne laughed. No two sisters could be more different and no sisters closer. Although they bickered, teased, and needled each other, they shared a deep bond that was elastic enough to allow differing opinions and stalwart enough to weather anything.

"This looks like a sweet gathering of nice people," a new voice added. "Or is it a nice gathering of sweet people?" Gates, John, and Anne had left the evening service half an hour earlier and came to the Tree Top Café for dessert. It was a Sunday tradition.

"You're the wordsmith," Anne said to Ross Sassmon, who now stood by the edge of the booth. "Sit down, join us. Were just having a little after-church pie." Gates scooted along the booth's bench seat to make room for Ross.

"It doesn't look like our good doctor is enjoying hers," Ross said, looking at the untouched wedge of pumpkin pie. "Not nutritious enough for you, Doc?"

"The pie's fine," Gates answered. "I'm just a little distracted."

"I can imagine," Ross responded. "Your

life seems to have become a little more complex."

"Somewhat." Gates was making an effort to be noncommittal. "Is this a business visit or are you planning on writing a feature story on neglected pies?"

Ross snickered. "Business, I guess. Actually I came in for a late dinner — life of the bachelor, you know — and saw you three sitting here. I was hoping I could ask a few questions."

"Of me, or Anne?" Gates asked.

"Of you." A waitress approached and asked if Ross was going to order. "Not now, but I will have some dinner a little later." The waitress adroitly refilled the three cups of the others and left.

"There's not much I can tell you," Gates said, seizing the initiative. "I'm as much in the dark as everyone else."

"Perhaps," Ross said, "but you are far more acquainted with Norman Meade than the rest of us. I've been doing a little research, running down articles on the Internet and the like, but while I can get a history of Meade's activities related to euthanasia, I can find very little on the man himself. Can you tell me anything about him as a person? It'd be a big help for next week's paper."

The unsettling feeling that had been haunting Gates the last two days returned. She didn't really want to talk about Norman. What she did want was a little time to unwind and to sort things out. Now she was becoming the source of information for all those who wanted deeper insights into the enigmatic Norman Meade. Carl had questions, Ross had questions, even Anne had been probing.

"Gates?" Ross said. "Are you all right?"

"Uh, fine. Just woolgathering. Ross, I know you have a newspaper to put out and that this is big news for our town . . ."

"It's big news for any place," Anne interjected.

"Regardless of how big the story is," Gates continued, "there's very little I can add to it."

"But didn't you go to school with him?" Ross asked.

"Yes, we both went to UCLA," Gates answered. "We took many of the same classes and even doubled as lab partners for some of them, like Gross Anatomy."

"Gross Anatomy?" Anne said. "That sounds repulsive."

"Since the student spends hours slowly cutting up a preserved human cadaver it can be a little repulsive — even for med students," Gates elaborated, and watched as Anne looked down at her pie in disgust, clearly losing her appetite. "Anyway, we doubled as

179

partners in that class and others. We also were part of the same study group."

"You told me that you dated," Anne added.

Gates frowned. The last thing she wanted to do was have private conversation in a public place while seated next to the town's editor. "I also told you it was only a couple of times. Sometimes we would go out for coffee, but there's not much free time when you're in medical school. It absorbs your whole life."

"Did he ever do anything or say anything that made you think that he might become Dr. Death?" Ross probed.

"We *are* off the record here, aren't we Ross?" Gates asked pointedly.

"Oh, come on Gates. Help me out here."

"I'm not going on record. I don't want to be quoted in your paper or anyone else's. This whole thing affects me on several levels, including both personal and business. I don't want to spend the next year doing damage control because of one or two articles that appear in the paper."

"But I have a job to do," Ross retorted irritably. "It's hard enough keeping this paper afloat. Work with me. The paper could use an increase in sales and this story just may do the trick."

"Paper still struggling, is it?" John asked.

180

"Always. When I bought it, I thought I was setting up a leisurely transition into retirement. Instead I'm being consumed by my own business. I'm still putting more money in it than I'm taking out. A good story would be a big help."

"I understand your financial troubles, Ross, but I don't want to be center stage on this thing."

There was an uncomfortable silence before Ross spoke. "What do you feel comfortable telling me?"

"Off the record?"

Ross nodded reluctantly then conceded, "Off the record."

Gates sighed and pushed her untouched pie away. "Norman Meade — the Norman Meade I knew in school — was one of the kindest and most caring men I've met. He was giving almost to a fault. To answer your question, no, I never saw anything that would indicate the course he would follow. In many ways I'm still amazed by the whole thing."

"What did you talk about?" Ross inquired.

Shrugging, Gates said, "Nothing significant. We talked about school mostly. The workload, specialties we might pursue. That sort of thing."

"He never talked about helping patients die?" Ross pressed.

Gates shook her head. "Not to me anyway. I do remember that he participated in a heated discussion in a medical ethics class. There was some debate about how much information a patient should be allowed to have about their own situation. For example, should a patient be allowed access to their own charts? Not many people know that a patient has no legal right to view his or her own chart. Well, Norman spoke strongly that patients should have more rights than what they currently receive. That was well over a decade ago and some things have changed."

"What do you mean 'heated discussion'?"

"Just the usual bluster from study-weary students trying to make the best grade possible in a highly competitive field. That's all. He didn't go off the deep end, if that's what you're asking."

"I'm just trying to get a handle on this thing, Gates, that's all."

"I know, Ross, and I'm sorry to be so difficult, but this is not easy for me."

"I don't think it's going to get any better for Dr. Meade," Ross said. "I came across a few articles in my research. The last time he was arrested for a physician-assisted suicide the jail was besieged by protestors. He was only in jail a couple of days, but that was enough time for the anti-Dr. Death crowd to make their presence known."

"Where was this?" John asked as he finished the last bite of his pie and quaffed his coffee.

"Nevada," Ross answered. "Earlier this year."

"That's all we need," Anne intoned somberly. "A bunch of outsiders picketing in front of the jail."

"By the way," Ross said. "How's old man Crews doing?"

Gates gasped. "I was going to call the hospital to find out. I can't believe I forgot to do that. I need to make that call."

She started to excuse herself when John reached down by his side and pulled out a cell phone. "Here, use this," he said, and then: "You gonna' eat that pumpkin pie?"

"You can have it, John." Gates dialed 411 to get the hospital's phone number and then quickly placed her call. "Good evening," she said when the hospital switchboard picked up. "I'm Dr. Gates McClure. Could you tell me what room Eugene Crews is in?"

Room 212, the hospital operator answered.

"Would you please connect me to the nurses' station that services that room?"

"One moment." There was a brief pause while the call was transferred.

"Second floor, west."

"Hi, this is Dr. Gates McClure, and I was calling on a patient by the name of Eugene Crews."

"Yes, Doctor, he's in room 212. We gave him a sedative a little while ago, but I think he's still awake. Are you one of his doctors?"

"No," Gates replied, knowing that the nurse was being careful about the information she gave over the phone. Anyone could call and say that they were a doctor. "I'm the one who called the ambulance. I know that you can't tell me much, but can you say if he's resting comfortably?"

"Yes, he's doing fine. We have him on telemetry to monitor his heart as a precaution, but his physician thinks Mr. Crews had an anxiety attack."

"Well, it's good to hear that it wasn't his heart," Gates said. "May I ask who his doctor is?"

"That would be Dr. Eric Pooly. He's part of the HMO here."

"You've been a big help," Gates said. "By the way, has anyone been by to see him?"

"Not to my knowledge," the nurse replied. "Do you want me to connect you?"

"Yes, thank you." Gates looked at the others who were huddled in the cramped booth with her. They were listening intently to the one-sided conversation. The phone on the other end rang once, then twice before it was picked up. Gates heard a loud thump, and a muffled curse. Eugene must have dropped the phone on the bed.

"Yeah," a gruff and ragged voice said. "Who's this?"

"Hi, Mr. Crews," Gates said, attempting to sound upbeat and cheerful. "This is Dr. Gates McClure. Do you remember me?"

"Oh yeah, I remember you. Of course I remember you."

"I was calling to see how you are feeling."

"Pretty good, I guess. The Doc says it ain't my heart. I just got shook up a little, with my daughter yellin' at me and my losing Darlene." His voice cracked with emotion.

"I'm sure it was a real tough day for you, but you're in good hands right now," Gates reassured him.

"But I gotta' get outa' here soon, Doc. I can't stay."

"Why is that, Mr. Crews? You need your rest."

"You don't understand. I got work to do. I mean, I gotta' take care of my Darlene."

Darlene? Was Crews having a mental break with reality? He just acknowledged Darlene's death. "I'm afraid I don't understand."

"Well, I ain't gonna' leave her in no coroner's morgue forever. I gotta' get her . . . buried." Again his voice choked with a sadness that not even distance, radio waves, and electronic switching equipment could diminish.

"Oh, you're talking about the funeral." Gates realized that Eugene Crews was probably as alone as a man could get. He had no help and could expect none from his daughter.

"I don't think my daughter will want to help. She's pretty sore at me."

That was an understatement. Gates thought quickly, then she had an idea. "Listen, Mr. Crews. I know somebody who knows a lot about these things and I'm sure he'd be willing to help. Do you want me to call him for you?"

"I don't know. Do you trust him?"

Gates smiled and hoped the smirk would be carried over the phone. "Yes, I trust him a great deal. He's my pastor. His name is Paul Chapman, and I bet he would be glad to help."

"A preacher, huh? I ain't been to church in years. You really think he might help? Considering how Darlene died, I mean."

Gates hadn't thought about that. She had no idea how Pastor Chapman would respond to the request. In almost any other circumstance she would have been highly confident about her minister's answer, but Darlene did commit suicide with Norman's and Eugene's help. Suddenly she felt like she had just offered money she didn't have. "I can ask him for you."

"Okay, that would be great. You'll let me know, won't you?"

"I'll talk to him tomorrow and then I'll call you. How's that?"

"Fine. Real fine. Thanks, Doc. I owe you."

"No you don't, Mr. Crews. You don't owe me anything. I think you should rest now. I hear they gave you a sedative."

"Yeah, I'm gettin' kinda' sleepy."

"That's the medication. I'll talk to you tomorrow. Okay?"

"Okay." Without another word, he hung up.

"Thanks." Gates handed the small cellular phone back to John.

"So he's doing okay?" John asked.

"Seems to be. I don't have any information of course. But his doctor thinks it was just an anxiety attack."

"Why did you ask about visitors?" Anne inquired.

"I was wondering if his daughter had stopped by. I had my doubts that she would. It's probably for the best."

Ross nodded. "I heard about that from

Carl. Not a nice woman by his description. I wonder how she found out about Darlene Crews."

"That's a good question," Gates said. "Maybe you could do a little research. Do you keep back issues? Maybe you could learn a few things from those. You know, birth announcements, graduation, that sort of thing."

"Why?" Ross asked with bewilderment. "What's all this have to do with Norman Meade and the murder of Ed Warren?"

"I don't know that it does," Gates said flatly. "But I've got a feeling that we should be turning over as many stones as possible."

"You think Meade is innocent, don't you?" Ross asked pointedly.

"Yes, I do," Gates said, surprised that her former hesitancy was gone. "And before you ask, let me say, no, I don't know why I believe that, other than the obvious fact that the way Warren was murdered was too incriminating. Meade would have to be as stupid as a stump to kill Warren that way, and Norman is far from stupid."

"Stranger things have happened," Ross said. "Crimes committed in anger can take strange directions."

"You know what all this means, don't you?" Anne said solemnly. "If Gates is right, then the real killer is still running free."

Chapter Eleven

Monday, November 3
8:00 A.M.

The office was quiet and she was alone. Gates locked the door behind her and walked through the lobby and around the Formica-topped counter that separated the office from the brightly painted patient waiting room. Behind the counter were shelves filled with medical folders dutifully marked with color-coded tabs. At 8:30 Gates' staff would arrive and begin their work. That left her half an hour of silent solitude to collect her thoughts and prepare for the day. Glancing at the appointment book, it looked like she would be busy most of the day. She tossed Saturday's mail, which she had picked up off the floor under the mail slot, on the appointment book. Nancy and Valerie, both competent and skilled nurses, would take care of it.

In addition to the waiting and reception areas, the office complex consisted of three exam rooms, an x-ray room, and a small open area where Nancy and Valerie would draw blood or package other biological medical specimens to be shipped to testing labs down the hill.

In the back corner of the suite was a small, wood-paneled office where Gates would fill out forms, consult with patients and their families, and capture a few moments alone. It was to this room that Gates marched and then shut the door behind her. In her hand was the morning edition of the *Los Angeles Times* which she had gathered off the front step. It, like all newspapers, felt dry and dusty in her hands. She plopped down behind her inexpensive simulated-oak desk.

It had been a good night for Gates. After leaving the Tree Top Café she made her way home, disrobed, smeared a fresh layer of ointment on her legs, grabbed a book, and read until sleep overwhelmed her. She had expected another fitful night, but her sleep was blissfully deep and unmarred by disruptive dreams. When her alarm had sounded at six that morning, she felt refreshed. Her legs, although still burned, were far less sensitive, and even showering was bearable. Grateful that the November weather, while cool at night, was still conducive to light clothing, she slipped into a pair of gray cotton twill pants and a long-sleeved black polo shirt.

Gates opened the paper and began searching the headlines for any news about Norman Meade. She wasn't disappointed. Warren's death had made the front page below the fold. The headline read, "Death in Jail." The article, which covered only four column inches on the front page but continued on deeper in the section, was written in the *Times*' usual free-flowing but detailed style. Gates preferred gathering her news from quality papers like the *Times* or from the local PBS station. Both provided unbiased and in-depth reports that were sadly missing from commercial news. While the article offered nothing new about the murder itself, it did provide a comprehensive background on both Meade and Warren. Gates, driven by a compulsion for detail that she had possessed all her life, took a tablet of yellow paper and began scratching out notes in two columns. In column one she listed information about Meade:

thirty-five years old.
Single.
Born and reared in Albuquerque, New Mexico.
Graduate of University of New Mexico and UCLA medical school.
Internist. Practiced medicine Albuquerque.
Founded Dignity in Death in 1994.

Participated in sixteen known physician-assisted suicides.
Arrested numerous times, but never convicted.
Medical license revoked in New York, Florida, and Illinois.

Apart from the number of suicides in which Norman participated and the revocation of his right to practice medicine in three states, there was very little that Gates hadn't already known. That was not the case with Ed Warren. She scribbled his information down:

forty-eight years old.
Widower.
Born and reared in California.
Graduate of UC Irvine and University of California San Diego.
Director of pediatrics at University City Hospital.
Adjunct professor of anatomy UCSD.
Board member of Contemporary Medical Ethics.
Outspoken opponent of euthanasia.
Arrested three times for disturbing the peace at anti-Meade rallies.

There was no mention of Warren's family, only that he had been married. Still, she knew more about the dead man than she did before reading the article. A picture of Warren accompanied the article. In the photo Warren appeared scholarly, wearing a white lab coat, arms crossed, holding in one hand the now universal symbol of medicine, a stethoscope. He looked gentlemanly, mild mannered, and professional. Gates had seen the other side of Dr. Ed Warren — vitriolic, wrathful, abusive.

There was the puzzle. Warren had achieved a degree of fame in his profession, directing the pediatrics department at a big city hospital and teaching at one of the premiere medical schools in the country. Why would such a man behave the way Gates had seen him do last Friday night? The man Gates saw was out of control, his anger blazing like a three-alarm fire. There was no professional detachment; no forethought about what results his actions might bring.

Closing her eyes, Gates relived that night at the Halloween party. Warren had stormed in, face red like a cherry, neck tight, voice loud. When Norman tried to calm him by introducing him to Gates, Warren reacted brutally and called her . . . she struggled to remember the exact words . . . it came back to her. He had said, "I don't want to meet any of your cronies, Meade."

Cronies. Warren had lumped Gates into

Norman's camp without knowing a thing about her. Then there was the caustic repartee between the two men. Norman first calling for civility, and Warren responding with insults. What was it they had said? "It's still murder to right-thinking, decent people," Warren had shouted. Then something unusual. Norman's response had been to laugh and then ask, "How would you know what was decent?"

Odd.

Gates repeated Norman's rejoinder aloud: "How would you know what was decent?" The implication was clear even then in the lava-hot moment of confrontation: Norman was saying that Warren was something other than decent. Perhaps it was just heated bluster, bile-laced anger, but then again, it could mean that Norman knew something about Warren that others didn't. There was only one way to find the truth of that matter, and that was to ask Norman Meade himself.

"Good morning, Doctor," a pleasant voice said, accompanied by a knocking on the office door. It was Nancy, her nurse.

"Come in," Gates said loud enough to be heard through the door.

A pretty, round face peeked in and smiled. "I hope I'm not interrupting anything, but I just wanted you to know that Val and I are in, and that Mr. Preston is here for his checkup. Shall I put him in exam room one?"

Gates glanced at the small battery-powered clock on her desk. It read five-past-nine. "I can't believe it's after nine already. It seems like I just sat down. Yes, Nancy, that will be fine. Would you also bring me his chart?"

"Sure," she replied sweetly. "It looks like this is going to be a busy one."

"Well, that's what we're here for," Gates said, standing and walking to the wooden coat rack in the corner of her office. She removed the white smock hanging there and donned it. "We'd better get started." Nancy nodded and started to leave. "Oh, Nancy," Gates said, calling her back. "Call over to the Community Church and see if Pastor Chapman might have time for me around four-thirty or so."

"Okay," Nancy answered as a smile crossed her lips. "Planning a wedding?"

"Cute, Nancy, cute."

"It never hurts to ask."

"I wouldn't be so sure about that," Gates replied humorously. "Just show Mr. Preston into the exam room."

"Okay, Doctor."

"Ross Sassmon is on the phone for you, Dr. McClure," Valerie said as Gates walked out of the exam room at the side of a teenage boy whose wrist was wrapped in gauze. "He says that you asked him to call."

"Thanks, Valerie," Gates replied, "I'll take it in my office. In the meantime, please schedule young Mr. Thompson here for another appointment in a week."

Plunking down in her desk chair, Gates exhaled audibly. She was exhausted and it was only two o'clock. If she hadn't made that promise to Eugene Crews about speaking to Pastor Chapman she would cancel the four-thirty appointment she had made. A white light on the desk phone flashed insistently, demanding attention. She picked up the handset and punched the button:

"Ross, how are you today?"

"Fair to partly cloudy," he said then laughed at his own joke. "I did that research you talked about. You know, the past articles on the Crews that you mentioned at the diner last night."

"I remember, but I think I just mentioned Martha Crews."

"You did, but I checked on all of them. Fortunately, it's not all that hard anymore. A couple of years ago, I would have had to plumb the depths of the morgue and look for articles, but about a year ago we hired a couple of high school students to feed all the information into a computer database. We're high-tech now."

"Morgue?" Gates asked, puzzled.

"That's an old newspaper term, Doc. The morgue is the place we keep all past issues of the paper. A newspaper is only good for a few days. After that, the news is old. We keep physical copies back about two years. The rest are on microfiche."

"Oh," Gates rubbed her weary eyes. The day had been busy, as expected, and made all the more hectic by three unscheduled exams. "Find anything of interest?"

"Not really. I did find a short article about Eugene Crews. About twelve years ago, he retired from a trucking company. Some of his friends gave him a party at the community center. I've only been editor for eight years, so this predates me. There's a little background on him and his family, but not much. The whole article is about four column inches."

"What about Martha?"

"Found her too. Wedding announcement dated in August of 1972. I also found her name in the graduating class of the high school for that year. It seems she graduated high school and married that summer."

"That's it?"

"That's it. The wedding announcement said that the couple planned on moving to

San Diego where the groom was stationed for basic training. Apparently he had just enlisted in the navy."

"She told Carl that she lived in Baker, California. She must have moved. I wonder if she's still married."

"If Eugene Crews is any example of how she treats the men in her family, then I doubt it. Pretty young woman."

"Pretty?" Gates thought of the obese woman with oily hair and filthy language. "The word 'pretty' seems incongruous. Who'd she marry?"

"A boy by the name of Robert Lemonick. He was on the track team."

"Robert Lemonick?" Gates wondered aloud. "Bob Lemonick? When did you say they were married?"

"August of '72."

"Let see. If they were eighteen when they graduated from high school and it's been twenty-six years since then, that would make them about forty-five now. Right?"

"Forty-four, forty-five, depending on how old they were when they graduated. Why?"

"I have a patient by the name of Bob Lemonick and he's about that age."

"You think it's the same guy?"

"Probably. How many forty-five-year-old Bob Lemonicks can there be in Ridgeline?"

"Well if she told Carl that she was living . . . where in Baker did she say she was living?"

"You're being a newspaper man again, Ross," Gates needled him. "She said that she was living in a trailer on someone's property which means . . ."

"That they are no longer married or she lied to Carl."

"It also means that we may know who informed her about her mother."

"Interesting, but does it mean anything?"

Wearily Gates rubbed her eyes. "Who knows, Ross? Who knows? She certainly had a right to know about her mother's death even if she did become abusive. And if her husband or ex-husband or whatever he may be told her, then again, so what?"

"So I wasted my time?" Ross sounded peeved.

"Not really," Gates answered. "Now you have some more background on Eugene Crews and his family for your story."

"True, I guess. I just wish I had more."

There was a gentle knock on the door. "Ross, I've got patients hanging out the windows here and a four-thirty meeting to make. I hate to cut this short, but I've really got to run."

"I understand," Ross said. "You will keep me posted, won't you."

"I'll do what I can," Gates said non-committally. "And Ross — thanks."

"You're welcome, Doc, but remember, one good turn deserves another."

"Now, Ross. You know the best favors are those done without the expectation of personal gain."

Ross laughed. "I know no such thing. I'm a reporter, remember?" He laughed again and then hung up.

There was another knock. Gates stood, opened the door, and found Nancy standing sheepishly outside. "George Tanner is on the line and wants to know if you can squeeze him in. He says he's been throwing up all morning."

Gates shook her head. "Okay, tell him to come on down. And you'd better call Pastor Chapman again and see if we can't push that meeting back to five."

"Consider it done."

Stepping from her office, Gates crossed the threshold of exam room two and wondered how long this day would last.

Chapter Twelve

Monday, November 3
5:25 P.M.

"Thank you for waiting, Pastor," Gates said to Paul Chapman as she entered his office. "This has been one of those crazy days, and I'm running behind."

"No problem at all," Chapman said as he motioned to one of four upholstered chairs positioned around a coffee table. "I got the call from your office, so I knew that you'd be late." Gates sat down and quickly glanced around the office. The room was large and on every wall was simulated-walnut paneling. The furnishings divided the room in half, with the four chairs and coffee table defining a casual meeting place where discussions about church business and counseling took place; an ash desk and floor-to-ceiling bookshelves set apart the study area of the room. A few unremarkable paintings hung on the walls, and a large window overlooking the back lot of the church property made the office feel open and inviting.

"I hope I'm not keeping you from anything," Gates said apologetically.

"Not at all," Chapman said as he seated himself opposite Gates. "Sally and I are going out to dinner later, but that's not for a while yet, so we have some time."

"Well, I appreciate this," Gates offered. "I wanted to talk to you about helping someone that has a need. I'm a little embarrassed to say that I may have offered your services before I should have. I think I got the cart before the horse."

"I will help any way I can," Chapman said smoothly. Unlike Sunday, he was dressed casually, wearing a light flannel shirt and pleated brown pants. Gates couldn't help being reminded how comfortable a man Paul Chapman was to be around. He virtually oozed patience and serenity. The few times that Gates had been in the office over the last few years, she immediately felt welcome and at home.

"I knew you would feel that way, but this situation is a little different than most."

"Oh? How so?" Chapman crossed his legs.

"You're aware of the situation with Darlene and Eugene Crews?"

"I don't know them, but I am aware of what happened last Friday night." The pastor revealed no emotion. "Everyone who was at the party knows."

"What you may not know, Pastor, is that Eugene is in the hospital. It appears that he's going to be fine, but he is an elderly man who endured two rather horrendous events over a short period of time. In addition to his wife's . . . death, he was attacked by his own daughter."

"Attacked?" Chapman's brow furrowed.

"Yes. She was upset about her mother's suicide and she unloaded on him; verbally at first then physically. I happened to be there. He went down in a heap. I thought he might be having a heart attack, but it looks like it was just severe anxiety. Anyway, I called the hospital to check up on him, and he shared his concern about the funeral for his wife. He has no one to help him in these matters. Before I realized what I was saying, I suggested that you might be willing to help."

Gates watched as Chapman's head nodded in thought. "And because of the way in which Darlene died and Eugene's . . . it is Eugene isn't it . . . ?" Gates nodded. ". . . and Eugene's participation in the suicide you feel that I might find involvement difficult."

"The thought did cross my mind."

"I'll help any way I can," Chapman said flatly.

A wave of surprise rolled through Gates. "I'm glad to hear that. I know Mr. Crews will be relieved."

"But you're surprised."

"Frankly, yes. I thought you would have reservations about the whole matter." She shifted in her seat.

"I do, but that doesn't matter at the moment."

This time it was Gates' brow that furrowed.

A smile, broad and sincere, spread across the pastor's face. "Surely you're not puzzled, Doctor. Let me explain." Chapman uncrossed his legs and leaned forward. "I believe you said you were at the Crews' house when this incident between Eugene and his daughter occurred. In other words, you saw it happen?"

"Yes, some of it. I witnessed the slap that downed Mr. Crews."

"What did you do then?"

"Well, Carl Berner grabbed the woman and I went to aid Mr. Crews."

"Do you believe that physician-assisted suicide is ethical and that Mr. Crews' participation in it was good and right?"

"I do not," Gates said defensively. "Not by any stretch of the imagination. I oppose it at every level."

"Then why did you help him when he was in pain?"

"Because I'm a doctor. That's my job."

Pastor Chapman let his smile widen, leaned back in the chair and raised his palms. "Well, there you have it. That's why I'm willing to help Mr. Crews. He's in pain, and it's my job."

Shifting her vision from her pastor to the blue carpet on the floor, Gates let the thought percolate in her mind. As a doctor she was able to separate a person from his deeds. It was not required that she like her patients, only that she provide professional and competent care. Gates was amiable enough to get along with most people, and genuinely liked most of her patients. But in those few cases where she was required to treat people who were difficult, self-centered and even self-destructive, she was able to place her feelings aside and focus on the disease. Was that what she was doing with Eugene Crews? She didn't think so. The few moments that she had spent with the man in person and on the phone, coupled with what she saw of him on the videotape and the way in which he unashamedly oozed love for his wife, made Gates appreciate, if not admire, the elderly man.

"Let me say something else," Chapman said, interrupting her reverie. "I know I'm preaching to the choir when I say this, but Christ taught us not only how to love God and live for Him, but also how to love our neighbors. You know as well as I do that loving others is a very difficult task, but it is nonetheless the thing that distinguishes Christians from others. I have people in my office from time to time who have committed serious sins: adultery, theft, hatred, and even child abuse. Their sins trouble me. I don't like to hear about it and in my heart I wish they would go away. But then Christ's words come to me: 'For I did not come to call the righteous, but sinners.' "

Gates recognized the verse. "In which Gospel is that found?"

"Matthew, chapter nine," Chapman answered. "When I was in seminary, Gates, there was a small group of students who believed that Christians should distance themselves as far as possible from unbelievers. They were promoting what seemed to me at least, an elitist Gospel. But I couldn't reconcile that with what I was learning from the Bible. How can we be the salt of the earth if we are kept in the salt shaker? What good is light if it never dispels darkness? Do you understand what I'm getting at here?"

"I think so."

"The thing that I have to keep reminding

myself of is this: Jesus hung out with sinners; it was the religious people He had trouble with. To be brutally honest, Jesus was most critical of people with my job — religious leaders, I mean."

"So by helping Mr. Crews with the funeral arrangements, you may be helping him in other important ways."

"Hopefully."

"That makes sense. But I want to make sure that I understand something. I wanted to ask you this Sunday, but . . . well, I know how busy you are on Sundays. You are opposed to what Norman Meade did?"

To Gates' surprise, Pastor Chapman didn't answer immediately. Instead, he chewed his lower lip and stared off into the distance. Silence hung in the air like a slowly descending mist. "I'm not as convinced as you," Chapman finally replied.

"I don't understand," Gates said seriously. She felt suddenly let down. "I thought all Christians believed in the sanctity of life."

"Well, I can't speak for all Christians, but I certainly believe that life is precious and a gift from God."

"Then how can you . . ."

"Let me explain . . . or try to explain," Chapman leaned forward again, his expression serious. "In principle we are in full agreement, but sometimes things go beyond the simple principle — there's the individual to consider. For example, we can sit here talking about the Christian and medical ethics of voluntary euthanasia; we can gather the literature, read the books of theology and philosophy, and spend years in the process. While we do that, however, there may be someone down the street in unimaginable pain with no hope for release, or facing a certain and terrifying death. Academically I agree with you, but when I think of the poor soul who suffers so much while others debate his or her condition . . . well it gives me pause. In other words, when I think of the individual and the reality of anguish, then I'm slower to agree."

"I must admit, I'm amazed to hear this," Gates said. In truth she was more than merely amazed, she was shocked, astounded. She had assumed that Pastor Chapman would rally to her side without question.

"I know you are," Chapman said, "and to be truthful with you, I'm a little surprised to hear it myself. My fear is, Gates, that we can stand on principle and lose sight of the individual. It would be easy for me to stand in the pulpit and denounce what happened at the Crews' house, but I'm not in Darlene's situation. I know this is shocking, and I don't want to be misunderstood. You'll never hear me promote voluntary euthanasia or physician-assisted suicide from the pulpit — never. If we could take any one hundred Christians at random and line them up, about seventy of them would side with you; another two might state their uncertainty, and only one would come forward and say that physician-assisted suicide is appropriate."

"But it's not biblical at all," Gates objected. "The Bible is clearly against suicide."

"Is it?"

"Are you telling me the Bible doesn't speak against suicide?" Gates asked more sharply than she intended. If Pastor Chapman was offended, he didn't show it.

"The word 'suicide' never appears in the Bible, nor are there any laws against suicide specifically mentioned. Now don't misunderstand me here, and please don't go misquoting me either. The word 'cocaine' doesn't appear in the Bible, nor are there any specific laws against its use, but that doesn't mean that drug use is not a sin. We have many verses that provide guidelines that would prohibit the use of recreational drugs. My point is that we need to be careful using the Bible to defend our views when the Bible is silent on those issues."

"What about the verse that says, 'The Lord

giveth, and the Lord taketh away'?"

"Job, chapter one, and that's not a reference to life but to the things that Job lost. We could also use those verses that teach us that we are made in God's image and that our bodies are the temple of the Holy Spirit. You can make a strong case against physician-assisted suicide and you'd probably be right. But remember that those are arguments of logic and not clearly laid down biblical laws."

Chapman continued: "One of the verses that supports your view the best, at least in my mind, is Romans 14:7–8: 'For not one of us lives for himself, and not one dies for himself; for if we live, we live for the Lord, or if we die, we die for the Lord; therefore whether we live or die, we are the Lord's.' "

"That's exactly my point," Gates said. "None of us lives or dies for ourself."

"However," Chapman said, raising a finger, "there are those who would argue that the Apostle Paul considered suicide for himself."

"Where could they come up with that?" Gates asked bewildered.

"I don't buy it myself. Too much of a stretch for me, but just so that you hear some of the other side . . ." Chapman rose from his seat, went to the bookshelves behind his desk, and removed two books. As he brought them over to the seating area, Gates could see that they were Bibles. "Again, this is a stretch, but it is an interesting stretch. Find Philippians chapter one." Gates thumbed through the pages of the New Testament until she found the reference. "Okay now start with verse 21. Do you want to read it out loud, or shall I?"

Clearing her throat, Gates read, " 'For to me, to live is Christ, and to die is gain. But if I am to live on in the flesh, this will mean fruitful labor for me; and I do not know which to choose. But I am hard-pressed from both directions, having the desire to depart and be with Christ, for that is very much better; yet to remain on in the flesh is more necessary for your sake.' "

"You see what they're getting at?" Chapman asked.

"The word 'choose'?"

"Exactly. They would say that Paul was struggling with the choice of dying or continuing to live, and that his motivation was to be with the Lord. Interesting spin."

"Interesting, but not conclusive, Pastor."

"Agreed. Remember, I'm not arguing for physician-assisted suicide, I'm just explaining why I'm a little reluctant to be dogmatic about it. It's a difficult thing for me to say, 'I know you're in horrendous pain, but you're just going to have to deal with it.' The flip side of that is this: I can't bring myself to say that voluntary euthanasia is proper. It doesn't sit well with me."

"So we are in agreement?"

"Mostly. I'm not suggesting that you change your opinion, but I am suggesting that you pour a healthy stream of compassion over your fervency."

The word compassion rang like a bell in Gates' mind. She was a humane person, deeply so. Had she really set aside compassion on this issue? Despite her sympathy for Eugene Crews at his house that frightening night and when she called him at the hospital, she had felt an undertow of resentment, punctuated by moments of indignation. How could she not feel these emotions. Euthanasia, voluntary or otherwise, was the very antithesis of her beliefs and of her training. Opposition to such ideas was even part of the Hippocratic Oath which stated: "I will do no harm." She knew that many medical schools had made taking the oath voluntary, and some had even allowed the graduating class to create their own oath. Gates, however, had taken the oath and valued its precepts.

"You okay, Gates?" Pastor Chapman asked softly.

Gates, drawn up from the well of her thoughts, again focused her attention on her pastor. "Yes, I'm fine. Just thinking about what you've said. I guess this topic is just one of my hot buttons."

"It should be," Chapman offered. "It affects not only your profession but your philosophy of life. How could you not be moved by the situation?"

Gates nodded her agreement.

"How's your friend, Norman Meade?" Chapman inquired.

"Getting by," Gates answered. "His attorney thinks that he'll be out on bail by the middle of the week."

"Then what?"

Gates was puzzled. "What do you mean?"

"What happens once he's out on bail? Does he go home and wait for trial? Or does he hang around Ridgeline?"

"I don't really, know," Gates said with a shrug. "I never really thought about it."

Chapman nodded. "Well, anyway, I'll go down and visit Mr. Crews in the hospital tomorrow and then start making arrangements for him. I'm not sure what to do about his daughter. That could be touchy. I guess I'll just have to play it by ear."

"I appreciate this, Pastor. I'm sorry for offering your services without first consulting you."

"No harm done," Chapman said. "Who

knows what good God will bring out of all of this."

Gates wondered if any good could come out of a suicide and murder.

Chapter Thirteen

Monday, November 3
6:45 P.M.

Professional detachment had always been the defense mechanism of choice for Gates McClure. The discipline allowed her to dismiss emotion and view problems from a safe distance. Emotions blurred the boundaries between good and bad decisions. In medicine, people either had diseases or they didn't. There were times, more times than Gates cared to admit, in which the doctor had no idea what disease afflicted his or her patient, but that usually succumbed to diligent inquiry, if the physician didn't become emotionally involved. At least, that's what she had been taught.

Emotions were expensive things that took their payment by troubling the thoughts of the doctor. To prevent this, it was best not to let feelings be involved in treatment. Discover the disease and treat it. Anything — everything — else was ancillary.

Of course it never worked that way. Physicians were human, and humans carried a whole truckload of emotional baggage. Despite all appearances, no doctor could inform a mother that her child has leukemia; or a husband that his wife would never come home again and not be touched by the soul-rending sorrow she witnessed. Those doctors who had succeeded in fully insulating themselves from all emotion often became failures in their personal and family lives — a high price to pay.

Gates struggled to keep objectivity and emotion in balance. To be a good doctor she had to care for those she treated; to be an efficient doctor she had to be able to set aside emotions that might fog her thinking. Unfortunately and fortunately, creation had not equipped the soul with an on/off switch. If such a toggle switch did exist, then Gates was stuck in the middle.

Driving down Highway 22 from the church toward her home, her headlights pushing back the inky blackness of the mountain night, she struggled with the swirling thoughts and emotions sweeping through her mind. The storm in her soul seemed to be picking up energy.

When Gates was eight years old, she and her sister Anne were traveling cross-country with their parents to visit some distant relatives in Nebraska. It had been a warm evening and the sky was quickly filling with slate gray clouds that tumbled through the atmosphere. Her parents drove in silence but were visibly concerned as they listened to the radio. Gates heard the words "tornado warning" uttered several times by the radio newscaster, and each time the phrase was uttered her mother would look at her father seated behind the wheel.

Gates, already deeply in love with all things scientific, found it exhilarating. She asked question after question about tornadoes until her mother finally demanded quiet. Gazing out the window, Gates watched in rapt attention as a dark funnel began to drop from the sky some distance north of them. She felt the car speed up. The funnel grew closer and closer to the ground, waving randomly as it did like the loose end of string flapping in a breeze. Then, as suddenly as it appeared, the funnel dissipated. Gates was sad; her parents ecstatic.

There was a funnel cloud of emotion spinning in Gates' head right now. Each hour that passed made the funnel drop closer to the ground zero of her psyche. Like real tornadoes the real damage came when spinning, swirling wind met stiff ground and unbending buildings. Except here the danger was not damaged property, but damaged beliefs.

Much of what Paul Chapman had said to Gates made sense. She didn't like it, but it still made sense. Life was so much easier when hued in black and white. Perhaps she was being too harsh. Not that her belief was wrong, she was certain that all forms of suicide were immoral, but that her expression was improper. Still that was the trick, wasn't it? That's where the genius lay: in knowing how to stand up for a belief without crushing dissenters in the process. There were times when that simply was not possible. Crimes could not be tolerated simply to protect compassion.

As she drove, Gates made a commitment to be more compassionate with the issue, but no sooner than she formed those words in her mind she felt . . . wrong. *Perhaps I shouldn't change my approach at all,* she reasoned. That mental statement brought a rerun of the same feeling . . . wrong. So what should she do? She had no answer for herself, and that made her angry.

Rounding a wide easy bend, she directed her car farther up the mountain. From there it would only be another ten minutes to her house where she . . .

Bright lights stabbed her eyes with a painfully piercing whiteness. Gates winced and instinctively put her foot on the brake. A shadow, silhouetted against the backdrop glare of the lights moved in front of her. Car? Animal? Person? Gates couldn't see, but her subconscious impression screamed that something was wrong. Gates slammed the brake pedal down. The rubber tires squealed in protest against the sudden stop.

A bump rumbled through the car. At first Gates thought she had hit the shadowy image, but the impact came from behind her, not in front. There was more noise as other tires emitted loud protestation against the pavement. Her heart pounded frantically. What had she done?

The lights moved, dancing slightly from side to side, but remained fixed on Gates.

"Turn that off! Now!" The voice was familiar. It was Carl Berner. A moment later the lights dimmed and then winked out. Gates realized that she must be in front of the police station. "On the sidewalk, right now!" Gates could tell from Carl's inflection that he was angry . . . more than angry, he was livid.

As her eyes attempted to adjust to the returning night, she heard more conversation.

"But officer . . ."

"No buts. You get out of the street and onto the sidewalk or I will personally escort you there — in handcuffs."

Blinking, Gates let her eyes adjust and tried to make sense of what had just happened. Now that the offensive light was out of her eyes, she could see people walking back and forth across the street. *This is crazy,* Gates thought. *This is a four-lane state highway, you don't just walk across the street.*

"You all right?" Carl asked, his voice muffled.

Gates turned to see him standing at the side of her car. She rolled the window down. The cool night air poured in freely. "I think so. I don't feel hurt. What happened?"

"Some brain-dead cameraman was setting up his camera to take a shot of all the action. He was crossing the highway when he turned on the camera's light. The idiot had it pointed right into oncoming traffic. You happened to be in the lead."

"That explains the light," Gates said. "But I felt a bump. Did I hit something?"

"No, someone hit you." Carl nodded behind her. "You got rear-ended."

Gates reached for the door handle. "Is anyone hurt?"

"Settle down," Carl said authoritatively. "I don't think so, but I'll check. First thing we have to do is clear this street or there's going to be more trouble." Carl turned and shouted across the street. "Wells, clear the driveway, I want these two cars in the parking lot. I also want the clown with the camera in my office immediately."

Peering through the darkness, Gates could see a crowd, far larger than what she had seen earlier. A few were carrying signs. Several police officers scurried to carry out Carl's orders.

"Look, Doc," Carl said. "I want you to pull into the parking lot and we can sort this thing out. Be careful, there are a lot of people there, most of whom have left their brains at home. One of my officers has stopped oncoming traffic, so it's safe to turn."

Twisting the wheel, Gates exited the road and slowly pulled through the curb-cut and onto the parking lot. Another car followed close behind. No parking stalls were empty, so Gates pulled as far forward in the lot as possible and switched off the car.

A moment later she was outside trying to make sense of what she was seeing. The crowd of media had grown, but now there were others. Scores of people, most toting hand-painted signs, were on the sidewalk.

"I'm so sorry," a woman's voice said. "I guess I was following too close and when you stopped so suddenly . . . well, I hit your car."

Gates turned to see a young woman no older than twenty, eyes red and moist, standing next to her. "Are you all right?" Gates asked concerned. "Did you hit your head?"

The girl shook her head. "No, I don't think we hit that hard. My parents are going to kill me. This is their car." She motioned to the white Ford Taurus.

"Well, the collision didn't feel that bad. Maybe there's no damage. Let's see." Walking to the front of the car the two women studied the grill and bumper. The parking lot lights cast harsh shadows across the area but it was easy to see that no damage was done. "Not even a broken headlight," Gates said. "Apparently you had more time to stop than you think. It would be impossible to tell with that light in our eyes."

"But what about your car?"

"Let's take a look." There was no damage to the rear of Gates' car either. "We couldn't even call this a fender bender."

"I'm so sorry."

"It's not your fault," Gates said putting her hand on the woman's shoulder. "What's your name?"

"Marianne Sanders," she replied. "You know, like the old TV show 'Gilligan's Island' . . . 'the professor and Marianne . . .' " She sang the last few words and then giggled nervously.

Gates laughed. "Well, Marianne, I'm Dr.

222

Gates McClure and I don't think you have anything to worry about. Both cars are fine and if you hadn't been paying attention things could be a lot worse. Your parents will understand. How old are you, Marianne?"

"Nineteen."

"Okay, here's what we're going to do. We're going to exchange insurance information just like you were taught in driving school. That way all our bases are covered. Since there's no damage no one will have to make a claim, but if your parents ask, you can say that you did everything right."

Officer Dan Wells walked by, his hand firmly clamped on the arm of the cameraman who had precipitated the whole event.

"Everybody okay, Doc?" Wells asked.

"Fine," Gates said. "Just fine."

"Good." Wells guided his charge up the stairs and into the police station.

As she returned her attention to Marianne something caught Gates' attention. It was a person, a woman standing in the parking lot of the hardware store where Gates had parked the day before. She was staring at Gates, casting a vicious, bile-laced expression. It was Martha Crews and she looked every bit as angry as when Gates first saw her. Gates suddenly felt a wave of concern wash over her.

"Let's go in and take a report." It was Carl.

"It doesn't look like we really need one, but I want all the paperwork in order just in case we need it. Who knows, maybe you can sue the television station that hired that guy."

"I don't think we would have much of a case since there's no damage and no injuries," Gates said seriously.

"That's what attorneys are for," Carl said, then he let go a small chuckle. "I think you ought to sue just for the principle of the thing. That was one of the dumbest stunts I've ever seen."

"You don't think you're overreacting?" Gates asked.

"No," Carl said angrily. "This day and this case just keep getting worse. If I was overreacting, then I would have shot the . . ."

"Carl," Gates interrupted, "Marianne is shook up enough. She doesn't need to be hearing that from you."

"Okay, okay," Carl said. "I'm sorry, but this whole thing is really starting to work on my last nerve."

"What's going on?" Gates asked.

"You and Marianne come on inside. We'll talk there." Carl jogged up the wooden steps and into the police station.

The incident report took less than ten minutes to complete. Gates and Marianne exchanged insurance information and phone numbers. All the while the cameraman sat fidgeting uncomfortably on a wooden bench next to the wall. He attempted to speak several times, but was silenced by a piercing look from Carl. Once, the male reporter that worked with the cameraman attempted to enter the building but was quickly ushered out by Dan Wells, who resumed his guard position outside the front door. When the paperwork was finished, Marianne thanked everyone and left.

"So what's going on, Carl?" Gates asked. "It's starting to look like a convention out there."

Carl woefully shook his head. "It just keeps getting worse, Doc. I'm going to have to ask for help from the county sheriff if things don't ease up soon. I've got all my men on duty just trying to control that crowd out there."

"Who are they?"

"About half are media, the other half are from an anti-euthanasia group. They've been showing up all afternoon. They're here to protest Meade. The media love it. Gives them something to report." He paused and looked at the chagrined photographer on the bench. "When they're not out causing accidents, that is."

"What do they want from Meade?" Gates asked.

"A confession, I guess; I don't really know." Carl stacked the papers he had been working on and set them on a nearby desk. "They really don't like Meade. I would go so far as to say that some downright hate him."

"What are you going to do?" Gates inquired seriously.

"Not much I can do as long as they remain orderly. They're well organized. Some guy from their group is calling the shots. It's clear he's done this before. He won't let anyone in his group block the driveways or step into the street. They march in a systematic way and stay on the sidewalk." Again Carl looked at the journalist. "I wish we could get everyone to cooperate in the same way."

"Do you think they pose a threat to Norman?"

Carl shook his head. "No. I've talked with a few of the picketers and they're very respectful and polite. I think they just want to use this opportunity to get a point across."

"Not everyone out there is friendly," Gates said. "I saw Martha Crews in the next parking lot. She looks as angry as ever."

"Yeah, I saw her too."

"Is she with the group?"

"I doubt it, but I don't know. I've been a little busy here. I did let her know that I was aware of her presence and that I didn't want any trouble."

"You spoke to her?"

"For just a moment, but that's when your little accident happened."

Gates turned to face the man on the bench who was now studying his fingernails affecting a nonchalant image, an image that was betrayed by the rapid jiggling of his leg, which he bounced up and down like a piston in a race car. "What will happen to him?" Gates asked in a hushed tone.

Carl answered in a similar tone: "Not much, I'm afraid. I'll just write a citation for jay-walking or something. That's about all I can do."

"I suppose I owe you an apology," Gates said.

"For what?"

"If I hadn't asked you to let Norman stay here in jail until his hearing, you wouldn't be having all this trouble. I feel a little guilty."

"Good," Carl said. "But just a little guilt. Okay? It was my decision after all."

Gates nodded. "Well, I think I'm going to head home. I've had all of this day that I want."

"You're lucky," Carl said. "I wish I could

go home. Do you want to see Meade while you're here?"

Gates thought for a moment, then said, "No. I have some things to think about. Maybe tomorrow."

"Tomorrow might be good, since he's being arraigned Wednesday."

"A date's been set?" Gates was surprised that she hadn't thought to ask.

"Yup. Two-thirty at the county courthouse," Carl said. "Both coroners' reports should be ready tomorrow."

"Both?"

"Darlene Crews and Ed Warren."

"Can I see the reports when they come in?" Gates inquired.

"No. You're not officially involved."

"Will the media get to see the reports? If they do, then showing me isn't breaking a code of trust is it?"

"Go home, Gates," Carl said wearily. "I'll think about it, but not now, so you might as well go home."

Without further discussion, Carl turned to the photographer. "All right, buddy, let's see if we can't write you a ticket or something."

The phone in room 18 of the Lodge Pole Inn rang sharply, jolting Lea Ballew awake. Looking at the cheap radio-alarm clock that was glued to the top of the night stand, she read the green numbers: 12:00. Normally a night owl by nature, Lea had unexpectedly dozed off while watching her station's eleven o'clock news program. She had videotaped her story earlier that evening and had Jeff Penna uplink it to the station via the microwave dish. On television it appeared that she was giving a live report, when in actuality she was watching the program like countless other viewers.

There had been nothing new to report about the murder of Ed Warren, but there was good footage of the growing crowd of protesters that had flooded the walkway in front of the police station. A few "person-on-the-street" interviews sandwiched between a thirty second opening and closing made for a pretty decent report, but it still lacked the punch of hard, breaking news.

After the taping of the report she had Jeff drive her to her room at the Lodge Pole. Fortunately, because the town was just four miles down from the High Peak ski resort, there were a dozen different motels and inns in Ridgeline — every one of them filled with "newsies." Since she had been the first reporter on the scene and the first to file a story, she and Jeff had had no problem in securing accommodations. Others who arrived the following day had not been so lucky.

"Yeah," she said as she snapped up the phone. She listened. "Are you sure?" She listened again. "And you got all this through newspaper stories?" Listening. "Okay, great. This is really great. I can use this big time. I owe you lunch when I get back. Can you fax those to me?" She paused and picked up the phone and studied the back. "Yeah, it's got a plug-in module. I should be able to hook up in my laptop and then you can fax the docs right to it. Give me ten minutes to fire the thing up and plug in the modem, then send me the stuff." More listening. "Got it. Thanks again. I think we might just scoop everybody."

Hanging up the phone, Lea sat up on the bed and thought about what the diligent research assistant, who had sacrificed a night out with friends, had uncovered. Quickly walking to the chipped walnut dresser situated opposite her bed, she picked up the gray IBM laptop computer and set it next to the phone. It took only seconds to unplug the phone line from the telephone and reinsert the small plastic end into the modem port. Depressing the power button, the small computer came to life with subtle, quiet clicks and buzzes. A few key strokes later she was ready to receive the stream of data that would travel the 120 miles from Los Angeles.

Two minutes later the modem began to speak in chirps and whistles as it answered an incoming call. Lea watched as the computer inhaled the bits of data through the phone lines. In a short time, she would be looking at an exact facsimile of the documents the research assistant had discovered.

Oblivious to the fact that this was a no-smoking room, Lea lit the end of a cigarette, inhaled deeply, and then let the internalized smoke ooze slowly out of her mouth in gentle fog-like billows. Now she had something to go on; something to report, and it was being sent to her as she sat on her bed.

Technology was wonderful. Of course, Dr. Gates McClure might disagree tomorrow, but what did that matter? What mattered was finding and reporting the truth. That's what she did. That's why they called her a reporter. It was her job to dig for details and bring them to light. Wasn't that, after all, why people watched the news? Isn't that why they sat on their couches and in their overstuffed chairs, their dinner carefully balanced on their laps while they were spoon-fed story after story in two-minute, bite-size chunks? There was a time when the industry did more in-depth reporting, but most people weren't interested in fleshed-out accounts of events. They didn't want to listen to detailed descriptions and discussions. They wanted to suck the truth in through their eyes as video pictures poured into their living rooms. For those who wanted more, well they could read a magazine — of course, the news would be a week old.

A hollow bar that slowly filled with a blue ribbon finally reached its destination indicating that the faxed material had been successfully received. Lea reconnected the phone and then began to study the image of the documents as they displayed themselves upon the color monitor. She was looking at a newspaper story that had been run over a decade ago in the old *Los Angeles Herald*. Scanning the text quickly, she smiled at what she read.

"Well, Dr. McClure, it looks like you've been holding out on us." Lea drew heavily on the cigarette and then exhaled noisily. "What was in darkness shall now be in the light."

Chapter Fourteen

Tuesday, November 4
7:45 A.M.

Gates leaned back in her chair and slowly massaged her temples. She was tired despite a night's sleep, and she knew that was a sign of stress. She was internalizing the events of the last few days. Everything had been so unexpected, so out of the norm for her. Her mind raced. Her stomach churned endlessly and the muscles around her neck and shoulders were tightening into ribbons of stiff flesh. All of this was accompanied by an irrational feeling that the worse was yet to come; as if some ancient Greek muse of premonition were whispering in her ear, "You ain't seen nothin' yet."

Squeezing her eyes shut, she took several deep, cleansing breaths and then returned her attention to the computer screen in front of her. Last night, before drifting off to restless, dream-laced sleep, she had decided to arrive at the office early and search for information on physician-assisted suicide. Rising at five, she hastily showered and prepared for the day. By six she was seated in her office chair with the computer on and a stack of medical journals on the desk.

Deciding that it would be easier to let the computer do the searching, Gates logged onto the Internet, and using one of the many available search engines she entered the phrase "physician-aided suicide" into the appropriate place. Less than five seconds later she had six hits. Although not a computer expert, Gates knew her way around the Internet (which she used to search for information on everything from medications to medical journals) enough to be able to narrow her search so that it yielded the best possible results.

Each hit appeared as a title in blue with a brief description of subject covered at that web location. By directing her mouse pointer to the blue letters and clicking the mouse button, she was immediately transported to that site. Some of the references were useless, being outdated or written by nonprofessionals. She decided that "physician-aided suicide" may be too abstract so she did another search using the phrase "physician-assisted suicide," which yielded 135 references. She then tried "euthanasia." This time her computer screen filled with 3,369 references. An overwhelming gold mine of information.

Scanning the massive list, Gates realized that the search had offered everything from serious discussions by medical ethicists to unexpected articles on animal control. Selecting some of the more promising sites, she began to print out page after page of material. It had become clear to her that the subject was vast and far more than she could cover before patients started arriving.

She did, however, pick up a few things previously unknown to her. One striking discovery was the number of pro-euthanasia groups. There was even one web site called Death Central where the privilege to die was proclaimed as a legal right protected under the Constitution and the Bill of Rights. It also contained articles about individuals who had chosen to end their lives — they were heralded as heroes.

Equally interesting was the collection of anti-euthanasia sites whose number rivaled that of the supporters. Some of the groups were factions of the right-to-life movement which Gates had wrongly assumed was concerned only with abortion.

She also learned that the topic of euthanasia (which means "good death") had several levels. There was physician-assisted suicide (p.a.s.) in which a doctor helps a patient end his or her life; but there was also something called voluntary euthanasia and active euthanasia. In the former, a person, for whatever reason and not necessarily medical, chose to have their life ended. The basic difference between this and p.a.s. was the presence of a doctor. Active euthanasia was death brought about without the person's immediate consent. Very few promoted this idea, which included lethal injection of the elderly or severely handicapped. As she read from the screen she discovered that the idea of active euthanasia was appalling to all but the most calloused. Still, there were the gray areas in which the line between active and voluntary euthanasia was blurred.

Such was the case of a doctor in Oregon who administered a lethal dose of succinylcholine to a seventy-eight-year-old woman suffering from subarachnoid hemorrhage — bleeding into the brain. During her hospital residency, Gates had seen just such a case. The doctor in charge used the opportunity to train the medical students by informing them that such cases were almost always fatal, and the surgery was only rarely useful. She could clearly recall the doctor wave his hand over the elderly woman and say, "There is nothing that can be done for her."

A brief review of the web sites also brought to light the legal tussles going on. Oregon voters had passed Measure 16 in 1994 which not only permitted doctors to assist patients in suicide, but also set down guidelines for when such a procedure might be used. The measure was immediately swallowed whole by the courts.

It seemed that everyone had an opinion from Catholic priests to New Age gurus. There were even several strongly worded opinions from the American Medical Association.

But what really caught Gates' eye was the thirty or so allusions to the name "Dr. Norman Meade." She printed out each article that contained his name. Before long, Gates had a two-inch stack of paper, the compilation of the many Internet articles she sent to her laser printer. She felt good about obtaining the information, but she was overwhelmed by the amount of material she hadn't selected.

"Well, it's a start," she said to the empty room. Leaning back in the chair, she began to read.

The day had marched on at an even pace and Gates was glad for it. Compared to yesterday's frenetic activities, today's slow and steady stream of work was refreshing. To make matters even more enjoyable, each patient was polite and cooperative. There were no emergencies, no sudden appointments, and no serious diagnoses. If yesterday had been an uncontrolled trip down the white-water of medical practice, then today was a leisurely float on a peaceful lake.

Until 3:15.

Valerie, her face telegraphing the consternation she felt, had come into the exam room as Gates was writing a prescription for a middle-aged woman who was seated on the exam table. Gates looked up from the small pad of paper upon which she was writing. It was unusual for the nurse to interrupt an exam.

"What is it, Valerie?" Gates asked.

"There are some people here to see you, Doctor," Valerie spoke softly and cut her eyes to the door that led to the lobby. Gates understood that Valerie wanted to speak to her alone.

"Okay, just a minute." Tearing the prescription sheet from the pad, Gates turned and handed it to the patient. "Here you go, Mrs. Georgi. This is a prescription for some antibiotics that I want you to take. Follow the instructions on the label and be sure to continue taking the pills until they're all gone — even if you start feeling better right away. If you don't, the infection in your ear might come back and we'll have to start over. You should start feeling better in a day or two. If not, then call for another appointment. Okay?"

The woman nodded. "Thank you, Doctor." She scooted off the exam table and exited the room through the door that Valerie was holding open for her. As soon as the patient had crossed the threshold, Valerie closed the door behind her and walked to Gates.

"All right, what's going on?" Gates asked.

"That woman from the television station and her cameraman are in the lobby. They said that they want to talk to you . . . you know, do a story."

"Which woman? There are a lot of women on television."

"Lea Ballew. The one that did that first news report about the murder."

"And she wants to talk to me?" Anxiety began to boil in Gates' stomach. "Why would she want to talk to me? I'm not officially involved in the investigation."

Valerie shrugged. "I don't know, but she seems like the type who can really be persistent. I can ask them to come back at a more convenient time, but I don't think she'll want to."

"How many patients are in the waiting room?" Gates inquired.

"Just two now, but two more are due soon."

Gates looked at her watch. She was right on schedule and didn't want an interruption to put her behind. Patients deserved to be seen as close to their appointment times as possible. Apprehension began to cloak her thinking in a dark mist, like storm clouds over a mountain peak.

"You want me to tell them to go away?" Valerie asked. "I can be pretty insistent too. I'll treat them like unwanted salesmen."

"I know you can." Gates smiled. Valerie was right, she could be insistent and could probably succeed in expelling the news crew, but not without making a scene. Not speaking with them might imply some hidden impropriety on her part. Although she had no desire to speak to the media, she felt that doing so was the better part of valor. "No, Valerie. I'll take care of it. Let's do this: When I go out there, you ask the next patients . . ."

"Mr. Popolous and Mrs. Greenspan," Valerie said, providing the names.

"You ask Mr. Popolous and Mrs. Greenspan to step into exam rooms two and three. That will clear the lobby for a few minutes. I'll take our visitors into my office. I don't want to spend too much time with them. That would mess our schedule up. So I'll give them ten minutes. If I'm not out of my office in that time, you come get me. Okay?"

"Got it."

Gates led the way out of the exam room, followed closely by Valerie. Gates recognized Lea Ballew from the news report the other night. Seeing her reminded Gates how artificial and overly dramatic the report had been. Ballew was shorter than Gates had expected, but what she lacked in height she made up for in beauty. Her long brown hair draped down to rest on narrow shoulders. Her eyes were a lively brown, with gently curving brows. She wore an eggshell turtleneck and navy blue blazer. Gold earrings of concentric circles dangled from her lobes. A gold necklace linked with pearls graced her neck.

Standing with her was a pleasant-looking man with a camera in his hand. He wore jeans and a flannel shirt. His eyes were kind.

Before anyone could speak Valerie took the lead. "Mr. Popolous, Mrs. Greenspan, we're ready for you now. Would you please follow me?" An elderly man with coal-black hair rose from his seat, winced in pain, and then slowly stepped toward Valerie, crossing between Lea and Gates. Following him was an equally elderly woman.

No sooner than the two patients had passed Gates, Lea spoke: "Dr. McClure, I'm Lea

Ballew from KGLA-TV and this is my cameraman Jeff Penna." Gates wondered how Penna felt being referred to as *my* cameraman. "I wonder if we might trouble you for some time?"

"What would KGLA need with me?" Gates asked pointedly. She turned to look at Nancy who was seated behind the reception desk.

"We're following up on the Ed Warren murder," Lea said sweetly. Gates sensed insincerity.

"I'm afraid I know very little about Dr. Warren's murder," Gates explained. "I have nothing to offer you."

"Actually, we're more interested in Dr. Norman Meade," Lea answered. "You do know him, don't you?"

Swell, Gates thought. *I don't need this today.* "Yes, I know him, but I still don't see how I can be of help to you, or offer you anything that would interest your viewers."

Lea smiled, but the sweetness was gone. "I'll be happy to explain that."

Gates turned to Nancy. "May I have the appointment book, please?" Nancy handed the large black book to her. Gates studied the pages for a few moments, slowly shaking her head. "Things look pretty full, Ms. Ballew, what day were you thinking?"

"Today. Right now would be fine."

"I'm afraid I have patients to see."

"We promise not to take very long."

This was going nowhere. Gates had hoped that they would simply go away. She had hoped that, but knew it was unlikely. She looked down at the appointment book, shook her head, then handed the book back to Nancy. "Ten minutes."

"It may take longer than that," Lea said.

"Ten minutes is all I can afford right now," Gates said firmly. "My office is back here." Gates started down the hall.

"It would be better if we stayed out here," Lea replied. "It's hard to shoot in a small room."

Gates sighed. "If you wish to speak to me, you can do so for ten minutes in my office."

"Dr. McClure," Lea said testily. "I don't think you understand. We've come a long way to be here and have gone through some trouble. We would appreciate it if you would cooperate."

That was it. Over the last few days, Gates' life had been turned upside down. A friend she had not seen in years suddenly appeared and was accused of murder. She had been harshly thrown to the floor, burned her legs with steaming hot soup and been tail-ended on Highway 22. She had witnessed an out-of-control woman brutally attack her frail, elderly father and she was being associated with a medical philosophy with which she did not agree. Now a pushy woman had waltzed into her office, cameraman in tow, and began making demands. Temper was a strong part of Gates' personality, one which she worked very hard to control. She was almost always successful in stifling her ire, but the swelling emotion within her indicated that a failing was inescapable.

Slowly Gates turned to the reporter. "Do you have an appointment?"

"You know I don't."

"Did I ask you here?"

"Well, no . . ."

"All right, then this is how it works. You may follow me into my office or you may leave my lobby, but you may not — will not — prance in here and assume control of my time, my staff, or my work."

"Dr. McClure . . ."

"Ridgeline is a small town and that may have led you to believe that we are all backwoods hicks with no refinement, dignity or self-possession. Well, you're wrong."

"I didn't mean to imply . . ."

"You only have two choices now," Gates interrupted as her temper flared. "Ten minutes in my office or as much time as you like on the street. What's it going to be?"

"I have a job to do, Doctor . . ."

"And it's interfering with my work," Gates snapped. Quickly she turned to Nancy. "Nancy, call the police and tell them that we have trespassers on the property." Nancy immediately snapped up the phone and began dialing.

"Okay, okay," Lea Ballew said raising her hands. "Ten minutes, in your office."

Without a word, Gates turned and walked down the hall. Lea and Jeff followed behind. Valerie was exiting exam room three when Gates saw her. Gates tapped her watch and silently mouthed, "Ten minutes." Valerie nodded and looked at her own watch.

Inside the small office, Gates sat down at her desk and motioned to the two chairs that stood opposite her. The cameraman walked to the farthest corner and propped the video camera on his shoulder. A moment later a bright light mounted to the top of the camera flooded the room.

Gates blinked against the glare. "Is that necessary?"

"Since we have so little time, Doctor," Lea said, ignoring the question, "we need to do away with any pleasantries and get right to the point."

"I'd prefer that." Looking at the camera that was deftly balanced on the cameraman's shoulder, Gates noticed a dark, tapered cylindrical device which she took to be a microphone. She would not only be seen, but heard as well.

"Dr. McClure, in doing background research for the ongoing story of Ed Warren's murder by Dr. Meade, we came across some information that we thought you might like the privilege of responding to."

"I wasn't aware that Dr. Meade had been convicted, Ms. Ballew. Don't you think we should wait for the evidence and trial, if there is one?"

"Your defense of him is admirable, Doctor and understandable."

Gates felt like the crew from "60 Minutes" had just shown up on her doorstep wanting an interview. "Understandable?"

"Yes, understandable. Our research shows that you're connected to Dr. Meade."

Nodding, Gates said, "There's no secret that we went to the same medical school — along with several hundred other people."

"UCLA, isn't that correct?"

"Yes."

"Dr. McClure," Lea said as she leaned back in the chair and steepled her fingers, "an article appeared in the *Los Angeles Herald* a few years back that tells of a young woman — a medical student — who was attacked one night not far from the UCLA campus. The woman in that article was named Gates McClure. That's an unusual name; Gates, I mean. That woman was you wasn't it?"

The ground opened up and swallowed Gates like some hungry fissure in an earthquake. She could feel the blood drain from her face, and her stomach tightened into a knot the size of a man's fist. In the land of constant crime only one paper had bothered to carry the story; a fact for which Gates had been grateful. Lea Ballew had discovered that single article.

"There are certain inaccuracies in the article," Gates managed to utter, her voice lacking its previous fire.

"But it was accurate about you, wasn't it?" Lea pressed. It was clear she was enjoying the moment. It was a fine way for her to get even with Gates for the scene in the lobby.

"My family is unaware of the event and I prefer to keep it that way," Gates said sourly.

"I can imagine. It must have been a horrible thing to endure."

"You have no idea."

"Such events happen frequently in Los Angeles," Lea said with mock concern. "As a woman, I know the fear of such horrendous crimes." She paused for effect. "You had a rescuer, didn't you, Doctor?"

Careful, Gates told herself, *careful. The questions could be loaded or slanted to achieve a certain response. Don't give her that satisfaction.* "I would prefer not to discuss a matter so personal as this. Surely you understand that — being a woman and all."

"I do, I do." Lea pushed on anyway. Gates knew that videotape could be edited so that Lea's surliness could be portrayed as sensitivity. "The man who came to your aid was Norman Meade, wasn't it?"

Gates said nothing. It had been Norman, but she didn't want to say so.

"I imagine you feel you owe him quite a bit."

"You seem to be having trouble with English today, Ms. Ballew. This is a personal matter and I wish to keep it so. What happened over ten years ago has no bearing on events of the last few days. Surely even you can see that. I suggest we end this right now."

"I have a few more questions."

"And they will go unanswered," Gates snapped. "I suggest you go out and find news rather than waste my time and yours trying to create it."

"This is news."

"It's long dead history and nothing more." Gates stood and opened the door. Valerie was on the other side with her hand raised ready to knock. She jumped when the door suddenly swung open. "Oh, good. Valerie, our unwanted guests were just leaving."

"Actually we would like to stay and pursue this."

"Life is full of disappointment," Gates answered quickly. "Turn the camera off and get out."

Slowly Lea rose from her chair and nodded to Jeff, who switched off the camera and light. "Dr. McClure, despite what you think, this is news and we will run the story. It would have been better if you had decided to be helpful instead of being so intractable."

"Expect a lawsuit, Ms. Ballew, and as far as my being intractable it was a natural response to your overt arrogance. Now get out of my office and don't come back."

"As you wish," Lea said, and left the room followed closely by Jeff. Valerie followed behind them like a dog herding sheep.

Slowly, Gates closed the door and sank down in her seat. She was furious; she was devastated. She wanted revenge; she wanted to hide. She felt like screaming; she felt like crying. Instead she folded her arms on her desk and laid her head down.

A lone tear rolled from her eye, down her cheek and fell silently to the surface of the desk.

Chapter Fifteen

Tuesday, November 4
4:00 P.M.

"You're scaring me," Maggie McClure said as she pressed a ground beef, crackers, flour, and egg concoction into the familiar shape of meat loaf. An identical loaf was situated in a deep baking pan that sat upon the counter. "Why can't you just tell me right now?"

"Because, Mother, I don't want to repeat myself." Gates was tearing dark green leaves off a head of romaine lettuce and tossing them into a crystal salad bowl. Orange shavings of carrots sat in a pile on the kitchen cutting board. The room was filled with the ghostly smells of fresh-cut onion. "Pastor Chapman and Carl will be here any minute. That's when we'll talk."

"You were always the hardheaded one," Maggie said as she plopped the hand-pressed meat loaf next to its twin in the pan. "You always did things your way, even as a child."

"Amen," Anne interjected. She was removing dishes and glass tumblers from the dishwasher. "But I have to agree with Gates, Mom."

"I know," Maggie agreed. She turned to the sink and began to wash the raw meat from her hands. "It just sounds so serious. I mean, how often does one of my daughters call for a family meeting and include the pastor and the town's police chief?" She returned to the counter and began to carefully pour a seasoned tomato sauce over the loaves.

The doorbell rang. Tom and Maggie McClure lived in one of the larger homes in Ridgeline, something they were able to achieve through forward thinking, planning, and saving as much money as possible from their salaries as teachers in the San Bernardino Unified School District. They had retired just two years ago and were enjoying the life of travel and freedom for which they had worked so hard.

"I got it." Thomas McClure rose from his favorite, highly worn easy chair and made his way to the front door and opened it. Cool air rushed in carrying the scent of pine with it, which mingled in an oddly pleasant way with the aroma of food from the kitchen. "Come in. Boy, did you all ride together, or something?"

Since the house had been designed as an open floor plan, Gates, Anne, and Maggie were able to watch as the guests entered the large living room. No walls, only counters, separated the kitchen from the combined living and dining area.

"Just coincidence, Tom," Pastor Paul Chapman said as he and his wife Sally crossed the threshold. "Chief Berner pulled in right behind us."

"I've been following you, Reverend," Carl kidded. He was holding hands with his wife, Sharee. "I've got a great picture of you hanging up on my wall at the station."

"See," Chapman said to his wife, "and you thought I was just being paranoid."

"I gave him the picture," Sally retorted and everyone laughed.

Gates crossed the large living room and hugged Sally and Sharee. "Thanks for coming, everyone. I do appreciate this. Come on in and sit down."

"Can we help in the kitchen?" Sharee asked.

"Oh, no," Maggie answered. "There's three women working in here right now, and that's two too many."

"Okay, I quit," Anne said, closing the dishwasher.

"Not until you're done unloading that," Maggie commanded. "Outside this house you may be mayor, but in this house you're just one of the McClure women."

"And proud of it," Anne replied dryly, returning to her duty.

The great room was amply furnished with a large brown, U-shaped couch, a matching love seat and Tom's old recliner. The gathering took seats while Gates offered them coffee or juice.

"As soon as the meat loaf is in the oven . . ." Gates began.

"It's in." A small squeak was followed by a cushioned thud as the oven door slammed shut. Maggie was eager to get things started. "We have some time, so why don't we get down to business?"

Maggie and Anne exited the kitchen and took seats on the couch. Gates pulled a dining-room chair over and situated it so that she could sit and see everyone in the room. Her mouth was dry and her heart fluttered with anxiety. She hadn't been this nervous since her surgical rotation during the third year of medical school.

Gates cleared her throat and looked at the small audience that was staring at her with apprehensive curiosity. Each was there at her invitation. Carl had been the hardest to convince. With the ever-burgeoning crowd in front of his police station, he was reluctant to leave. Gates had made his request a personal one — a favor. Carl didn't refuse.

Swallowing hard, Gates began: "I appreciate you all coming on such short notice. I know some of you had to make sacrifices to be here. As you've probably guessed, this is more than a dinner gathering. I need to share something with each of you that is . . . well, difficult to speak about. In fact, I've not talked about this for over ten years."

She stopped and took in the small crowd. Her mother was leaning forward, arms crossed over her stomach in a classic anxiety pose; her father rocked slowly in the recliner, listening intently; Pastor Chapman and Carl sat stoically, patiently waiting for her to continue. Gates looked at her watch. It was ten minutes past four.

"Most likely," she started, "the five o'clock news show on KGLA will have a story about the Norman Meade affair. That story will include me. If the report doesn't air at five, then I'm sure it will on the eleven o'clock show." She inhaled deeply like a swimmer who had been underwater too long, and then released it. "Earlier today, Lea Ballew bowled her way into my office for an interview. We didn't hit it off very well. I found her arrogant and demanding, and I can be a little quick tempered. I didn't want her there at all, but I couldn't get her to leave. I gave her ten minutes. I wanted to talk to you before the report aired."

"Why did she want to talk to you?" Maggie asked, her voice dripping with concern.

"At first, I thought it was because I know Dr. Meade, but she had more on her mind." Another deep inhalation and release. Her heart fluttered like a leaf in a tornado and her stomach was an ocean of acid. "Something happened to me when I was in medical school and it involves Norman Meade. This Ballew woman found out about it through an old newspaper story."

"Newspaper story?" Anne asked.

Gates nodded. "Only one paper carried the account and it was a small article written by an undergraduate journalism student who stumbled on to it through the campus police. Even then, he got most of the details wrong, but the essence of the account was true."

"Is this what you alluded to the other day," Carl asked, "when you said you owed Meade something?"

Nodding, Gates said, "Yes. I didn't want to talk about it then, and to be utterly truthful, I don't want to talk about it now, but I no longer have a choice."

Hands, hard and rough.

Gates licked her dry lips. Her mouth was arid and hot like the oven in the kitchen. "We, the study group to which Norman and I belonged, were working at the library late one night. I think we were cramming for a pharmacology exam. Anyway, I felt pretty confident about the material so I left early. I was living off campus so I needed to drive home. I was walking to my car, which was a hundred yards or so down one of the big parking lots. I had to pass along some of the other school buildings . . ."

Breath, stale and putrid. She stopped suddenly and lowered her head. "I was . . . I mean . . ."

"Take your time," Pastor Chapman said. "We're not going anywhere."

"Thanks," Gates said quietly. She looked down at the floor, then at her hands that she had been unconsciously wringing. "I . . . I was attacked."

Maggie and Anne gasped. "Oh, my baby . . ." Maggie began, but Gates raised a hand to quiet her.

"Let me get through this before we get emotional." Gates looked up. "Two men, older teenagers I think, I'm not sure. It was dark, they came out of an alley formed by two of the buildings and grabbed me by the hair . . ." Hands, hard and rough. "They pulled me into the alley. One had his hand over my mouth and he was telling me to shut up or he would cut me . . ." Breath, stale and putrid.

"They . . . they said horrible things, frightening things . . ." Words, hushed and harsh; violent and offensive. "They pinned me to the wall and one of them held a knife to my throat. I could feel its point digging into my skin . . ." Pain, piercing, throbbing. "I struggled at first, but they were too strong . . . and there was the knife." Gates cut her eyes away. "I've never been so scared . . ." Helpless, hopeless, lost.

Returning her gaze back to her friends she saw the raw emotion that the story was ripping from their minds. Both Anne and Maggie were covering their mouths with their hands; tears were running down her mother's face. Tom McClure had tears in his eyes too, but there was also pure, undiluted fury there. Carl's jaw was set tight, and the veins in his neck were becoming pronounced; his wife and Gates' good friend, Sharee sat silently, eyes wide, mouth open. Both Pastor Chapman and Sally oozed compassion.

"It was clear what they wanted," Gates continued. "While one held me the other ripped open my blouse." Gates wanted to close her eyes so that she wouldn't have to see the faces of her family and friends, but when her eyes were closed the event came to life again as a ghostly specter of vivid, undeniable, uncontrollable memory.

"That's when I heard another sound," Gates went on. "At first I thought they had another friend, but I could tell that I was wrong by their expressions. I heard footsteps, then they stopped. Both men looked to the entrance of the alley. One raised a finger to his mouth, turned and went to investigate. That's when I saw him: Norman Meade. Even silhouetted as he was by the street lights in the parking lot, I could recognize him. His shadow fell on the men.

"Norman took a step forward," Gates went on, "but the attacker flashed this large knife. He said with a strong accent, 'Go home man. This doesn't concern you. This is our party.' Norman stopped for a moment and stared at the man. This time the guy shouted obscenities and said, 'I'll cut you man. I'll cut you real bad.' Norman looked down the alley and saw me pinned to the wall by the other attacker, the knife still at my throat. I was bleeding a little, but I don't know if Norman saw that. I think he did though because . . . he changed. I've heard of this happening, but I had never seen it before or since. Something snapped in Norman. I had always known him to be gentlemanly, kind, a real sweetheart, but something threw a switch in his brain." Gates stopped.

No one spoke, allowing Gates the privilege

of gathering her thoughts.

"Norman took another step forward and the attacker said, 'I'm warning you man.' Norman was on him before he could finish the sentence. I saw a foot, Norman's foot come screaming up from the ground catching the man in the stomach. I could hear his breath knocked from him. Next, Norman grabbed the man's arm — the one with the knife — lifted it over his head, turned and twisted so that the man was doubled over, his arm held out to the side by Norman. Norman kicked him again, this time in the face." Gates shook her head. "Just like I could hear the man's breath being expelled by the fist kick, I could hear his jaw snap. He dropped to the ground, screaming in pain.

"The man who was holding me looked at Norman, then at me, then at Norman. When he saw his buddy on the ground he released me and charged. I shouted a warning to Norman who had his back turned to us. Just as the attacker reached Norman, Norman spun, arm raised, and landed an elbow to the man's face. The man dropped to his knees. That's when Norman really came unhinged. He started punching and kicking and punching. I thought he was going to kill him, but then he stopped and turned toward me. I'm afraid I was pretty useless. I just stood next to the wall clutching my blouse shut and shaking."

Silence and stillness percolated through the room. Anne broke the silence. "So Norman rescued you."

"He did more than that. He saved my life," Gates said. "I don't think those two would have let me live."

"Why didn't you tell us?" Tom asked. "We're your family. We would have understood and rallied to your side."

Gates shrugged. "I should have, but I just wanted to put the whole thing behind me. You know how private I am. Besides, there was nothing you could do."

"What happened to the perps — your attackers?" Carl asked.

"Both were beaten pretty badly, but they had enough adrenaline or fear, or both, to run when Norman came over to me. Norman drove me home. I refused to go to the hospital — after all, all I had was a little cut. He waited with me while the police took a report. The two men were never found. I was sure the police would find them in some hospital ER, but they didn't. That was the end of it."

Again silence.

"I'm so glad you're all right," Maggie said, visibly shaken by thought of her daughter's ordeal. "We owe Dr. Meade a great deal."

"Is that why you've been helping him?" Carl asked.

"Partly. But I'm not sure you could say that I'm really helping him. I just asked for a few favors, that's all."

"Did he bring all this up again?" Carl inquired suspiciously.

Shaking her head, Gates answered, "No. He hasn't mentioned it. He never has. After that night, we never talked about it again. I think he feels bad about the way he lost control."

"I think we should pin a medal on him," Tom said loudly. "He saved my baby."

"I haven't been a baby in a long, long time," Gates said with a smile.

"You will always be our baby," Maggie said, wiping tears with the back of her hand.

"Thanks, Mom." Gates looked at the others. "This will affect you all, I'm afraid, so I wanted you to hear the story — the real story — from me. As I said, the newspaper article is wrong on several counts, so what Ballew says may be erroneous in detail, but it will be correct in substance."

"Why does she want to run this story?" Anne asked. "What does she get out of it?"

"I'm not certain," responded Gates. "Background on Norman, maybe. A little more mystery. At any rate, it's going to tie me to him in people's minds. I don't know if that's good or bad. Anyway, I didn't want you to get word of this over the television. It didn't seem right."

"I'm glad you told us," Anne said. "It wasn't easy to hear and had to be even harder to tell, but at least we know the truth of the matter." Tears were welling up in Anne's eyes. "You've held on to this secret for so long, Gates. I don't know how you did it."

"Neither do I."

"You are a courageous woman, Gates," Chapman said. "It takes tremendous strength to share what you just shared. I think you will be all the better for it now that it's done."

"I'm not sure that it is done, Pastor. I'm not sure at all."

A fresh coat of darkness painted the mountain community. Lights radiated with yellow warmth from the windows of neighboring houses as if they were attempting to aid the waning moon in its futile effort to illuminate the world. The wind, chilly, but not cuttingly cold, rolled through the trees and down the street. Limbs of trees moaned lightly as they danced with the breeze. In the distance, dogs barked; nearby a late-working woodpecker hammered on the trunk of a ponderosa pine.

Gates sat in a large fan-shaped wicker chair

and watched day surrender to night. She crossed her arms as if hugging herself and tried to ignore the evening chill on the outside and the fearful chill on the inside. Goosebumps rippled along her skin, encouraged both by the cool breeze that licked at her flesh and the ice of uncertainty that filled her being.

The news report was just what Gates thought it would be. Lea Ballew stood before the camera looking professional, sincere, and enthused by the news she was sharing. Describing the account as an "unusual turn of events," Lea Ballew went on to link Gates with Norman Meade, implying a romantic relationship without directly saying so. By the time the three-minute report was over a great many people in Southern California believed that Gates and Norman Meade were tied tightly together, with Gates owing the suspected murderer her very life, and therefore, her undying allegiance and support. Gates knew that no explanation she offered would unwind the tight knot created by that report. A hollowness expanded within Gates; a hollowness that seemed to be consuming her from within.

The front door opened allowing the subdued chatter of people and the clanking, clinking of the dishes being loaded in the sink to pour unhindered into the quiet of Gates' night. Turning, she saw Carl step onto the wood deck that ran the length of Tom and Maggie's house. After closing the door behind him, Carl walked to the white-painted rail that circumscribed the porch, looked up and down the street, then turned to face Gates.

"Nice night," he said as he leaned against the railing. "Won't be long and it'll be too chilly to sit out here."

Gates nodded but didn't speak.

"You okay?" Carl asked softly.

"Yeah," Gates answered, shifting in her chair. The wicker creaked mildly as she moved. "I'll be fine."

"Don't go through this alone, Gates. You've got friends and a great family. We're here for you now and always will be."

"I know, Carl, and I appreciate that. I just came out here to let my emotions settle a little."

It was Carl's turn to nod. "I want you to know how much I appreciate you including me tonight. It helps me understand your interest in Norman and in Warren's murder. For what it's worth, I'm really glad that Meade was there when you needed help."

Gates offered a weak smile. "Me too."

"This may be a bad time," Carl began as he too crossed his arms in an effort to ward off the evening's chill. "I got the autopsy reports today. I thought you might be interested. Do you want to hear about it, or would you rather be alone?"

"In for a penny, in for a pound. Did the reports have anything useful to say?"

"You tell me. Darlene Crews died from an overdose of diazepam and morphine."

"That's not all that surprising," Gates said. "Norman said as much in the video. Well, except he told Darlene Crews that the meds were valium and morphine. Diazepam is better known as valium and isn't truly a barbiturate, but close enough in layman's terms. Doctors and pharmacists would make a distinction."

"Was he lying to Darlene?" Carl asked.

"I doubt it," Gates replied. "The two drugs are from different families, but used for many of the same things. Valium and the others are easier to control and have fewer side effects. What about Warren?"

"Warren was different. The coroner found traces of succy . . . soco . . . ."

"Succinylcholine?" Gates prompted.

"That's it. I don't know how you pronounce these words. They're real tongue twisters."

"Actually, that's one of the easier ones." Gates was surprised. "Are you sure the report said succinylcholine?" Gates spelled the word.

"Positive. Why?"

"It's a neuromuscular block. Normally it's used in short surgical procedures to facilitate intubation. It works fast too — thirty to sixty seconds — but then it wears off in three to five minutes."

"Does that mean that the drug couldn't be the cause of death?" Carl looked puzzled.

"I don't mean that at all. When used properly the drug wears off quickly. An overdose can easily be lethal in two ways. First succinylcholine can paralyze the respiratory system, too much and the patient suffocates. Second, it sometimes leads to malignant hyperthermia."

"What's that?"

"Basically it means that the body overheats. The patient presents with muscle rigidity and high temperature. Blood pressure increases as does the heart rate. In surgery the doctors would attempt to counter with Dantrolene which blocks the release of calcium ions from the sarcoplasmic reticulum."

"I don't pretend to understand any of that, but I do know that Warren was not in surgery."

"Exactly, and that's what makes what happened to him all the more horrible." Gates stared into the night as unwanted images flickered in her mind. "Succinylcholine is not an anesthetic. It doesn't put you to sleep. If Warren received a lethal dose of the drug, then he would almost instantly have muscle seizures and his breathing would stop. During all of that he would be fully conscious and aware of what was going on around him."

"That's sick," Carl reacted.

Gates shrugged. "I'm probably a little too exhausted to think straight, but it doesn't seem to fit, does it? I mean, why would Norman use succinylcholine? Even if he did, then why go through all the trouble of setting up the IV stand, pump, and trigger?"

"That's the way he does things?"

"With his patients he . . ."

"Victims," Carl corrected.

"Don't start with me, Carl. You know I don't approve of what he does. My point is this: Norman uses the IV and trigger to allow the valium and morphine to be introduced into the body in a controlled manner. My guess is that he does this for the comfort of his patient. The sudden introduction of drugs into the body can be traumatic. Judging by what we've seen on the video, Norman does everything to ease suffering, not cause it. He even offered to wait until Darlene had rested. I know that sounds odd, but he seemed consumed with her comfort."

"So?"

"If Norman was angry enough to kill Warren, then I doubt that he would go through the steps to make him comfortable, hook up an IV and then load Warren up with succinylcholine. That's an unlikely scenario for murder, Carl. I have felt all along that despite what Norman does with the terminally ill, he couldn't murder someone, even someone as vile as Warren."

"Wait a minute, Gates. Earlier this evening you said that you watched as something snapped in Meade when he was beating up your attackers. Maybe something snapped again."

Not answering, Gates simply stared at Carl.

"What?" Carl asked. "What?"

"The two events aren't even close to being the same. You can't compare a man defending himself and his friend against a couple of thugs with a knife to premeditated murder. Come on, Carl, the one thing that is crystal clear about all of this is the use of the Norman's IV and trigger. It's too incriminating. I'll bet my dollars to your donuts that if you could test the equipment found in Warren's hotel room, especially the plastic line that ran directly to the needle, that you wouldn't be able to find a trace of succinylcholine. Is that something you can test for?"

"Check the IV line itself? I doubt it, but I could check."

"It couldn't hurt, but as I think of it, I doubt you'd find anything anyway. The saline solution in the IV bag would have continued to run and probably cleaned out the line."

"That would make it impossible."

"I told you I was tired." Gates thought for a moment, then asked: "Do you know if the coroner checked for recent injections?"

Carl shook his head. "No I don't. You mean like if someone had given him a shot?"

"Exactly. It would be pretty small, depending on the needle's bore size."

"You don't think something in the IV killed him?"

"Warren had to be unconscious prior to the IV. Warren was far too belligerent to submit to an unwanted IV. We talked about this, remember? Either someone helped in the murder by forcing Warren to hold still while someone else administered the IV, or Warren was unconscious or already dead when the IV was placed."

"I'm sure the homicide detectives have thought of that," Carl offered.

"I wouldn't assume that. I don't want to tell you how to do your job, but if it were me, I'd check. I assume the detectives have other cases they're pursuing."

"That's true enough, I guess. It couldn't hurt to make a call."

Again the door opened, accompanied by the sound of the television and subdued conversation. It was Pastor Chapman followed closely by his wife Sally.

"I hope we're not interrupting anything," Chapman said.

"You're not," Gates said. "Carl and I were just trying to solve the world's problems from the front porch."

"Well, I wish we could help you, but we need to be leaving. Busy day tomorrow."

"Thank you for coming," Gates said.

"Are you doing okay?" Sally asked sweetly. "Is there anything we can do?"

"I'm fine," Gates said. "If I need anything, then I'll be sure to call."

"You do that," Paul Chapman said. "By the way, I went to see Eugene Crews."

The day's event had almost squeezed Eugene from Gates' mind. "How is he?"

"Better. I think he's being released tomorrow. I spoke with him about the funeral and then I spoke to folks over at the funeral home. There are a few more details to work out, but it looks like the service will be Saturday. It will be graveside only. I think he would like to see you again."

"I'll be there if I can," Gates said. "I appreciate you taking the time to help."

"I'm glad that we could. Well, I guess we need to say our good-byes."

Rising from the wicker chair, Gates hugged both Sally and Paul, thanked them again, and then watched as they walked to their car which was parked on the street.

"He seems like he has his act together," Carl said. "This is the first time that I've spent any time with him."

"That's easy to repair," Gates said with a smile. "Just show up at church this Sunday."

"I may be busy."

"You're always going to be busy, Carl. Some things need to be given a priority."

"You sound like my wife."

"She's a smart woman. You'd do well to listen to her."

Carl laughed. "What? And ruin centuries of tradition? I could be expelled from the Union of Male Chauvinists. Then what would I do?"

"You make it sound like a bad thing," Gates jested. "It really does make a difference in a person's life. My faith has made a big difference for me."

"Is it helping you now?" Carl asked with no animosity.

Gates thought for a moment and wondered

how much praying she had done about the recent events that were so affecting her life. To be honest, she hadn't applied her faith to the matter at all. Gates had always been quick to act, and to do so with a singleness of purpose. Usually she prayed after the event, a habit she knew was backward. Still, she felt the comfort of her faith; the constant abiding peace and purpose. She was still subject to the ups and downs of emotions, but her faith, like the rudder of a ship, kept her on course and assured that she wouldn't capsize.

"Yes, it has helped, and I think it will help even more in the days ahead."

"That's good to hear," Carl said. "You may need it. You just may need it."

Carl's words had the frightening ring of truth to them.

Chapter Sixteen

Wednesday, November 5
7:00 A.M.

Weariness was going to be Gates' companion today. Sleep, deep but impotent, had come quickly and she slept the sleep of the dead: no dreams, no movement, no rest — black numbness. She had been worried that nightmares of her attack would return and prowl the corridors of her weary and troubled mind. Instead, sleep covered her like an avalanche. When she awoke her eyes were gritty and her thoughts clouded. Instead of waking refreshed, she felt a compelling need for a nap.

Following her usual routine, she showered with only mild discomfort from her burned legs, ate a bowl of corn flakes, drank a cup of coffee, and dressed for the day. Gates then stepped from her house and walked to her Honda Civic which she had left in the driveway the night before.

At first the sight of the car did not register with her. It took a moment for what she was seeing to seep through her already churning thoughts. Something was wrong. A second later she began to slowly circle the vehicle. All four tires were flat; a ragged slice in each of the sidewalls. In addition, someone had "keyed" her car — dragging the pointed end of a key along the paint, leaving an enormous scratch that reached to the primer coat. On the hood there were more scratches and this time they formed words: "Thou shalt not kill."

"I don't need this," Gates said to herself angrily. "In fact, this is the last thing I need." Quickly she turned and reentered the house. She picked up the phone and dialed the Police Department. Carl was already on the job. After Gates identified herself, she was put immediately through to the Police Chief.

"I'll be there in ten minutes," was all Carl said, then he hung up.

Over the last few days, Gates had experienced almost every possible human emotion from unexpected joy to searing anger. Now she was furious. The attack on her car was unwarranted and grossly misplaced. Her only crime, and it was certainly no crime in her eyes, was that she knew Norman Meade. But that simple truth alone was enough for someone to vandalize her car.

Deep within Gates a new emotion began to

rise: apathy. She wanted to throw her hands up and scream, "I don't care anymore. I don't care what people think. I don't care what happens to Norman. All I want to do is pack up and leave; to go someplace where no one knows me." The emotion was a lie. It would be easier for Gates if she could be indifferent to it all, but she couldn't. She never could stop caring regardless of the personal price. Others had been able to do so, she had seen them shut themselves off from those around them. As much as Gates might want to emulate them, she knew she would never be able to do so.

Carl arrived in precisely ten minutes just as he had said he would. Gates, who had been watching for his arrival, stepped out of the house to meet him.

"Ouch." Carl grimaced. "They sure did a number on you."

"I see no benefit in admiring vandalism," Gates snapped.

"Easy, Doctor. I'm on your side."

"Sorry," Gates frowned at her behavior. "I'm more than a little upset at this. Why me? Why vandalize me?"

"Guilt by association, Gates. I was afraid that something might happen after that report last night. Meade was still locked up in my jail and therefore protected. You on the other hand . . . well, you're an easy target."

"What do you mean Meade was locked up in jail? You said, 'was still locked up'."

"I had Dan Wells take him down the hill to his arraignment. They left early this morning."

"I almost forgot," Gates said, chagrined. "What time is the hearing?"

"Eleven," Carl answered. "We'll know something a couple of hours after that." Turning, Carl walked back to his car, opened the trunk and returned with a black leather bag. A few moments later, he was standing by the Honda with a Nikon 35-millimeter camera in his hand, which he had removed from the bag. He began taking pictures at the front of the car. Systematically, he worked his way clockwise around the vehicle snapping pictures from different angles.

"Will you dust for fingerprints?" Gates asked.

Carl shook his head. "I could, but I doubt it would do any good. Besides, it would leave your car a mess. That stuff is a pain to clean up."

"A mess? My car's already a mess. What more could you do to it?"

"Gates, even if we could lift a good print off the car, and even if we could run it through the computer system, and even if there was a record of the person who did this, the best we could do is charge them with misdemeanor property damage. But you would be hard-pressed to prove that the presence of a finger-print was proof that the owner of the print had been the one who actually did the damage. What you really need is a witness, and I doubt there is one of those."

"So what do I do?"

"File an insurance claim, pay the deductible, and get it fixed."

"That's it?"

"Unfortunately, that's it. If I thought we could find the perpetrator then I would pursue the matter, but the odds are really against that happening. I'll write a report; that will help with the insurance company, but that's about all I can do for now. If I were you, I'd start parking my car in the garage."

"You haven't seen the inside of my garage — it looks like a war has recently been waged in there."

"Hire a teenager to come in and straighten it up. Next time they might break out the windows or something. If you make too many claims your insurance company might up and cancel you. I don't think you need that right now." Carl put the camera away. "I'll have these developed today and give you a copy for your files. Your insurance may want to see them. By the way, how are the locks on your doors?"

"Why? Do you think I may be in danger?" Gates felt her heart skip a beat at the question.

"Probably not, but then why take chances? Some people use the causes of right to commit wrongs. I just want to be sure that you're safe."

"I've got good locks on the door. My dad insisted on that."

"Good for him. I don't do this for everybody, but let me take you to work. You can call the body shop from there. I'll drop the keys off and they can take the car over to the shop. In two or three days, your car will be as good as new."

"Perhaps, but I'm not sure that I will be."

Looking up from the papers on physician-assisted suicide that she had printed out the day before, Gates studied her desk clock. It read 9:15. A strong sense of disquiet settled over her. Immediately after entering the office she had scanned the appointment book. The day was full and began with a 9:00 A.M. appointment, yet neither Nancy nor Valerie had come to let her know that the first patient had arrived. While it was not unusual for a patient to be late, she still felt uneasy. Setting the papers on the desk, Gates rose, donned her white smock, and stepped from her private office into the hall that led to the reception area and lobby.

Valerie was seated behind the counter and Nancy stood close by. Both turned to face Gates when she approached. "Patients running a little late?" Gates asked.

A look of disappointment clouded Valerie's face. "Mr. Jackson canceled."

"Did he reschedule?" Gates inquired, wondering about Valerie's expression.

Shaking her head, Valerie said, "No. He didn't want to reschedule. In fact, he seemed upset. So did Mrs. Arnold. She canceled too."

"Upset? About what?"

Valerie looked at Nancy. "They didn't say specifically, but we think they're upset over what the reporter said last night on the television."

Gates sighed heavily and her stomach tightened. "I don't believe this. I get attacked years ago and am rescued by Norman Meade who goes on to become Dr. Death and people get mad at me. Keep me posted." Gates spun on her heels and stormed back to her office.

It was ten o'clock when Gates' first patient arrived. May Grier was a rail-thin woman of fifty-plus years who wore a perpetual sour expression on her face. A social worker turned business woman, she had no shortage of opinions and no compunctions about sharing them. Quick with her tongue, she let people know exactly what she thought and why she thought it whether the listener cared to hear it or not, and would do so with words delivered in machine-gun fashion. She was the last woman Gates wanted to see today.

"I keep my appointments, I do," Grier intoned with the imperial air of a queen addressing her subjects. "It's disgraceful not to do so. I know you're a busy woman, Dr. Gates, and as a conscientious woman I feel that I have a duty to be where I say I'm going to be."

"That's very admirable of you . . ." Gates began.

"I'll bet you've had some patients cancel today and I think that is just plain wrong. Not that I approve of your relationship with . . . with . . . that man. Still, I'm a woman of principle."

"There's no relationship, Mrs. Grier . . ."

"What a person does in their personal life is her business and none of mine. That's the way I was taught and that's the way I believe. Although . . ."

Uh, oh, Gates thought, *here it comes.*

". . . how you can associate with someone who travels around the country killing the

280

weak and frail is beyond me. I think they ought to send him off to Leavenworth and throw away the key. I think he should be put away forever, and not for just what he did to that Dr. Warren, but for everything else."

"He hasn't been convicted yet, Mrs. Grier," Gates said evenly as she placed the business end of a stethoscope on the bare skin of the woman's back. Grier arched at the touch of cold. Gates felt mildly ashamed that she was drawing a small measure of satisfaction at the woman's discomfort. "Breathe in deeply please."

"Leavenworth might be too good for him . . ."

"No talking please," Gates said. "It makes it hard for me to hear. Now take a deep breath and then let it out slowly." Grier complied, but as soon as Gates pulled the stethoscope away she continued her diatribe. "Lost all sense of life, we have. Human life is sacred and shouldn't be tossed away because of a little pain or inconvenience."

"The people he deals with have more than a little pain," Gates said then wished she hadn't. Every time Gates spoke it encouraged Grier to take the conversation to the next level.

"What difference does that make? Life is still sacred. Always has been. Always will be.

I'm surprised that you can agree with a man like that."

Gates felt herself slipping from professional health-care provider to irritated citizen. "What makes you think that I agree with him?" Gates' inflection carried more anger than she wanted it to, but the swelling tide of anger was getting the best of her. Normally she could quell the harsh emotion she was feeling, but last night's report, her vandalized car, patients canceling, and now the fierce dart-like words of this chronically ill-tempered woman were becoming unbearable.

"I just assumed . . ."

"That's the whole problem, Mrs. Grier. People like you find it easier and more satisfying to assume something than to make the effort to find the truth."

"But the news report . . ."

"How do you know that report is true? Do you believe it just because it appears on the television?"

"Of course not, I just . . ."

"The story was basically true, but you, of course, don't know that since you've not bothered to ask anyone like myself who was directly involved in the event. It's people like you who make life difficult. You hear something, usually at some gossip session, and then you formulate your opinions which you share freely with everyone who lacks the character to tell you to shut up. And to make matters worse, people like you formulate those opinions without the benefit of reason and thought. You care nothing for how your words wound others, just so long as you have an opportunity to hear yourself talk."

"Well," Grier said with a huff, "I never!"

"That's obvious," Gates snapped. "Just for the record, Mrs. Grier, I not only strongly disagree with Dr. Meade, I have told him so to his face. That, however, is not sufficient reason for me to assume his guilt in the murder of Dr. Warren. The truth of the matter is that Dr. Meade did not kill Dr. Warren. I'm sure that truth will come to light soon. I know how much that may disappoint you."

"I don't have to take this," she said, hopping off the table and walking behind the modesty screen where patients changed into examination gowns when necessary. "I've been a patient of yours for a lot of years. I can't believe you're talking to me like this."

"Mrs. Grier, I'm just talking to you the way you talk about others." Gates immediately regretted the words.

A moment later, the woman stomped out from behind the screen and marched to the exam room door. Once the door was open she turned and said loud enough for the whole office to hear, "You're not the only doctor in town, you know. There are several who would love to have my business."

"Don't bet on it," Gates said under her breath, but Grier was gone.

Gates felt lousy. She was angry at the day's events, at Mrs. Grier, but most of all at herself. She had sacrificed her professionalism for the opportunity to vent some anger. Doctors did not behave this way, but then very few doctors had been through what she had.

Valerie stepped into the room. "What was that all about?"

"My quick temper met her big mouth," Gates replied. "It's the old problem of an irresistible force meeting an immovable object."

"She sure looked angry," Valerie said. "I don't think I've ever seen her move so fast." Valerie looked at Gates and then let slip an insidious little smile. "Way to go, Doc. Way to go. I'll give you a minute to settle down while I show the next patient into room three."

It's not bad enough that my patients are canceling on me, Gates said to herself, "now I'm driving them out of my office. Pretty soon, I'll be out of business."

Gates was seated in her private office, her feet propped up on the desk and her head laid back against the high-backed desk chair. She was staring at the ceiling and breathing slowly. On her lap was the stack of papers she had retrieved from the Internet search. The day had worn on slowly. Only two other patients had canceled; actually, they were "no shows."

She was having trouble concentrating and a dull headache had begun to insidiously work its way from the back of her neck forward toward her temples. She was debating whether to take a couple of pain killers when a buzzing sound sprang from her phone. Placing her feet back on the floor, Gates leaned forward and pressed the button that would activate the speaker phone. "Yes?"

"Carl Berner is on line two for you," Nancy said. "Shall I tell him you're busy?"

"No thanks, Nancy, I'll take it." Gates picked up the hand piece of the phone, placed it to her ear and punched the button with its blinking light. "Hello, Carl."

"Hey, Doc. Having a good day?"

"You don't want to know."

"Oh. Well, I know what that's like. Did you hear from the auto-body shop, yet?"

"Nine hundred dollars plus the cost of four new tires," Gates said. "And I have a five-hundred-dollar deductible."

"Ouch. You might be able to get it done cheaper down the hill. You know things like that cost more up here."

"No, I've already told them to go ahead and do the work. I should get my car back in two days."

"You wanna' borrow Sharee's car?" Carl asked. "She can drive my car and I'll just take one of the patrol cars home for a couple of days."

"Thanks, Carl, I may take you up on it. Is that why you called?"

"Actually, no. I thought you might be interested in knowing that Meade made bail. He's out while the investigation goes on. He has to stay in the state though, which is what he was planning anyway."

Gates felt a refreshing sense of gladness run through her. Somehow she knew that Norman was innocent. He didn't deserve to be in jail for Warren's murder. Yet the feeling was muted by the work that Norman did and the events of the day. "What do you mean?"

"Well, not to put too fine a point on it, Doc, he's coming back to Ridgeline."

"You're kidding. I thought he would get as far from this place as possible, even if he does have to stay in the state."

"You and me both, but your Dr. Meade is an odd one. I wouldn't be surprised if he looks you up."

Gates was silent as she wondered how she

might respond if Norman showed up at her home or office.

"You still there, Gates?"

"Yeah, I'm here. Just thinking."

"Well, at least he's out of my jail. Now maybe that crowd in front of my office will finally go home."

"Maybe," Gates said. "Why do I feel that I've just started down this rocky road, Carl?"

"Because you have, Doc. Because you have."

Gates needed to be here; she needed to be in this place at this time.

She had arrived at church for the mid-week prayer meeting earlier than usual. The sanctuary was empty and quiet with only the low drone of the heat pumps vibrating their presence through the walls. It was 6:45 and in a short time people would begin to enter the building. The crowd would be small as it was each Wednesday, but that was fine with Gates too. She wasn't here to socialize; she was here to gather strength.

Outside, the night was turning cool as the sun surrendered to the encroaching darkness. Cold and dark. Gates felt cold and dark. So much had happened and there was so much raw emotion galloping up and down her mind like horses on a track. Except the race never

287

seemed to end. All she wanted was to know the truth. The truth would set her free, she knew that, but the truth was elusive and came at a price. She had been falsely accused by those who couldn't spare the mental energy to evaluate the truth of the situation; she had been victimized by some angry zealot with a sharp key and a hateful attitude; her practice was beginning to suffer; she had lost her temper with a patient; and she had been forced to relive the painful attack that had occurred so many years ago — an attack that had been broadcast over much of Southern California.

This was not a happy time for Dr. Gates McClure. Already her mind was doing what it always did when she was under a great stress: it alternated between thoughts of packing up and running away, and sinking into depression. She loathed both ideas.

As she sat on the padded pew in the quiet room at the back of the church, she let her mind float free of direction. It bubbled and simmered and churned and stewed. There was a tempest in her mind, a hurricane of hurt and anger that blew viciously against the frail structures of reason and conviction. Like storm-battered buildings on a coast hammered by a cyclone, the edifices of her composure rattled and shook. All but one, that is.

One part of her, one mental-emotional

building was standing firm, unaffected by the onslaught of depression and anxiety: her faith. That was why this place, this church was so special. She knew that there was nothing magical in the room itself; nothing mystical about the furnishings. This was just a place where she was reminded that the biggest storms of life are nothing but gentle breezes to God.

As she sat meditatively, a phrase that had been floating around her consciousness rose to the surface once again: "I must hold on." Somehow she knew that was wrong. She didn't need to hold on to her faith, because her faith held on to her and did so with a viselike grip. That's when the refreshing breeze of realization blew through Gates. She would get through all of this, not because she was strong, but because God was strong. Nothing could change that, nor could anything endanger it.

Gates nodded her head so slightly that had any observer been present, he would have been unable to notice. She nodded because she knew that the truth was still out there and that the truth would set her free. Regardless of what might come her way she would persevere. What did it matter that her family now knew of the attack, or that the whole world knew? She had done nothing wrong. She had been faithful in all things. If any charge could be laid at her feet it could only be that she cared enough to become involved.

The storm in Gates' heart began to ease. The tumult was diminishing, fading, and being replaced with a renewed sense of confidence and purpose. This was what Gates had come for; this was what she needed.

The side door that led from the sanctuary into the education wing of the building opened and closed. Gates turned to see Pastor Chapman enter. He was wearing casual slacks and a dress shirt with a sweater vest. Since prayer meeting was a relaxed time, he wore no tie. "Hello, Gates."

"Evening, Pastor, how are you?"

"Great, but the real question is: How are you?"

"Better," Gates answered honestly. "It's been a little rough, but sitting here has been good for me."

"Well, we've been praying for you. Is there anything I can do to help?"

"Keep praying, I suppose."

"That never hurts. I heard about your car. Do you have adequate transportation?"

"I'm driving Sharee's car. My Honda should be ready in a couple of days."

The lobby door that led to the vestibule opened and the sounds of people talking and laughing filled the church. As a steady stream of people entered, Paul greeted each one with a handshake and broad smile. They filed down the central aisle to take places near the front. Some greeted Gates with smiles, others offered only subdued nods that revealed an underlying uncertainty about her.

The service began as it always did with requests for prayer. Over the next twenty minutes the small gathering brought reports on friends and family that were in need of prayer. There were requests for healing for those with physical affliction; wisdom for those facing decisions; intervention for those with family problems; and salvation for lost loved ones. The pastor then had the congregation stand as he voiced an intercessory prayer. Paul Chapman was a man who took his prayer seriously and that earnestness came through in every word. He prayed for each person mentioned by name, and entreated God's action in their lives. After the prayer, the congregation was seated.

"Before I begin tonight's Bible study," he began, "let's do as is our custom and see if you have any general or specific questions that may have come to you from your personal Bible study."

"Yeah," someone blurted out. "Is this Dr. Meade right or wrong with this physician-assisted suicide thing? I mean, is that a sin?"

"Of course it is," a man said. "Suicide is murder."

"I don't know," a woman said. "If I were in a lot of pain and beyond help, I think I'd rather die and get it over with. At least, I'd be in heaven."

"Not if you commit suicide . . ."

Paul Chapman raised his hands to settle the gathering down. Such interaction was not at all unusual on a Wednesday night when people felt free to ask questions and share personal beliefs. Gates, however, felt that this time might be more emotional — too emotional for her.

"Let's take one question at a time," Chapman said with a chuckle. "If we don't, then we will have a lot of talk and no answers."

The pastor began to address the questions put to him about suicide, pain, and death. His answers were clever, casual, and laced with humor. Gates knew that Pastor Chapman understood how volatile the questions were. With each answer, she was reminded of the conversation she and her pastor had had just a few days ago. Much of what he was saying now, he had said then. With each answer he gave came several more questions which he gracefully fielded.

This, however, was not what Gates had

come to church for. The more she listened the more anxious she became. The peace she had felt earlier was being disturbed by what was for her a rehash of the difficult subject of physician-assisted suicide. The source of her rising anxiety was a fear that someone would turn to her and ask her "professional" opinion. Normally, she had no problem sharing her views, but tonight was not normal.

As Paul Chapman was speaking, Gates rose silently and slipped from the building.

Gates did not park in the driveway of her home. Since her garage was too cluttered to allow room for the car, and not wanting a repeat of last night's vandalism (especially since she was driving Sharee's car), Gates chose to park on the street a block down from her house and walk home, hoping that no one would associate the car with her. Carl would have advised against it stating that it would be unsafe for her to walk alone at night. Someone or several people might be angry enough to cause her harm. But Gates didn't care. It was only a block, after all, and she was a big girl.

After enduring the attack in medical school, Gates had struggled not to withdraw into herself; not to become timid and frightened every time the wind howled or she heard footsteps behind her. She would not become reckless, but she was determined not to become a recluse. Life was meant to be lived and unconfronted fear sucked the joy of life from people — Gates had seen that before. She would not let it happen to her.

Still, as she walked on the sidewalk she could feel herself tense, her senses heighten. She could hear the breeze rustle in the trees and the sound of cars a street or two over. Each step she took made a distinctive thud that she was sure anyone could hear. Unconsciously she began to walk faster.

The short stroll was uneventful and Gates entered her home safely. She was greeted with the flashing light on her answering machine indicating that a message was waiting for her. Dropping her sweater on the sofa, Gates punched the "Play Messages" button. The voice of Norman Meade filled the room: "Hi, Gates. I guess you heard that I got out on bail. That's some good news at least, but there's still a long way to go." There was a short pause as if Norman was undecided about what to say next. "I need to speak to you. Tonight if possible, and if not tonight, then first thing in the morning. It's important. So please call me. I'm staying at the bed-and-breakfast again." He gave the number. "Call even if it's late." A dial tone replaced Meade's voice.

Gates closed her eyes and sighed. "Not tonight," she said wearily to the empty room. "Not tonight."

Turning off the lights, Gates went straight to her bedroom. Five minutes later she was asleep in bed.

Chapter Seventeen

Thursday, November 6
7:00 A.M.

The shrill ring of the phone sheared the sleep away from Gates, causing her to bolt upright in bed, her heart pounding. The phone rang again. Blinking hard and struggling to make sense of what was happening, Gates looked at the phone situated on her nightstand, grabbed the hand piece and put it to her ear. "Uh, hello." The clock read 7:00. Normally she would have been up and dressed by now, but she decided last night that some extra sleep would do her good.

"Dr. McClure?" the disembodied voice said. "Is this Dr. McClure?"

"Yes, who is this please?"

"I'm sorry to call you at home so early, Doctor, but I wanted to reach you before you started your day. This is Colleen Platt." Her voice was strained but not panicked.

Colleen Platt and her husband Philip had been longtime patients. Philip was very ill and confined to bed. Gates visited the house every two weeks to check on him and to encourage Colleen in the home-care she provided for her husband.

"What is it, Colleen? Is something wrong with Philip?" Gates repositioned herself so that she was seated on the bed.

"I wonder if you might come over this morning," Colleen said. "About eight-thirty, if you can."

"I don't understand. Has Philip taken a turn for the worse?"

"Yes, somewhat, but I can explain better over here. I know this isn't the day you normally come, but you have been so good to me and Philip and . . . well, it would mean a lot to us if you could make it."

"All right, Colleen, I'll be there by eight-thirty."

"Thank you, Doctor. Thank you," Colleen exuded. "It means so much to us. Good-bye." She hung up.

"Now what?" Gates asked aloud.

The Platt's house was typical of many of the smaller homes in Ridgeline and not very different from Gates' own place. It had a sharply pitched roof, and hand-cut fascia boards that had been painted to match the balustrade that circumscribed the front porch. Shutters painted a bright blue gave the house a cheerful Swiss-château look. Gates had been in the house enough to know that there was less cheer here than the exterior might lead a visitor to believe.

Gates had no sooner shut the door of her borrowed car than Colleen was out the front door and down the porch steps. She was a short, thin woman in her mid-fifties with dark hair that was liberally streaked with gray. Her eyes were wide and tinted pink from tears. "I'm so glad you could come, Dr. McClure."

"What's going on, Colleen?" Gates asked without preamble.

"It's Philip, he's worse."

"Have you called an ambulance?"

"That's the problem, he won't let me. He says he's tired of it all."

Tempted as she was, Gates resisted saying, "Philip isn't physically capable of preventing you from calling an ambulance." Instead she offered: "Let's take a look."

Inside the quaint house a fierce but quiet battle was being waged, not with guns or words, but at the microscopic level. The battlefield was the frail body of Philip Platt, retired civil engineer. Colleen led Gates through the front door and down a narrow hall. The corridor was lined with pictures of the couple's life. The photos always caught her eye. There were group pictures of Colleen and Philip with their three children, all now grown and living out of state. There were the photos of Philip's graduation from college as well as those of his children receiving their diplomas. The hall was a museum of a couple's life; a life lived happily and productively until five years ago when Philip's own body turned against him.

Stepping into the master bedroom, Gates saw Philip reclined on a rented hospital bed. He cut his eyes to watch her as she entered. His face emotionless, projecting no fear, no anxiety, no anger; but then that was the nature of the disease. Philip couldn't offer a facial expression no matter how much he wished to do so.

Shortly after Philip's fiftieth birthday he began to complain of weakness. During the warmer months, he would spend his weekends working in his yard or puttering in his garage. It was one such weekend that Philip began to notice a general weakness and unexpected fatigue. After working on some shelves he was building for the spare bedroom he noticed that he was having trouble lifting a gallon can of paint. Having always been healthy, he immediately became concerned. That following Monday he was in Gates' office asking if he had contracted some flu bug.

Gates remembered the day vividly. "So you're feeling weak and tired?" Gates asked.

"Yeah, Doctor. Real tired. As a civil engineer I spend a lot of time in the office, but I've always felt that I was in shape. I shouldn't be tiring this easily."

"Well, let's see what we can see," Gates had said. Raising a finger she held it in front of Philip's eyes. "Please focus on my finger, Mr. Platt." Moving her finger, she watched Philip's eyes struggle to track the movement. In large part he was successful, but the smooth motion that was typical of a healthy person was absent. "Are you taking any medications?"

Philip shook his head, "No. Not even aspirin."

"Hold out your arm," Gates said. "Bend it at the elbow like you're about to curl a dumbbell in the gym." Philip complied. Gates then had him form a fist, which she held in her hand. "Now pull against my hand like you're lifting a weight. I'll resist. Okay?"

"Okay." Philip began to move his forearm up at the elbow like a weightlifter hoisting a dumbbell. Gates pushed firmly in the opposite direction. At first, Philip was able to lift against the resistance, but a few moments later his arm gave out. "That's odd," Philip had said. "It was like my muscle just ran out of steam. What's wrong with me, Doc?"

"It could be anything, Mr. Platt," Gates had responded. "It's too early to tell. I need to conduct a few more tests." Despite her unconcerned tone, she had already run a series of possibilities through her head: Eaton-Lambert syndrome, botulism, Guillain Barré syndrome, enteroviral infections, hypermagnesemia, and half a dozen other possibilities. For the next twenty minutes, Gates asked questions and ran the standard battery of office tests.

When she was done, Philip asked, "Well?"

Gates remembered sighing. "Well, Mr. Platt, I'm afraid I can't give you a definitive answer. My first guess is that something is interfering with the way your nerves activate the muscle tissue. There are scores of reasons for such things. The best course of action here is to have you seen by a neurologist and let him run a couple of tests." She began scribbling something on a pad of paper. "I want you to call Dr. Nelson Peeman. He has an office down the hill in San Bernardino. He's a very capable physician."

"Surely you must have some idea as to what my problem is."

Gates shook her head. "At this point I would only be guessing and it's too easy to guess wrong without hard data."

301

"Humor me," Philip said strongly.

"As I've said it could be a number of things."

Philip stared harshly at Gates. It had been clear to her that the man had wanted an answer. Patients were always impatient; that was understandable. Not being medically trained, most people took a "let's run some tests" comment from their physician to mean that something was horribly wrong. That, of course, was usually not the case. The simple truth was that a doctor's office, especially a small-town office like Gates', was not equipped to run sophisticated tests other than the most basic x-rays and drawing blood. More technical tests had to be referred to a specialist.

"All right, Mr. Platt, my best guess — and that is all that this is at this moment, a guess — is that you have developed a neurological condition. There are many kinds and causes for such disorders. That's why we need more tests."

"It sounds serious." Philip's face had begun to pale.

"Not necessarily," Gates replied evenly. "It could be a very minor and temporary problem. The whole thing could clear up in a couple of days. But we need to run tests to be sure."

"What kind of tests?"

"That will be up to the neurologist. He'll do basically the same exam I did, but he'll add to it. In addition, he may conduct an EMG . . ."

"EMG?"

"Electromyography. It's a way of testing the constancy of your muscle response. In addition, he'll run a simple test in which you will receive a small amount of a compound called edrophonium. If your muscle activity improves after receiving the drug, then it may indicate that you have what's called myasthenia gravis. The key indicator is muscle fatigue that improves with rest. But again, I don't know that that's the case. It's only a suspicion at the moment."

"How serious is it? Am I in danger?"

"The disease, if that is indeed what you have, varies. Like most diseases it can range from a simple annoyance to much worse. The common cold kills hundreds of people every year in our country, so as far as I'm concerned, every disease is serious. However, while MG can be severe, it can usually be managed."

"What is it?"

"It all has to do with the way your nerves deliver signals to the muscle. Normally the nerve sends an electric signal down its length, which causes the muscle to contract — similar to current in a wire. There is a substance in our bodies that makes that possible. It's called acetylcholine, and it's a neurotransmitter. MG is an autoimmune disorder that produces antibodies that attack certain proteins in the body. Those proteins are call antigens. Normally, these antibodies only attack foreign substances, but occasionally they will attack the body itself. There are a whole host of these diseases, AIDS being one of them. Don't misunderstand me here," Gates said forcefully, "I'm not saying you have AIDS. In MG the antibodies block and destroy the normal acetylcholine receptors leaving fewer nerves to do the job.

"It's a rare disorder," Gates continued. "About one person in 20,000 contracts it, and most of those are women between the age of twenty and forty. Men usually don't contract the disorder until they're fifty or older."

"I turned fifty last week. How bad can this get?"

"Mr. Platt, that's the wrong question. This is why I'm hesitant even to talk about this with you until I know for certain that you have myasthenia gravis. The real question is whether or not you even have the disease, and if so, to what degree? Asking how bad it can get at this stage is like asking how bad an accident you could be involved in every time you pull the car out of the garage. Could you have a serious collision? Sure. Are you likely to if you drive carefully? Most likely not. Let's wait and see, shall we, Mr. Platt?" Gates stepped over to him and put a comforting hand on his shoulder. At the moment it was all she could offer.

Looking at Philip now reminded her how serious a disease can become. The edrophonium test had come back positive, as had both the electromyography and the blood tests. That in itself had not been alarming. Many people with myasthenia gravis live normal lives by taking advantage of peak energy times and following a schedule of rest periods. In addition, there were drug therapies designed to increase the amount of nerve chemicals. Unfortunately Philip's MG proved to be progressive. Now, five years later, he was sufficiently weak to require bed rest most of the time. It was not unusual for his breathing to become labored and swallowing difficult. His eyelids drooped as if they had been frozen mid-blink, and a small trickle of drool ran from the corner of his mouth.

"I hear you're having a rough time, Mr. Platt," Gates said as she stepped to the side of the bed and placed two fingers on his wrist to check his pulse. As she did so she also watched the labored rise and fall of the ailing man's chest. He was struggling to breathe as if some large animal was sitting on his chest. A soft wheezing sound accompanied each inhalation and exhalation.

When Platt had been diagnosed with MG, Gates made an effort to learn as much as she could about the disease. Philip's neurologist would provide much of his care, but since he would be living in the relatively isolated Ridgeline, it would be good for her to know as much as possible. On her frequent visits she would note his continually degrading condition. It took only a moment for Gates to realize that on the Osserman Classification scale of myasthenia gravis Philip was crossing over from a Grade III (severe generalization) to Grade IV (crisis with life-threatening impairment of ventilation).

"Mr. Platt, I think it's best for you to go to the hospital right away," Gates said.

Slowly, weakly, Philip shook his head no. The muscles of his face, too impotent to respond, made no expression. "No," he croaked nasally.

There was a knock on the door. "I'll be right back," Colleen said as she turned to leave.

"Mr. Platt," Gates said firmly. "You need to be in the hospital. They can help you there and make your breathing easier."

"No."

"We've talked about these events before, Mr. Platt. We knew there would be days like this. The hospital is better able to help than I am."

"No."

"He seems persistent, doesn't he?" a familiar voice said.

Gates turned to see a man standing in the doorway to the bedroom. It was Norman Meade. Behind him stood Colleen. "Hello, Gates. You didn't return my phone call."

"What are you doing here . . . ?" She let the question fade. It was suddenly obvious why he was here. The unwelcome realization hit her hard like a punch to the stomach.

"I was asked to come." Meade stepped into the room. "Mrs. Platt called me at the bed-and-breakfast . . ."

"I didn't know where he might be," Colleen interrupted, her face filled with concern, "so I called over to the newspaper and asked Ross Sassmon. He wrote that article you know. Anyway, I've known Ross for a lot of years, so he told me that Dr. Meade had been staying at the bed-and-breakfast before his arrest . . . oh, I'm sorry. Perhaps I shouldn't mention that." Colleen was a simple and innocent woman who became flustered easily.

"That's all right, Mrs. Platt," Meade said, offering a small smile. "You didn't say anything that wasn't true."

"Well, when I saw on last night's news that Dr. Meade had been released on bail, I mentioned it to Philip. He wanted me to call — begged me to call Dr. Meade."

A new sense of fury swelled in Gates. Like a black tornado that was building strength and ready to touch the earth leaving a trail of scattered debris in its wake, anger twirled in her mind and reached down to her soul. Gates felt her jaw clench in a tetanal-like seizure. Her heart pounded. There was only one reason Colleen would call Norman Meade and that was to ask his help in aiding Philip's suicide. Everything was stripped away now. All the reading she had done on medically aided suicide, all the effort she had expended on Meade's behalf took a back seat to the single screaming truth that this was her patient. Anger grew geometrically in Gates.

"Are you all right, Gates?" Norman asked.

"You don't belong here, Norman. This is my patient."

"But I asked him to be here," Colleen objected.

Gates ignored her. "I draw the line here, Norman. I'm not going to let this happen. Do you understand? This is not going to happen."

Norman said nothing in response. Instead he gazed at Gates through woeful eyes that broadly beamed his own inner turmoil. His face was drawn and creased. He appeared tired, near exhaustion. If she were Catholic, she would suspect that he had just returned from exile in purgatory.

"It's what I want," croaked Philip from the bed. The words were immediately followed by violent coughing. A moment later he spoke again, "I want to die. Too tired . . . so very tired."

"See," Colleen said. "I don't know what to do. He begged me to call you, Dr. Meade, so I did. Then I immediately called you, Dr. McClure. I just don't know what to do." Tears came to her eyes and she raised a shaky hand to her mouth.

"What's the diagnosis?" Meade asked Gates. As he spoke he fixed a steady gaze on her, a gaze that was not a challenge, but one that would communicate resolutely his intention not to be intimidated.

Reluctantly Gates answered. "Myasthenia gravis, Grade III on the Osserman — normally. I feel he's dropping to Grade IV and will soon be in myasthenic crisis."

"What does that mean?" Colleen asked seriously, her eyes darting back and forth between Gates and Norman.

"It means that your husband is getting worse and needs to go to the hospital where he can receive better care," Gates said.

"Dr. Meade," Philip whispered. He attempted to swallow, an action he had to repeat several times before succeeding.

Norman stepped closer. "I'm here, Mr. Platt."

"Please . . ." Platt's eyes widened slightly, just the small amount allowed by the disease. His gaze communicated more than his words. His dim blue eyes reflected a weary soul, the creation of a tormented body. "I don't want . . . to go on. Not fair to Colleen. Not fair to me."

"Norman," Gates said strongly. "This goes beyond our friendship. I warn you . . ." She stopped when she saw Meade's upraised hand.

Turning from Philip for a moment he looked at Gates. "Gates, please, shut up." The words were quiet, respectful, and firm as concrete.

The tornado of emotion touched down in Gates' mind. She was ready to unleash everything on him, for this was the ultimate indignity. How dare he come to the house of her patient. She was willing to defend his innocence regarding the murder of Ed Warren, but she would not defend his other practices and she certainly wasn't going to stand by here and watch as he led one of her patients down suicide's path. But before she could speak, Norman turned back to Philip.

"Mr. Platt, I'm so sorry for your discomfort and your pain. I understand why you wanted to see me, but I must say no."

Gates' heart tumbled to a stop. Had she heard correctly? She started to ask Norman to repeat himself when he continued, "I help people who are in the worst of all possible situations find relief. I agonize over each one of them. I've been hounded, spat upon, and jailed for what I do, but none of that matters. All that matters to me is helping the incurable sufferers die with dignity. It's the second hardest thing I do. The most difficult thing for me to do is to tell someone like you, someone who suffers so very much, that . . . his suffering is not enough."

"Please . . ." Philip said. Tears were welling up in his eyes. From her position Gates could see a tiny rivulet of tears wash down Norman's cheek. "No more . . ."

"Mr. Platt," Norman began, his voice choked with compassion. "You have a terrible disease, and your particular case is extreme. I'm familiar with your affliction. No one knows why or how it starts, and none of that is really important now. What is important is that you get yourself down to the hospital where they can ease the discomfort you feel. In a few days, your breathing will be easier. Mr. Platt, you still have life to live, thoughts to think, love to give and receive." Meade wiped away the tears. "You may hate me now, but you may find yourself grateful this time next week."

"No . . ."

"Mr. Platt, you must go to the hospital and you must go now. If you refuse, your doctor can declare you incompetent and have you taken there against your will. None of us wants that."

Philip did nothing at first, then a few moments later, he nodded.

"Gates, call for an ambulance please."

The phone was in Gates' hand a second later and she placed the call.

Together Gates and Norman watched as the ambulance pulled away. Gates felt wasted by the event. The emotions that had raged in her had taken their toll. She was spent and it was still early in the day. Looking at Norman she could see that he too was exhausted. He stood slump-shouldered and his eyes were red from the tears he had shed.

"Did you do that for me?" Gates asked.

"What?"

"Refuse to set up the suicide, of course."

"No, Gates, I didn't. He wasn't a candidate. As bad as MG can be, his suffering can be relieved. Ultimately it may take his life, but not today."

"Do you regret turning him down?"

Norman shifted his gaze to Gates. "I don't enjoy this, Gates. I never have."

"Then why do it?"

"Because I can't *not* do it. That probably doesn't make sense to you, but it's the only way I can explain it. To gaze upon hopeless suffering and do nothing seems wrong."

"I'm sorry if I was a little rough in there," Gates said. "This has been a torturous week and when I saw you walk in and made the connection between my patient and . . . and . . . what you do, well, I started to come unhinged."

"That's what makes you a good doctor. So many physicians I meet today view their patients as income and not humans. There are still a great many professionals out there who genuinely care for the people who come to them for help. You're one of them."

"Thanks." A shrill beep sounded and Gates looked down at her pager. "It's my office."

"So you need a phone."

"No, I'll just drive over there. It's not far from here."

"I need to talk to you, Gates," Norman blurted out. "It's important. I don't know how much longer I can stay in Ridgeline. I've stayed so that we can talk."

"Okay. How about the Tree Top Café . . . no, the owner is not one of our biggest fans. Let's meet at Middy's in the Blue Sky Motel. It's a little upscale, but it should be quiet and you won't get mugged by the owner."

"That's a plus in a restaurant. I've always preferred eating establishments that don't serve violence."

"All right, then. Let's meet at six." Gates walked to the car she had parked at the curb. Once again her emotions were jumbled with on-again-off-again anxiety. One moment the thought of dinner with Norman seemed wonderful, the next repulsive. It was as if someone were flipping a switch on and off. "What are you doing for transportation? How did you get here?"

"I still have the rental car I got when I first came to town. I'll be able to get there just fine."

A minute later, Gates was on her way to the office, leaving the mysterious Norman Meade behind her.

Chapter Eighteen

Thursday, November 6
9:10 A.M.

Gates had been possessed by an uneasy feeling from the moment her beeper had sounded. On the ten-minute drive from the Platts' house to her office she sensed a tingling of apprehension. It wasn't that she had been paged, for that happened frequently as both friends, family, and the office would contact her this way, but the trepidation was still there. At first she calmed herself by rationalizing the premonition as nothing more than frayed nerves that had been tattered all the more by the sudden appearance of Norman Meade at the Platts' residence. The immediate fear and anger she had felt then, she told herself, had left her filled with disquiet. After all, this had been more than a grueling week.

As she rounded the street on which her office was located, her apprehension heightened. Parked in front of the office were two police cars. Pulling into the paved lot in front

315

of her office, she quickly exited the vehicle and sprinted up the stairs. Before she passed the threshold something caught her eye. The large picture window that overlooked the parking lot had been shattered. Shards of glass were strewn everywhere. Once inside, she saw more glass fragments, splinters that glistened in the morning light. There was more glass on the floor inside the office than lay outside on the ground. She didn't have to be a detective to know that the window had been shattered by an object from the outside. A moment later she saw the offending projectile: a large stone the size of a football lay in the broken remains of the glass.

Gates felt her breath leave her. Questions bounced around in her mind like a score of bees trapped in a large glass jar. Would this never end? All she had ever wanted out of life was to be a doctor. She had trained and worked years to achieve that goal; she had no training in how to tolerate terrorism.

"Oh, Doctor, I'm glad you're here." It was Valerie. "I'm sorry you had to walk into this, but I thought you would want to know as soon as possible, so after I called the police, I paged you."

"What happened?" Gates knew it was a dumb question, but it was the only thought in her mind that she could articulate.

"Nancy and I both arrived a little late this morning, just before nine." Valerie's words were quick and breathy, betraying the anxiety she felt. "I didn't see it at first, you know how wrapped up I can be in my own thoughts, but Nancy did. She gasped and then I saw it too. Someone had thrown a big rock through the window. Who would do that, Doctor?"

"I'm not sure, but I have an idea," Gates replied through clenched teeth. "Where's Nancy now?"

"She's showing Chief Berner the back offices. They're checking to see if there's more damage or if anything's been stolen."

"There's more bad news, isn't there, Valerie?" The nurse nodded. "Let's hear it. I might as well know it all now as later."

"He . . . she . . . they . . . whoever, smashed the computer, cut all the upholstery in the offices, including the exam tables. Your instruments are scattered everywhere."

"The drug cabinet?"

"Untouched." Valerie paused, "That's odd isn't it? I hadn't thought about it before, but the drug cabinet is still secure; nothing is missing."

"Which tells us a lot." Gates turned to face Carl Berner and Dan Wells, Nancy stood just behind them. It seemed odd to Gates to have two uniformed officers standing in her office.

"You okay?" Carl asked.

"I've been a whole lot better, Carl," Gates replied, making no effort to conceal her distress. "Can you tell me what's going on besides the obvious fact that someone has broken my window and vandalized my office?"

"First, I need to show you something," Carl answered. Turning to Wells, he said, "Dan, why don't you make a cast of the footprint outside and get someone over here to help you dust the place for prints."

"Okay, Chief." Dan was gone in a moment.

"Should we start cleaning up?" Valerie asked.

"No," Carl answered. "I want everything left alone. As it is, there are too many people in here now."

"Valerie, why don't you take the appointment book home and start calling patients. Cancel whatever we have for today and tomorrow. They can take the appointment book, can't they?" Gates asked Carl.

"I guess that will be okay, but nothing else."

Gates nodded. "Nancy, could you wait out front and talk to any patients that might have been scheduled for this morning?"

"Sure, but there's only one. The rest canceled."

Gates bowed her head and rubbed her eyes.

"I wish it weren't so," Carl said kindly, "but this isn't the end of it. I suggest you see the rest . . . you know, get it over with. Then you can go home and leave the rest to us. Maybe Nancy or Valerie can call your insurance company for you."

"I'm not going to like what I see, am I, Carl?"

"No, ma'am, you're not. And like I said, I wish there was some other way, but there's not. Let me walk you to your office." Carl motioned to the hall that led from the reception area to Gates' office. It took less than a dozen steps to traverse the distance, but it seemed like a mile to her. With a heavy, clinging dread, she followed behind Carl. The office door was open. "Please don't touch anything," he said as he stepped into the private sanctuary that was Gates' office.

While still in the hall, Gates had determined to remain unmoved by what awaited her. She gasped anyway. The office was a shambles: books and magazines were scattered everywhere; a small aquarium that rested on a stand near her desk had been shattered, soaking her desk and everything on it — dead fish lay strewn about, their tiny corpses rigid in the alien environment of air; the monitor to her computer had been smashed leaving a gaping wound where once glass had been; the wood of her desk had been scarred in similar fashion to the way her car had been keyed; but the ultimate indignity were the words that had been spray painted on her wall and over the framed degrees of her college and medical school — "Thou shalt not kill!"

For a moment, just a moment, Gates felt as if she might faint, but that was replaced by stoic determination. Her first desire was to scream, to kick something, anything. Instead she began to shut her emotions down like a worker shutting off overhead stage lights. Reaction was useless, she reasoned. She would not give the perpetrator any satisfaction in knowing that Gates had either crumbled or exploded. A sadness streamed through her. This had been her office, the place where she worked her profession. This was a healing place, a hopeful place. Much of Gates' psyche was tied up in this very office as well as each exam room, and now someone had maliciously, viciously violated and sullied it, and had done so with extreme prejudice.

"She sure did a number in here," Carl said. "This took time to do."

"She?"

"It's a guess right now, but we found a few shoeprints outside the front window and around the building. They're fairly small, so they probably belong to a woman. Dan's out there taking impressions now. We'll compare them to the shoes you and your nurses wear. It might come in handy."

"She," Gates said softly to herself. "Martha Crews? Do you think she did this?"

"She has motive. She's in the area." Carl shrugged. "I have nothing on which to arrest her, but she leads the list on my hit parade. Whoever did it probably associates you with Dr. Meade. Look here," Carl pointed at the aquarium-soaked desk. "You were collecting articles on physician-assisted suicide, right?"

"Yes, I was doing research."

"Well, whoever broke in here saw that and began ripping up the articles. That shows not only hostility, but a degree of premeditation on their part. They want you to know what all this is about. In some ways, it's both a message and a way to punish you."

"Punish me? But I haven't done anything. I'm not a proponent of medically aided suicide or any other suicide."

"That doesn't matter, Gates. The truth doesn't matter. All that matters is that this person thinks you are part of the enemy."

"So what do we do now?" Gates asked, suddenly weary despite how early in the day it was.

"We? We don't do anything. I do something. You, well you get to go home, put your feet up, read a book and try to put it out of your mind for a while. Let the insurance company do its work, and let us do ours."

"Are you going to arrest her?"

"Martha Crews? If I can prove she's the one who did this. That may be difficult, but I will have a talk with her, that's for sure. If I can find her."

"I still don't know how she can think that I approve of what happened to her mother."

"You helped her dad, that's all she needs. And before you say it, I know that helping her father has nothing to do with what Meade did, but it may in her mind. One of the first things I learned as a cop, Gates, is that perception is far more powerful than truth. If she or someone else thinks you're buddy-buddy with Dr. Death, then they will transfer that hate to you. Reason has nothing to do with it. Only emotion matters to people like that."

"You paint a bleak picture, Carl."

"That's because my experience has left me with nothing but dark colors."

"Anybody back here?" a voice called. Both Gates and Carl stepped into the hall. Ross Sassmon was walking their way. "What a mess. Are you all right, Doctor?"

"I've been better, Ross. Thanks for asking."

"I heard the call over the police scanner," Ross said, looking around. "I can't believe someone would do this to you. Any ideas who it might have been?"

Carl spoke up quickly: "We're still investigating, Ross, so it's a little premature to be naming names."

"Any estimate of damages?" Ross asked, pulling a pad of paper from his shirt pocket.

"No," Carl answered. "It's too early for anything but the gathering of evidence."

"Why you, Gates?" Ross inquired.

"I don't know, Ross, I just don't know."

"Come on, Ross," Carl said pointedly. "You know the answer to that as well as anyone. The TV report linked the doctor here with Norman Meade, just like you did in your article. I have to tell you, Ross, I don't think that report was balanced."

Ross looked offended. Article? Colleen Platt had mentioned the article, but Gates hadn't given it any thought. The town paper — Ross' paper — came out on Wednesday. Today was Thursday, but she had been so preoccupied that she hadn't bothered to read the paper.

"What do you mean, Carl?" Gates asked.

"Ask Ross, he wrote the thing."

"I didn't know you were a newspaper critic, Chief," Ross said in a huff. "How many journalism classes did you take in college?"

"I've read enough newspapers in my day to recognize a hatchet job when I see one." Carl was becoming angry and defensive of Gates.

"Would someone just tell me what's going on," Gates demanded.

"Ross did in his article the same thing that Ballew woman did on television — linked you to Meade in such a fashion that people would think that you were a couple."

"I did no such thing," Ross objected. "I just printed the facts."

"Facts can be juggled, Ross, and you know it." Carl pointed an accusatory finger at Ross. "That article could have been a lot clearer and told the truth."

"It was all true."

"The facts perhaps, but not the underlying premise. Maybe shoddy reporting is why your paper is so desperate for cash."

"Gentlemen . . ." Gates interrupted.

"You're paranoid," Ross snapped. "Next thing you know, you'll be blaming me for all of this." He waved an arm over all the destruction. "And my paper is doing just fine."

"Gentlemen . . ." Gates attempted again.

"Maybe you are responsible, indirectly."

"I am not responsible, directly or indirectly,

and if you so much as whisper to anyone that I am, I'll file a defamation of character lawsuit faster than you can make it down to the doughnut shop."

"Enough!" Gates shouted. "I've had enough of my life destroyed today, I don't need you two slugging it out in my office. Ross, leave."

"But . . ."

"Just go," Gates prompted. "There's nothing here yet. Call me later — tomorrow, maybe — perhaps then I'll know something."

"Gates," Ross began, "I never meant you any harm. I just reported a story."

"Please leave, Ross. I haven't read the article, so I have no opinion. Just leave. Let Carl do his work and let me try to pull my life back together."

Slowly, like a scolded puppy, Ross put away his pad, turned, and walked away.

"I'm sorry, Gates," Carl said. "I've never been a big admirer of the media. Ross' paper is such a small-town publication that it's usually benign, but when I saw that article it irritated me no end."

"I'm leaving now, Carl," Gates said wearily. "I've got to get out of this place. This is all too 'Twilight Zone' for me."

"You should go home and rest," Carl agreed. "This stuff can really take it out of you. By the way, I'm assigning all my officers to patrol your street more often. I don't want to take any chances."

"Do you think I might be in danger?" Worry now joined the other emotions rumbling in Gates.

"I'm just a cautious man and I don't want to take chances." Carl smiled. "If I let anything happen to you, my wife would kill me and that would be a significant loss to the whole world."

Gates chuckled. "You really should work on your poor self-esteem, Carl."

Carl laughed. "Get out of here, will ya'. I have work to do. I'll call someone to come in and replace the window when we're done. If you need help cleaning the place up let me know, I might be able to find a couple of teenagers doing community service."

"Thanks, Carl. I'll leave those decisions for later."

A few minutes later, Gates was in the car driving up Highway 22, uncertain of what to do next. One thing she did know, she wasn't going home to rest.

Gates did not go home. Instead she went three miles up Highway 22 to the local McDonalds, the only fast-food establishment in Ridgeline, ordered a coffee, took a seat in the plastic and simulated-wood booth, and stared out the window. The sun had continued its daily climb up the sky, shortening the long shadows of morning. Brown sparrows hopped along the ground searching for seeds and the occasional stray French-fry left by previous customers. Each bird — there were about eight of them — bounced from place to place pecking at the ground as they continued their day-long search for food.

As she watched the little bird ballet, Gates mindlessly turned the thick paper cup in her hand. She didn't really want coffee, she simply wanted a place to sit and think. Watching the birds filled her with an odd sense of envy. Their lives seemed so simple: hop, peck, hop, hop, peck, peck. Her rational mind tried to remind her that their lives were short and always in danger from larger animals. Still, they seemed untroubled: peck, peck, hop, hop. For a moment, Gates wished that her life was composed of nothing more than searching for seeds on the ground. It was an odd thought for her, for she was normally so driven to achieve, to do, to be involved.

She recognized what she was doing: She was seeking escape from the constant pressures of the day. Birds didn't worry about ethical and philosophical issues. They cared nothing for matters of law. They simply looked for food and did what sparrows did all over the world, living on the fringe of humanity yet untouched by it. Watching the birds reminded her of a passage of Scripture that she had read: "Consider the ravens, for they neither sow nor reap; and they have no storeroom nor barn; and yet God feeds them; how much more valuable you are than the birds!"

How much more valuable I am than the birds. Gates mulled the words over in her mind. *True,* she thought, *God does feed them, but they have to leave the nest and look for the food. Perhaps that is what I need to do.*

She wondered. She wondered if Martha Crews had indeed demolished her office. She also wondered if there would be enough evidence to arrest and convict her if she had. Carl would be looking for Martha, but would be lucky to find her. Gates couldn't possibly hope to track her down. Besides, that would be insanity. The woman was much larger and had proven that she had an explosive temper. Finding the woman herself was absurd. Yet she felt the need to do something; to leave the nest and start helping herself. But what?

A name popped into her mind: Bob Lemonick. Ross Sassmon had told her that Bob and Martha had married right out of high school. Maybe he would know where she was, and if so, then Gates could pass the information on to Carl. And even if he didn't know, if their breakup was so complete as to sever all contact, then he still might be able to say if Martha was capable of such destructive behavior. No, she reasoned, they kept contact over the years. Most likely it was Bob Lemonick who had told Martha about her mother. Maybe, just maybe, he would know where to find her and Carl could arrest her, putting an end to the vandalism.

Would there be danger? Only if Martha was there at Bob's office. Gates had been Bob's doctor for a number of years and he had always seemed kind and even-tempered. There should be no danger from him. All she would have to do is drive to his work and talk to him there. That was a public place and Martha certainly wouldn't be there — she would be hiding. If, of course, she had been the one to vandalize her car and office.

Gates took a sip of coffee, watched the birds some more, and tried to remember where it was that Bob worked. After a few moments of stirring her memory the answer popped to the forefront of her mind like a cork: Bob Lemonick was a real estate agent in one of the larger agencies. But which one? Gates knew she would remember if she just saw the name of the firm. Rising from her seat she went to the counter and asked to borrow the local phone directory. Five minutes later she had what she needed.

Chapter Nineteen

Thursday, November 6
10:30 A.M.

Gates sat patiently in an uncomfortable, yellow simulated-leather chair and took in her surroundings. After leaving the McDonalds, she drove down Highway 22 until she reached the edge of town. There, barely in the city limits, was a small strip mall laid out in an L-shape with a black macadam parking lot in front. Several stores occupied the little center, including a doughnut shop, a dry cleaners, and a video rental store. None of those interested Gates. She was here to see Bob Lemonick, a real estate agent with Double Pine Realty, one of a dozen such offices in Ridgeline. Rather than calling ahead, Gates had decided to drop in unexpectedly. She was uncertain if Mr. Lemonick would speak to her. As luck would have it, he was out of the office looking over some property for a new listing, but the young red-haired receptionist assured Gates that he would be "right back." That was forty minutes ago.

The real estate office was an open area partitioned into cubicles by thin, freestanding walls. There were two enclosed offices which Gates assumed were occupied by the brokers who ran the firm. Through an open door, she could see a large conference table in one room.

"Are you sure I can't get you some coffee?" the receptionist asked as she peered into the cubicle where Gates was seated.

"No thanks," Gates replied. "I've had all the coffee I need for the day. Thanks anyway."

The receptionist nodded. "I'm sure he'll be back any minute, and . . . oh, here he is now."

Gates stood and faced the entry to the cubicle. The receptionist spoke: "Mr. Lemonick, this is Dr. Gates McClure . . ."

"Of course," Bob Lemonick said with a broad smile as he extended his hand. "I've known Dr. McClure for a long time." He entered the cubicle, set a battered leather briefcase on the equally battered desk, and sat down. He motioned for Gates to do the same. "This is a pleasant surprise, Dr. McClure. Did I miss an appointment or are you looking for some property?"

"Neither, actually." Gates sat down and studied Lemonick. He was a tall, thin man with a face marred by scars from a youthful struggle with acne. His voice was higher than one would expect from a man, but well below falsetto. His blue eyes were mottled with specks of gray. Despite the broad smile that revealed mildly crooked teeth that had yellowed from years of cigarette smoking, his eyes oozed a sadness of hidden pain. "Actually, I was hoping I could ask you a few questions."

"Questions? What sort of questions?" He opened his briefcase, pulled out a file folder and quickly placed it in the file drawer of his desk.

"About your wife," Gates said softly.

"I'm not married, Doctor."

"I'm talking about Martha." Gates couldn't miss the sudden stiffness that seized the man behind the desk.

"Is she ill?"

"Ill?" Gates was surprised by the question, then realized that he must be connecting her role as a doctor with Martha. "Oh, no. At least not that I know of, anyway."

"Then I don't understand."

"Last Saturday your wife and I . . . met."

"We divorced many years ago, Doctor. She no longer tells me her comings and goings. Last time I spoke to her, she was in Baker."

"She's in Ridgeline and has been for several days, at least since Saturday."

"Maybe we should find a place a little more

private," Lemonick said uneasily. "Let's go in the conference room." A moment later he was on his feet, striding out of the cubicle, across the office and into the enclosed conference room. Gates followed close behind. Once inside the room, Lemonick closed the door and motioned for Gates to be seated. She sat to one side of the large cherry wood table; Lemonick sat on the other side, situating the narrow width between them.

"All right, Doctor," he said pointedly, "what's this all about?"

Gates unraveled the account of Martha's attack on her father the Saturday before, her hatred for Norman Meade, and the vandalism of her car and office. "What I want to ask you, Mr. Lemonick, is this: Is your wife — excuse me, former wife — capable of such actions?"

Surprisingly, Lemonick laughed out loud. "She is capable of that and a whole lot more, Doctor. She is not a well woman — mentally, I mean. She . . . we . . . have been through some very hard times. Those events changed her."

"I see," Gates said.

"Let me explain," Lemonick began. "The Bob Lemonick you've known for the last few years is vastly different than one you would have met years ago. Today, I'm building a career as a real estate agent. Next year I hope to take the broker's test and then open my own business. Five years ago, I was a drunk living on disability payments from the state. I was never arrested for being drunk in public, but I should have been many times. Being the former football star of Ridgeline High had certain advantages then."

"I'm not meaning to pry," Gates said.

"You're not. I'm just giving some background so that you can better understand Martha. We were married right out of high school. We were in love, but the wedding was pushed up a couple of years when Martha discovered that she was pregnant. I'm not proud of that or anything else I'm about to tell you. I am proud of the way that I am now. Back then, in high school, both Martha and I were very popular. She was different then — pretty, good humored, a lot of fun to be with. So marrying early wasn't a problem for me, I was getting a good deal, and she thought she was too. I was young and still full of wild oats. My grades weren't so good, and while I was a star on the local football team, I knew that I lacked the talent for college ball. That's a whole different world. We needed a steady income, so I enlisted in the navy. After basic training, I was stationed in San Diego, so we moved there. I didn't have much sea duty, so

I got to go home each night. That was nice, especially after the baby was born. A little boy. He was great. And Martha was a great mom too." A nearly visible sadness began to hover over the man. "Do you have any kids, Doc?"

"I'm not married," Gates replied.

Bob Lemonick nodded and looked down at the table. "My boy was sick." He picked at a small spot on the table with his thumbnail. "Aplastic anemia."

"Oh, no," Gates said without thinking. Aplastic anemia was a condition that could erupt spontaneously. The disease resulted when a person's bone marrow was incapable of producing the proper amount and type of blood cells. The disease varies from person to person. In a young child or infant it could easily be fatal.

"Since I was in the navy we had Bobby — he was named after me — admitted to the navy's Balboa Hospital for treatment." Gates watched as Lemonick's eyes began to tear. "What he needed was a bone-marrow transplant, but I didn't think the navy was working fast enough or had enough experts working on my son. The only advantages I could see in keeping Bobby in the navy hospital was the money it saved us, and that I could visit him even while I worked. I don't know if I mentioned this or not, Doctor, but I was a medic in the navy. I worked in the hospital. But the money didn't matter, I wanted the best for my son. So we had him transferred to another hospital that had some of the best pediatricians available."

Lemonick stopped talking and looked off in the distance. Gates knew that his mind was now in another city and in another time. He took a deep breath and let it out noisily. "It didn't matter. He died anyway."

Gates' eyes began to burn, and she was blinking more frequently. The story had touched her deeply.

"Well," Lemonick went on, "I continued in the navy for a while, but I was never the same, and neither was Martha. We weren't strong enough to help each other, and we were too young to know how. We cut ourselves off from friends and family. Just the sight of them reminded us of our loss. We started drinking. We drank a lot. It wasn't long before I was kicked out of the navy with a dishonorable discharge. I tried several jobs — tow-truck driver, taxi driver, janitor — but sooner or later I'd be fired for being drunk on the job. Martha, well her drinking turned to drugs. She changed. She was so beautiful when I married her, so full of life, but the drugs and booze made her into a monster. It wasn't long before we were at each other's throats. The marriage ended." Lemonick let loose a snicker. "It's a wonder that we were sober enough to get a divorce."

Gates said nothing. She sat silently attempting to digest what she was hearing.

"Martha went to Baker to stay with some friends. I guess they had a motor home or mobile home or something where she could stay. I came back to Ridgeline and lived with my parents for a while. It wasn't long before they kicked me out. I had some money coming in because the state was paying me disability. Remember, I said I had been a tow-truck driver?"

"Yes."

"I wrecked the truck and was injured. My back. But then you know that, because I come to you when it flares up. Anyway, the money from the state let me rent a one-room cabin just outside of town. It wasn't much of a place, but it did have a fireplace to keep me warm in the winter, and a bed. I kept drinking, then one night — it might have been day, I was too drunk to tell — I had a dream. I saw Bobby."

Again, tears welled in his eyes and his voice cracked. Gates was nearly overwhelmed.

"I saw Bobby, except he wasn't an infant any more. He was a little boy, maybe eight years old. He was looking down on me from heaven and he had his arms crossed like this," he crossed his arms over his chest, "and was shaking his head like he was ashamed of me. My little boy was ashamed of me. Well that did it. I started going to AA meetings down at the Community Center and they helped me kick the habit. I haven't had a drink in over five years now."

"That's great," Gates said, still shocked by the story she was hearing.

"I took a couple of real estate courses so that I could take the test for my agent's license. Passed it first time. I've been working here ever since. I was top salesman last month."

"That's something about which you can be very proud." Gates was amazed. Here was a man that had been through it all, sunk to the bottom of life's ocean, and been able to swim to the surface again. "I'm sorry if my question stirred up painful memories."

"There's always something to stir up those memories, Doc. A day doesn't pass when I don't relive some moment of my past."

"I can't even imagine how hard all of that must have been on you."

"It was — is — rough, but things are going better now. I feel like I have a future."

"So you feel that your ex-wife could be responsible for the damage to my car and office?"

"It's possible. She's an explosive woman, Doc. She can't handle her emotions anymore. She's a very angry person. She hasn't been right in the head for a long time. She blows up at the least little thing. I haven't seen her in a lot of years, and don't want to. Those days are gone."

"Do you know where she might be staying in Ridgeline?"

"No idea whatsoever. I don't think she has much money, so I doubt she's staying in a hotel. Maybe she's sleeping in her car."

Gates rose from her seat. "Thank you, Mr. Lemonick . . ."

"Call me Bob."

"All right. Thank you, Bob. I know this wasn't easy for you."

"Sure you don't want to look at some property? I've got a couple of real beauties."

"No thanks, but if I change my mind, I'll be sure to look you up."

"You do that, Doc. You do that."

According to Gates' watch it was nearly noon, and although it was near lunchtime she was far from hungry. After meeting with Bob Lemonick, Gates had driven home and changed clothes. Setting aside her office attire, she slipped into a pair of jeans, a T-shirt, and a dark blue, plain sweatshirt. At first she puttered around the house, cleaning here and there, but soon became bored with the activity. She tried reading a novel, then a magazine, but neither could hold her attention. *This is silly,* she thought, *I can't sit around here when my office is a shambles.* A minute later she was in the car on her way to the office.

Her office reminded her of a war zone. A new window had been installed. Carl had said he would have a glazier fix the window, but Gates was surprised that the work had already been done. That was the good news. The bad news was that everything that had made Gates' office clean and orderly now lay cast about on the floor and furnishings. Patient files were scattered everywhere, making it almost impossible to walk without stepping on one. Judging by the footprints on some of the papers, people had done just that.

Everywhere there was a smooth light surface were smudges of dark powder used to expose fingerprints. White powder had been used on dark surfaces. Slowly Gates walked through the silence of defacement. Everything had been touched and therefore altered in some way, either by the vandal or by the police. Long gashes oozed stuffing out of chairs and exam tables. Unseen earlier today were deep scars in the drywall where a sharp instrument had been dragged along the surface. In the bathroom, which Gates had not inspected earlier, she found the ultimate insult: some of her medical instruments had been dropped in the toilet. The message was clear.

Her office was the most disturbing of all. This was the place where she counseled her patients, got away from the hectic day for brief respites, and in general operated her business. The destruction here was most painful.

Picking up a trash can, Gates slowly removed the water-soaked papers from her desk. Since she was meticulous about her filing, nothing of importance other than medical journals and the Internet research she had done was wet. She threw all the items away. She felt a sick feeling as she touched each slimy page knowing that someone hated her and that that someone had been handling these pages.

Setting the trash bin down, Gates left her office and entered one of the exam rooms. Quickly she glanced around and found the box for which she was searching. It was a pastel-colored cardboard box that looked similar to a box of facial tissue. Picking it up she extracted a pair of latex gloves and expertly stretched them over her hands like she did almost every day of her life. Filled with a bubbling cauldron of emotions, Gates decided to begin the arduous task of cleaning up. She knew that she could call Valerie and Nancy and, for that matter, her mother and father, to come down and help. But she didn't want help. Not at the moment, anyway. She wanted to be alone. The work would be therapeutic. The best way to cleanse the violation she felt was to scrub away every reminder, every nuance that would give witness to abuse. She wondered if that would be possible. Even the fresh paint that would be needed to obliterate the spray-painted words, "Thou shalt not kill" would be a reminder that someone hated her so much as to risk arrest and prosecution just to vent pent-up wrath.

It hurt Gates to think that someone actually hated her and for no good reason. If this was about Norman Meade, and she couldn't see that it was about anything else, then the ironic fact was that she was probably in agreement with the vandal's sentiments.

As she worked, Gates couldn't help but think about how ludicrous all this was. She had not sought out Norman Meade. All she had done was surrender to her sister's will and attend a costume party. Since then she had been victimized in a dozen different ways and all for the wrong reasons. Gates couldn't help feeling that if she had written all this out as a plot to a novel, no one would believe it.

The words came back to her: "You shall know the truth, and the truth shall set you free." It wasn't in Gates' Christian nature to doubt Scripture, but so far it seemed that the more truth she obtained, the less freedom she had. Still, she believed every word of that verse.

Where to begin? Profession first; personal later. Marching back to the bathroom, Gates stood looking down at the medical instruments in the toilet bowl and then reached in with both hands and began plucking them from their watery tomb. Each would have to be sterilized, each examined.

Once begun, the cleaning continued. She worked systematically from room to room and, on a pad of paper she had retrieved from the office, made a list of the items too damaged to ever be useful again. These would become part of the insurance claim. Hour after hour passed, but Gates ignored their passing as she ignored the pain in her back and knees as she knelt to gather up each file, each note, each prescription pad. Surprisingly soon, from Gates' perspective, darkness began to fall. Gates looked at her watch: 5:05. She had promised to meet Norman at Middy's at 6:00; that was less than an hour away. *I can't meet him like this,* she thought. She pictured herself arriving at Middy's, hair mussed, blue jeans, sweatshirt, latex gloves, and tennis shoes. The thought made her smile. *That would be a different look for me.* Still fifty-five minutes was not much time.

That's the good thing about living in a small town, Gates thought. *Ten minutes to drive home, thirty minutes to shower, and dress, and another ten minutes to drive to the restaurant. That should leave me five minutes to spare.*

As she walked through the front door, she paused and looked back at her office and wondered if it would be the target of Martha's — if it had truly been Martha in the first place — unmanaged anger again tonight. She checked that the door was locked, twice, and then left.

Chapter Twenty

Thursday, November 6
7:15 P.M.

Gates raised the coffee cup to her mouth and took a sip of the warm, black fluid. It not only tasted good, it felt good. She shifted her gaze to the man opposite her at the table. Norman, dressed in a long-sleeved dress shirt and dark pants, held a similar cup to his lips. The light in Middy's was dim and a single scentless candle burned in an ornamental glass container sending wisps of light dancing on the table and now-empty dinner plates. After a salad and a plate of steaming seafood pasta, Gates was feeling full and relaxed. The latter sensation was the most welcome for she had not felt at ease for nearly a week.

Meeting Norman for dinner had proved enjoyable. The restaurant, which could easily seat over fifty people, had been quiet and uncrowded. Only five other couples had shared the large open dining area. The hum of small talk from the other tables, the dark wood exterior, and the wonderful food had worked magic in Gates' recently tumultuous life. After leaving the office, she had hastily driven home, quickly showered, and then spent ten minutes wondering what to wear. She wanted to look nice, but felt uncomfortable dressing as if for a date. Finally she had decided on a red cotton twill blazer, white cotton blouse, and matching slacks. Dressy, but not too much.

The dinner had gone well, filled with idle talk and remembrances of medical school. Soon, however, the conversation had turned to the tribulations that had befallen Gates since Norman arrived in town. Norman, for his part, listened patiently, asked questions, and expressed deep dismay at all the events. When told in succession, the plague of problems seemed enormous. Now at the end of the meal, as they enjoyed coffee, Norman slowly shook his head in disbelief.

"I'm amazed," Norman said softly. "I had no idea the problems my presence would cause you. You have been battered, burned, mistreated, and terrorized. It isn't right. I never meant for you to be harmed in any way, Gates, I really didn't."

"I believe you, Norman," Gates said. "You're not responsible for everything that has happened, not directly anyway."

"What do you mean, not directly?"

"My father used to say that everything has a price. Nothing is free. Whatever we do or don't do will cost something. It might be time or effort, but something will be paid out."

"And you're paying for my being here?" The dim light could not shadow Norman's hurt.

"I guess so, but who could have predicted what would happen?"

"Trouble follows me wherever I go, Gates. I'm used to it. It's all part of the life I've chosen, but it bothers me deeply when that trouble spills over into the lives of others, especially those I care about — my friends."

Care about? The phrase caught Gates off guard. "Into every life some rain must fall."

"Don't trivialize these events with clichés, Gates. The attack on your office was an indirect attack on you. The news report hasn't helped your image in the community, and it's all because of me."

"I didn't agree to meet you for dinner to lay a guilt trip on you, Norman, but surely you must realize that what you do is going to affect a great many people and in a way that you could never anticipate. As long as you continue with your practice of physician-assisted suicide, then you must expect repercussions."

"I've always anticipated repercussions, but

they have always been directed at me and no one else."

Gates put her cup down and stared at Norman for a moment. "Are you sure?"

"Of course I'm sure."

"Let me ask you something, Norman. When you go into a town like ours or some city and do what you do, how long do you stay around? How long do you remain in the community?"

"Well," Norman said raising a dismissive hand, "my schedule being what it is requires that I move around a lot."

"How long?" Gates insisted.

Norman was silent for a moment. He scratched his chin and looked around the room at the empty tables. "Maybe a day, usually less."

"Then how do you know what repercussions your actions bring?"

"I keep tabs on things," Norman protested.

"There are some things that you can't measure: heartache, family stress, lingering doubt, and grief are intangibles. You could never see their effects at a distance. In fact, had Dr. Warren not been killed in a way that implicates you, then you would be someplace else in the country right now and you would never have known what has happened to me or Eugene Crews."

"That's not entirely fair," Norman answered. "I could be someplace else right now. I don't have to be in Ridgeline. I have to stay in the state, that's true, but California is a big state."

"True," Gates said. "So tell me, Norman, why *are* you here?"

Just as the question was asked, the waiter stepped to the table and refilled their cups. A moment after the man was gone, Norman answered: "To see you."

"Me?"

Norman leaned forward over the table and made eye contact with Gates. The light from the candle danced ethereal pirouettes on his face. He looked good, strong, attractive. Taking a deep breath, he spoke softly, easily, "Gates, I have very strong feelings for you and have had since we first met in medical school . . ."

Gates broke eye contact. "Uh, Norman, before you go on . . ."

Norman raised a hand. "Please, Gates, let me finish. There's nothing to worry about, but I need to say these things. Okay?"

Gates nodded in silence.

"I was very much attracted to you in school, and that feeling has not changed. When I saw you at the Halloween party last Friday, those emotions flooded my very being until I

350

thought I was going to drown in them. Back in school, I never felt that my feelings could be returned in like kind. You were so serious then, as you are now. I enjoyed — relished — each time we went out for coffee and each hour we spent studying. Now let me put your mind at ease. I know you have no interest in me, and even if you did our philosophical differences would never allow us to be a couple. I am aware that you hate what I do, and perhaps even hate me . . ."

"I don't hate you, Norman."

"That's good to hear, Gates, but I know you don't respect me. I can live with that. I have to live with that. But I want you to know that . . . well, that I care for you deeply, and seeing you these last few days has brought me a great deal of joy, despite my being jailed and accused of murder."

Gates shifted in her seat. She had not expected this, not after so many years. The truth was that there was a time when these words would have sent her spirit soaring. Now they frightened her.

Norman continued: "I'm not asking for a commitment on your part. I just wanted you to know. I try to live my life honestly, Gates. Many would argue that, but I do. It would be dishonest of me not to share these emotions."

In stunned silence, Gates studied Norman.

Her heart was pounding and her mouth, despite the coffee, was suddenly dry. Butterflies, the size of eagles, fluttered in her stomach. She couldn't tell if she was shocked, frightened, or thrilled. Intellectually she knew he was right — there never could be anything between them. But part of her — the schoolgirl part of her — wished it were different. Many nights in medical school were ended with her lying upon her bed thinking of the intense, driven, handsome student named Norman Meade and wishing he would take a deeper interest in her; each night she convinced herself that such a thing was impossible. Years of life had brought a maturity and experience to her life that forged a nearly unshakable self-confidence. Now she was confident in her intelligence; uncertain in relationships.

If only things were different. The dreaminess that had unexpectedly shrouded Gates' thinking was whisked away by the strong winds of reality. Feelings of years gone by could not produce fruit today. Only in romance novels, Gates told herself, could such a disparity of ethics be overcome. It was clear that Norman held no hope for such a miracle; Gates would harbor no such hopes either.

"Thank you for your candor," Gates said wishing she hadn't sounded so clinical. "I mean . . ."

"I know what you mean, Gates. I've put you in an awkward situation."

"There was a time when this would have been the greatest news, but we are so very different now. Our ethics are different. If we were talking about a relationship between a Republican and a Democrat, then we could make things work. But we are separated by something far more significant than that."

An uncomfortable silence fell between the two. Gates felt compelled to change the subject. "I've been meaning to ask you something, Norman. It's about something you said Friday night at the party."

"Ask away." He seemed relieved with the topic switch.

"I don't know if you remember, heated as the moment was . . ."

"I can be a little short tempered. My mouth has gotten me in trouble before."

"Well, in this case you said to Warren, 'How would you know what was decent?' Do you remember that?"

"Sure, he said something about what decent people think or believe or something. I remember."

"What did you mean by that?"

Norman shrugged. "Warren was an egotistical little man. In his day, he had been a good doctor, a fine pediatrician. But then he got involved in social causes and politics and his work began to suffer. Ultimately he would take extended leave of his position as director of pediatrics at University City Hospital in San Diego. It was that or be fired."

"Fired?"

"There were a couple of cases in which a child died under his care. No fault could be laid at his feet legally — although I don't know why — but rumor had it that he had bungled a diagnosis or two and the end result was that the children died. I don't know much beyond that. I do know that once he was out of day-to-day practice, he became a professional dissident, tilting at various windmills, including physician-assisted suicide. It wasn't long until I became his favorite target. I had read recently that he had signed up with a New York publisher to write a book. I guess following me around was a good way to gain publicity."

"The article I read on him stated that he was still with the hospital."

"Technically he is, he's just on indeterminate leave — ostensibly to do battle against people like me — but the hospital was relieved to have him off the floor."

"How do you know?"

"My organization includes a great many people from the medical profession, including some at his former hospital. Word got to me through them. As far as I'm concerned, it's useless information. I could never use it to defend myself against his charges, it would appear like pure bitterness. Besides, attacking him would just make me and the cause look bad. I had greater work to do."

Gates thought for a moment. "Then your comment about his not knowing what was and wasn't decent was a reference to those children that died?"

"And the cover-up that went with it."

Again Gates fell into silent contemplation. Something in her subconscious was trying to surface, but she couldn't identify it.

"Do you despise me?" Norman asked suddenly.

The question stunned Gates from her thoughts. "I've already said that I don't. However, I couldn't be more opposed to what you do. If I hate anything, it is this thinking that doctors have a right to take life."

Norman frowned. "Gates, you should know by now that I don't take lives . . ."

"I sit corrected," she interrupted. "You make it possible for people to take their own lives. That may make a difference in your thinking, but it's a small distinction in mine. I don't understand how you can do what you do. It's against the Hippocratic oath." Gates wondered if the turn in topics was an effort on her part to avoid the uncomfortable discussion of Norman's feelings for her.

To Gates' surprise, Norman laughed. "Hippocratic oath? Do you really believe that the medical community has confined itself to the Hippocratic oath?"

"It should."

"You don't believe that."

"I do," Gates protested firmly. "You and I took an oath that says, among other things, 'I will neither give a deadly drug to anybody if asked for, nor will I make a suggestion to this effect.' That's exactly what physician-assisted suicide does — no matter who actually administers the drug."

"Above all do no harm," Norman quoted. "It's a nice sentiment, Gates, but don't you think I thought that through? The Hippocratic oath also states that the physician will give 'no abortive remedy' but the law of the land has not only made abortion legal, but lucrative."

"And that's wrong."

"It may surprise you to discover that I agree. I am opposed to abortion and believe that it is taking a life and doing so without any compelling reason such as suffering. You should have another problem with the Hippocratic oath, especially considering your faith."

356

"What's my faith got to do with it?" Gates asked, puzzled.

"Oh, come on Gates, think. How does the Hippocratic oath begin?"

"I don't have it memorized."

"I do. It begins like this: 'I swear by Apollo Physician and Aesculapius and Hygeia and Panacea and all the gods and goddesses, making them my witnesses, that I will fulfill according to my ability and judgment this oath and covenant.' Am I to understand that you as a Christian are citing a document that begins with an oath to ancient Greek gods? Surely you don't believe such gods exist."

"I do not, but that is beside the point."

"Is it? Even if it is, the Hippocratic oath is not legally or even morally binding. The oath states 'above all do no harm'. If someone is in miserable suffering and terminal are we not doing harm by not easing that pain?"

"The world of medicine has changed a lot over the last few years. Pain is far more manageable. There are very few situations in which pain cannot be controlled."

"Then why is there so much pain?"

"Many doctors are not educated in the latest pain treatments."

"That doesn't help the patient much, now does it."

"That's not the point . . ."

"It is if you're the one in agony. Gates, I've seen patients in such pain that they would shoot themselves in the head if they had the opportunity, and their doctors can do nothing about it except give them enough morphine to put them in a coma, and sometimes that doesn't even work. I've seen patients receive morphine shots in the spine to block pain, and even that failed."

"That's rare."

"Does it matter if it's rare if you're the one who lives minute by minute in hell?"

"Doctors don't take life, they preserve life," Gates said strongly.

"Doctors take lives all the time. They botch surgeries, misdiagnose diseases, prescribe improper medication." Gates could see that Norman was getting heated.

"Look, I've done some research over the last few days and read some articles, and I think they bear out my point: physician-assisted suicide sets a dangerous precedent. In the Netherlands where euthanasia is legal . . ."

"Euthanasia is not legal in the Netherlands, it's just not prosecuted," Norman corrected.

"But it is widely accepted," Gates countered. "In the Netherlands, there have been cases when patients have received lethal doses of medication to free up beds in a crowded hospital. That's what I'm afraid will happen here if physician-assisted suicide were ever to become legal. It's the slippery slope argument. First patients tortured by disease are allowed to kill themselves, then soon doctors will be allowed to not only assist in a suicide but to commit the actual act of euthanasia. How many years after that before voluntary euthanasia becomes involuntary and the elderly, handicapped, and incapacitated are routinely disposed of to make room and save money? And don't say there's no slippery slope, Norman. We watched as early term abortions became legal to mid-term, and now partial-birth abortions are legal."

Again, Norman frowned. "Gates," he began softly, "I am aware of all the arguments pro and con. I've debated them for years. I've followed the legalization and subsequent court case surrounding the 1994 Oregon law as well as the law making voluntary euthanasia permissible in the Northwest Territory of Australia. I've followed the court cases of Vacco v. Quill, and Compassion in Dying v. Washington. I also know that medical journals have reported surveys that show that over 53 percent of AIDS doctors have helped at least one patient kill himself. My office is filled with every report, court case, debate, and anything else regarding the matter. I know the logic of the slippery slope. I am a walking encyclopedia on the subject, but none of that matters. All that matters, Gates, is the present suffering and lack of dignity for the terminally ill."

"I don't agree . . ."

Norman was gesturing sharply with his hands as he spoke. "People — lawyers, academicians, doctors, philosophers, ministers — sit around and debate the fine points of the issue while people like Darlene Crews choke on their own saliva. What's so ethical about that?"

"That's not fair, Norman," Gates rejoined, her words tinged with indignation. "You don't have a lock on sympathy. There are many people who care about the pain they see and it touches them deeply. I am as moved by the suffering of Darlene Crews as you. I just don't believe we should be helping her and those like her kill themselves."

"So you're willing to let her suffer in mind and body just so that you don't get your professional feelings hurt. That's not an act of professionalism, it's selfishness, pure and simple."

The words struck Gates like a slap in the face. The warmness and relaxation she had felt earlier was swept away. "How dare you. You waltz into my life uninvited and then insult me to my face because you suffer from a messiah complex. I was the only one in this town who believed you innocent in the killing of Dr. Warren. I alone took it upon myself to ask favors of Carl Berner on your behalf. You would have been locked up in a cell down in county if it weren't for me." Gates stood to her feet. "I didn't come here to hear you pontificate on your holy cause, nor will I sit here and listen to you insult me." In fluid motions, Gates snapped open the small purse she had brought with her, removed a twenty-dollar bill and tossed it on the table.

"Gates, wait. You don't have to do that."

But Gates had already turned to leave, ignoring the stares of the other patrons.

Chapter Twenty-One

Thursday, November 6
9:30 P.M.

It had taken ninety minutes of driving for Gates to settle down. When she was this angry she hated to be home alone where she would pace around the room stewing in the juices of exasperation which invariably left her feeling worse. Besides, Norman would call to apologize and she didn't want to talk to him just yet. So she drove, taking the sinuous road out of Ridgeline, up the mountain past High Peak ski resort. Since ski season had not started the road was only sparsely populated by other vehicles. It was on this road that Gates let her thoughts roam free.

With each turn in the road, and on this mountain there were many of them, she thought how her life had come to resemble the serpentine path. Her life, with only rare exception, had always been straightforward. Aside from the attack in medical school, nothing bad had ever happened to her. Now in a week's time she had had more trouble than she cared to have.

Norman had hurt her. His words had struck deep, but not because he was right. Eloquent as he was, he was still wrong about physician-assisted suicide. She replayed the scalding words: "So you're willing to let her suffer in mind and body just so that you don't get your professional feelings hurt. That's not an act of professionalism, it's selfishness, pure and simple." He had attacked her professionalism and her motivation. He had implied that she didn't care about the suffering of others when in fact few doctors cared more. Those words were like a steam burn to her soul. But why? She had been insulted before and not taken it this hard. Sure his words were unexpected and sharp, but had her words been any less pointed?

A new scene began to play on the screen of Gates' mind. As it flickered to life she saw herself castigating Mrs. Grier. Gates could hear her own voice vividly: "The story was basically true, but you, of course, don't know that since you've not bothered to ask anyone like myself who was directly involved in the event. It's people like you who make life difficult. You hear something, usually at some gossip session, and then you formulate your opinions, which you share freely with everyone who lacks the character to tell you to shut up. And to make matters worse, people like you formulate those opinions without the benefit of reason and thought. You care nothing for how your words wound others, just so long as you have an opportunity to hear yourself talk."

Mrs. Grier had stormed out of the office just as Gates had stormed out of the restaurant. "Way to go, Gates," she said to herself, "your dramatic exit achieved nothing. You're as guilty of offensive speech as Norman."

The question remained: Why did Norman's words sting so much? She was an adult. She was a professional. She was used to stress. So why? A thought sprang up like a flame from a match and demanded attention. Gates recognized it immediately and made an effort to ignore it, but it would not go away. Norman's words hurt her so much because she was still attracted to him. Despite tossing gallons of denial on the matter, the truth flared to life and shone even more brightly; and that truth brought her no peace.

At the crest of the mountain, just ten miles past the ski resort, was a county-maintained viewpoint called Vista Peak. During the day, tourists would stop here and gaze down at the city spread out below. At night, teenagers and romantic adults would park here to gaze at the moon, wonder at the stars, and watch the city lights flicker. Gates exited the road and parked as far from the other cars as possible.

She needed to be alone.

She needed to think.

She needed to pray.

A cool breeze swam around the car as Gates sat in a silence as dark as the night. Overhead, the moon hovered like a metallic mylar balloon. Gazing beyond the hood of her borrowed car and just beyond the metal guardrail that separated the gravel view area from the sheer drop of the mountain cliff, sparkles of light from the city glittered in the white of houses, and the red of stop lights. Here, high above the rest of the world, Gates felt alone and removed from the rest of the universe. It was a good feeling.

Despite the captivating vista, images less appealing and more confusing held sway. Images of Norman Meade, Darlene and Eugene Crews, of their abusive daughter Martha, and her ex-husband Bob Lemonick. She also saw the room in which Ed Warren had been murdered, her scarred automobile, and her vandalized office. She could feel the still-tender bruise on her hip where she had struck the concrete floor when Warren had pushed her; and that was accompanied by the now mildly tender skin of her legs where she had been burned when she had carelessly spilled soup on herself.

She not only saw these things but she heard things as well: her pastor's words when she sought his counsel, Ballew's incriminating and slanted news report, Philip Platt's pleas to be aided in death.

Images, sounds, thoughts, memories; swirling, churning, bubbling. Emotions: anger, fear, sadness, hope, indignation . . . love? Principles: truth, honesty, righteousness, ethics, professionalism. Demons: confusion, bitterness, doubt. All of these loose and free and soaring through her very being. No structure, no framework, no logic — chaos reigned for the moment as surely as it did before creation.

What to do? What to think? What to feel?

Her head bowed, Gates began to calm herself with rhythmic breathing, listening, focusing on the beating of her heart. She forced, commanded, compelled her mind to shed the blurring emotions and thoughts. Soon there was no vista to view, no breeze to hear. She was alone in singular thought, her mind directed toward heaven. It was here that she heard and felt and experienced the things she needed: unconditional acceptance, wisdom, love, purpose, power, direction. She needed to be here; needed to feel the presence of God, to touch the face of the Almighty.

At first the prayer was halting, faltering, disconnected; but as the moments floated past the words became directed and specific as if someone were helping her compose the supplication like a teacher tutoring a child. The prayer lacked sophistication and polish, but it was resplendent with sincerity and honesty. It was the perfect prayer and the perfect tonic for a tortured soul. Tears flowed without shame; laughter came without embarrassment; healing came without fanfare; direction was given without words.

Perfect communication.

Perfect prayer.

Clear objectives.

The clock in the car read 10:44 as Gates guided the vehicle down the road. That meant that she had spent more than two hours at Vista Peak. The drive back down the mountain to her home was the opposite of her drive up in more ways than direction and altitude. Her anger was gone, having been replaced by a peace. Instead of turmoil, Gates now felt an overriding fulfillment. She had returned to the single concept that had been her driving force for much of the last week: "You shall know the truth, and the truth shall set you free."

That's all that mattered now. What others

thought of her could not be controlled. If patients continued to cancel, then so be it. If the world knew of her attack in medical school, so what? And if people wanted to associate her with Norman Meade — Dr. Death — then there was nothing she could do about it. She would not let such things diminish her life. All that mattered was the pure, unadulterated truth.

She had some of that truth. She knew that Norman Meade was innocent of Warren's murder. She knew that no matter how eloquent and well rehearsed his impassioned arguments for the right to die were, they were wrong. He was to be admired for both his passion and his compassion, but Gates could not condone his work. And what of Norman's revelation about his feelings for Gates? That was the one area of uncertainty left. Had he been right when he said that their different views would keep them apart?

What kind of relationship could they have? Gates tried to imagine a romantic tie between them, and each time the fanciful image dissolved into absurdity. She would see them meeting at the end of the day and she would ask, "So dear, have a rough day at the office?" Gates could only shake her head at the thought. Yet being the object of someone's attention filled her with warmth. It was the one thing missing in her life.

As had become her custom, Gates drove a block down from her house, parked Sharee's car by the curb, and walked back to her home. The thoughts of the night were still fresh in her mind as she walked up the three steps that led to the front porch and slipped her key into the lock. So lost in introspection only her subconscious noticed that the lock on the door felt different than usual. It turned too easily, as if it had been left unlocked.

The hinges squeaked softly as she turned the knob and pushed open the door. *I should have left a light on,* Gates thought to herself. *That's what I get for waiting till the last minute to leave.* The open curtains let the light of the moon filter into the room bringing with it shadows from the large ponderosa pine in her front yard. The house was warm compared to the brisk breeze of the night. Unconsciously she let her eyes trace the room. The moonlight was insufficient to provide much detail. All Gates could see were the vague shapes of her furniture and the flashing light of her answering machine.

Gates stopped cold.

Something about the red light on the answering machine was wrong. At first she didn't know how or why, but it was wrong nonetheless. She gazed at it for a moment, fixated on the pulsing red flashes; then she realized that it was in the wrong place. The machine always rested on a small phone table that stood about three feet tall. But the blinking light was much lower than that — too low to be on the table. The only way it could be that low was if the answering machine were resting on the floor. But it was in its place when she left. That meant that it had to have fallen while she was gone, but what could have caused that? There had been no earthquake. She would have felt it if there had been. She had no pets to disturb her furniture. Maybe someone . . .

That thought triggered a wave of fear. Someone had been in her house. That's why she felt a sudden sense of disquiet. The dim images of her furniture, lit only by the weak light of the moon, were in the wrong place. Suddenly Gates felt the pit drop from her stomach. Someone had been in her house. Had? Maybe *was* in her house.

Quickly she reached for the light switch on the wall near the door. Where was it? She could feel the paint on the drywall but not the smooth hard plastic of the switch plate. She pawed at the wall, moving her hand quickly from side to side. There. She felt it and as soon as she did she heard something: the slight creak of the wood floor protesting the shifting weight of someone. Gates' heart hammered in her chest. The switch. She threw the switch and the room was bathed in the dim light of a lampstand across the room.

The sound. The squeak. A step.

Gates spun on her heels to face the now-lit room. She was greeted by a sneer crookedly pasted to the oily skin of Martha Crews. The next thing Gates saw was a fist as it crashed into her nose. Falling backward, Gates hit her head on the still partially opened door. The door crashed shut. Widening her eyes, Gates shook her head to keep from losing consciousness. Pain, hot and piercing, rifled through her. She blinked and looked up. Martha Crews stood above her.

"I've been waiting for you, Doc," she said, her voice laced with bitterness, madness.

"What . . ." Gates started to speak.

"Shut up!" Martha thundered. "I didn't come to talk." Viciously, Martha reached down and grabbed Gates by the hair and then yanked up. Gates let loose a cry of pain and instinctively grabbed Martha's wrist. Suddenly, and by the sheer strength of the crazed woman, Gates was standing on her feet. Martha spun to the side, pulling Gates by the hair. Then came the other fist. This one struck Gates squarely on the cheek, snapping her head to the side. Again, she crumpled to the floor. Again, Gates struggled to remain conscious. Again she felt piercing pain.

Using her hands and feet for leverage, Gates pushed backward along the carpeted floor. She could feel blood streaming from her nose and across her lips. Above her towered Martha Crews, her lips pulled back in a ghoulish sneer, small beads of perspiration dotting her brow. Back, back, Gates pushed herself, never taking her eyes from her attacker. Another sharp pain, this time in the back. She had backed over the fallen phone table. Gates winced. Martha sneered all the more.

"What do you want?" Gates demanded.

"Retribution, Doc. Vengeance." Her words were guttural, harsh, weighted with evil.

"I'm not responsible for your mother's death," Gates objected, still trying to distance herself from the approaching threat.

"Like I believe that. You're all the same." As she spoke, a small burst of spittle sprayed from her mouth.

"Who?" Gates asked hoping to strike some cord of reason in the woman.

"You doctors. Your friend Meade killed my mother. The only good thing he ever did was kill that doctor. One less of you to torture us, hurt us, and then charge us for the privilege of doing so."

Slowly Gates started to get to her feet. She began pushing herself up with her arms. If she could distract Martha long enough, she just might be able to escape outside. Martha was a large woman, obese. Surely, Gates could out-run her. "What's that got to do with me? I helped your father."

"My father is part of the problem. He struck a deal with the devil when he invited Dr. Death to come and kill my mother." Before Gates could even comprehend the sentence, Martha lurched forward and swiftly kicked Gates' left arm out from under her and she fell back to the floor. It was clear that Martha was not going to let Gates get up. Gates would have to be more forceful.

"What's that got to do with me?" Gates demanded, attempting to sound controlled and powerful from her position on the floor.

Martha laughed loudly, then hissed: "You're his girlfriend. Let's see how he likes it when someone he cares for . . ." she never finished the sentence. Instead she quickly stepped forward and kicked at Gates aiming for tender ribs. Gates saw it coming and pushed away. Martha's shoe just grazed Gates' rib cage. She could feel the heel of the shoe scrape at the flesh under her blouse. Taking initiative born of pure, unbridled fear, she grabbed Martha's right foot as it sailed by and held it tightly.

Looking up from the floor, she saw a puzzled look cross her attacker's face. It was clear that Martha had expected no resistance. Then, with as much force as she could muster, Gates did some kicking of her own, aiming at Martha's left ankle. It worked, Gates had kicked the other foot loose from its station on the floor. Martha waved her arms wildly and fell backward to the carpeted floor with a loud thud. Gates could feel the shock wave of the fall rumble beneath her.

Frantically, Gates scrambled to her feet and faced the front door. Martha, in movements that belied her size, was just getting to her feet. Her expression radiated fury. Since Martha stood between her and the door, Gates knew that she would need another way out. There was only one: the back door in the kitchen. Spinning quickly, Gates turned to sprint toward the kitchen. She fell, tripping over the broken remains of the telephone table and crashed hard on the floor. Once again Martha was standing and Gates was sprawled on the carpet. Behind her she heard a guttural snicker roll from some dark cavern in Martha.

Heart thundering, adrenaline-laced blood coursed through Gates' body. Her mind became sharp, her senses acute. Not once had Gates ever been in a fight; not in school and not with any of the children she grew up with.

She had never struck anyone. That was changing. Rolling on her back Gates looked up at the advancing behemoth called Martha Crews. She needed a weapon, but what? Glancing around the debris littered floor, Gates grabbed the first thing she could reach — the telephone. Without thought, she seized the hard plastic phone, sat up and threw it with all her might.

Martha was not ready for the act, the phone caught her just above the left eye, opening a large gash that began to freely flow with blood. Martha screamed in pain and stumbled backward until she made contact with the wall. The air filled with obscenities, but Gates had no intention of staying around to listen. She was on her feet again staggering toward the kitchen. Now in fight and flight mode, she could no longer feel the pain in her nose and cheek from the punches she had received, nor could she sense the stinging flesh above her ribs.

Unwanted pictures of the attack she endured years ago began to flood her mind. From the moment of that first attack, Gates had wondered if she had done enough to defend herself. She had struggled, but she hadn't really fought back. For months and years she had felt as though she had surrendered too easily and had become a passive victim. She balanced that with the understanding that there was no way that she could have overcome the two attackers, but the nagging question still remained. In the briefest moment of thought, Gates determined not to be passive again. If Martha Crews was going to harm her, even kill her, she was going to have to work to do so.

The hardwood kitchen floor was littered with pots, pans, broken glasses and plates. In one easy motion, Gates reached down and grabbed a heavy metal pot. Instead of running directly to the back door, she stopped, and turned to see Martha rounding the corner that separated the kitchen from the living room. No sooner than Martha had stepped into the kitchen, Gates swung the pot, putting her weight behind the motion. It caught Martha squarely on the chin. She staggered back a few steps, touched her face and then looked at the blood on her fingers. Why the woman didn't crumble to the ground was beyond Gates. At least the sneer was gone.

Gates looked to the back door and wondered if she could make a run for it. It would not be easy. The door was locked with both a standard doorknob lock and a dead bolt. It would take several seconds for her to undo both, seconds she didn't think she had. Turning back to Martha, Gates spoke loudly in hopes of sounding more vicious than she was: "Enough. You are barking up the wrong tree, Martha. I'm not who you want."

"Where is he?" Martha screamed. "Where is Meade?"

"There are better ways of dealing with this . . ."

"Where is he?" She took a step forward, Gates raised the pot. "The police will be here any moment," Gates bluffed and hoped that it was true. Hopefully a neighbor has noticed something wrong.

"It will be too late for you," Martha spat.

"Why me?"

"I told you, you're all the same."

"You're the one that keyed my car aren't you? You're the one who trashed my office."

Martha didn't answer, instead she charged, head low, arms outstretched, and a crazed scream emanating from her mouth. Gates tried to step aside and wield the pot once more, but Martha crashed into her like a football player making a bone-cracking tackle. Martha's shoulder caught Gates under the rib cage knocking the wind from her. The momentum lifted Gates from her feet and the two went crashing into the rear door. The force of the impact stunned Gates who was struggling to breathe. In a single motion, Martha lifted Gates from her feet and threw her over her shoulder and careening toward the hardwood floor. Gates thrust out her right hand to break the fall. She heard and felt something snap in her wrist.

Oblivious to the searing pain in her arm, Gates rolled over on her back as Martha turned around. Gates waited for no conversation, but struck out. Taking careful aim, she kicked as hard as she could at her target, the inside of Martha's knee right next to the patella, the kneecap. The small bony shield of the knee was held in place by cartilage and a sufficient kick could rip that away from the bone. It did. Martha screamed in pain and grabbed her knee.

Gates scrambled to her feet and slowly backed away. Unbelievably, Martha began to approach again, limping with each step. She bared her teeth in pain and anger. The woman would not quit. Bob Lemonick was right — the woman was crazy. Gates continued to walk backward until she had stepped from the kitchen and bumped into the table in the adjoining dining room. Her heart pounding and her breathing labored. Martha paused for a moment and looked around the kitchen. Things were scattered about as if a tornado had taken a detour through the place. Among the scattered utensils she spotted what she wanted: a large butcher's knife. She grabbed it.

"I was just going to rough you up some, Doc, but now you went and made me mad. Real mad."

"You were mad before you came here, Martha. Now you're just proving it."

"I don't need self-righteous talk from the likes of you." She took a step forward and flashed the knife.

"I agree." Gates projected false bravado. "You need professional help."

"You think I'm crazy? Do you, Doc?"

Emotionally Gates was over the edge. She no longer chose her words cautiously. "Oh, I don't know, Martha. Here you are having trashed my office, my car, and now my house, standing in my kitchen with a knife after attacking me, and you want to know if I think you're crazy. Yes, I think you're crazy and confused. You need more help than I can give you." Gates felt behind her and to the side. She felt the back of one of the dining-room chairs.

"I don't care what you think, Doc. Doctors are the real killers and they never have to pay the price for it."

"I know about your child, Martha. I know you lost him. I know everything fell apart after that, but I'm not the one who let you down."

"How do you know those things?" Another step closer.

Gates took hold of the chair. "I spoke with your ex-husband. He told me."

"He never could keep his mouth shut; he probably told you everything. Well that is just too bad for you." Martha charged, knife held high in the air. Her voice filled the room with a ululating scream. Gates in a fluid motion yanked the chair from its resting place and spun it along the floor hitting Martha in the legs. Like a giant oak, Martha came crashing to the ground face-first, her head made a sickening thump, the knife in her hand clattered along the floor.

Gates wasted no time. Quickly she grabbed the knife and ran toward the front door. The moment she was outside, she turned and threw the knife on the roof of her house, and hobbled down the steps from her porch. The pain in her head, side, and wrist would no longer be ignored. As if making up for lost time when it had been masked by the tidal wave of adrenaline, the pain began to blaze through her body. Tears filled her eyes and she began to pray as she ran down the sidewalk. She didn't know if Martha was behind her or not; didn't know if the fall over the chair had incapacitated the angry woman, but she did know that she needed help and needed it immediately. Gates could not withstand another attack.

Stepping into the street she began to pray for a passerby, someone who would take her into his car and drive her to safety. Headlights, bright and refracted by the tears of pain and fear in her eyes splashed down the street. Gates staggered to the middle of the road and raised one arm to wave. Her other arm, wrist broken, was tenderly cradled to her stomach.

Closer, the lights came. Brighter the lights beamed. A moment later the car stopped.

"Doc? Doc McClure, is that you?" Familiar voice. Friendly voice. Gates began to weep. "Doc, it's me, Dan Wells." Officer Wells. Gates remembered that Carl said he would have an officer drive by the house from time to time. She was angry that he hadn't been by sooner; she was overjoyed that he was here now.

"Martha Crews," Gates said breathlessly. "In my house. Attacked me."

"Let's get you into the patrol car." A moment later, Gates was seated in the front seat. Dan had called for backup.

Pain: piercing, fiery, ever-present.

Fear: thundering, permeating.

Confusion: swirling, deepening.

Blackness: welcome, embracing.

Chapter Twenty-Two

Friday, November 7
7:30 A.M.

Opening her eyes proved painful. Her mouth was dry. The room was bright. Slowly, like the dripping of a faucet, memories began to replace the sense of displaced confusion she felt. Above her was a ceiling that was not her own; below her was an unfamiliar bed. Blinking several times in rapid succession, Gates slowly turned her head.

"Oh, you're awake, dear. That's good."

A blurry image of a person seated next to the bed began to move. Gates willed her eyes to focus.

"How are you feeling?"

The image cleared and so did her sleep-hazed mind. "Hi, Mom. I feel okay, I guess. What time is it?"

"Just about 7:30," Maggie McClure said looking at her watch. "Your sister and father went over to the cafeteria for some breakfast."

Gates nodded. She remembered being brought into the hospital room after spending an hour in the ER. There had been x-rays and a general exam. Then there was the casting of her right wrist. Gates looked down at her arm as it rested on top of the white blanket. It was encased in a fiberglass cast. The skin of her arm itched. Shifting her weight in the bed sent peals of pain through her body. Her side ached and her head felt twice its size.

"Easy, dear," her mother said. "Just because you've been sleeping for a few hours doesn't mean that you're ready to go horseback riding." The image made Gates wince.

"I'll be going home soon," Gates said matter-of-factly.

"Not unless the doctor releases you."

"He will. I'm just in for observation, that's all. They'll cut me loose in a couple of hours."

"I don't know, dear, you took quite a beating from that woman."

"I'm fine, Mother. The x-rays were negative. I'm just a little battered."

"A little. Both your eyes are black, your nose is swollen twice its size, you have a couple of bruised ribs and a broken wrist."

"None of which is serious. I'll be up and around in a day."

Maggie frowned. "Why are doctors such lousy patients?"

"Because they're no good at practicing what they preach," a male voice said from the doorway. Quickly Gates turned her head to see who was speaking and immediately regretted it. The sudden motion sent more ripples of pain through her.

"I probably shouldn't say this," Carl Berner said as he entered the room. He was followed by Norman Meade who looked crestfallen. "But you look like you've been playing some pro football, without the benefit of a helmet."

Gates offering a weak smile, "You don't know how long I've been waiting for some handsome man to say that to me."

"How are you feeling, Gates?" Norman asked remorsefully.

"I feel . . . okay. Glad to be alive."

"I'm so very sorry for all this, Gates. I truly am."

Maggie chimed in. "He's been here all night. Wouldn't go home no matter how I prodded him."

"I appreciate that, Norman, and there's no need to apologize. You can't be held responsible for Martha Crews' actions."

Norman shook his head mournfully. "Not true. If I hadn't been so arrogant and selfish, I wouldn't have said the things that made you walk out. I would have seen you home. I would have been there."

Slowly, to avoid the introduction of more

pain, Gates shook her head. "We met at the restaurant, remember. We both had our cars. There was no way you were going to see me home."

"Still . . ."

"Leave yourself alone, Norman. You've got enough problems to worry about without feeling guilty over me. By the way, how did you find out?"

"I told him," Carl said. "When Dan Wells called to let me know that you were in the hospital and that he had arrested Martha Crews, I looked Dr. Meade up. I wanted to make sure he had nothing to do with all this."

"Why would he?"

Carl frowned. "In case you've forgotten, he's under suspicion for murder. Remember?"

"Of course, I remember," Gates rejoined. "And I've told you that he didn't do it."

"I'm just being thorough," Carl said defensively. "Besides, it shook me up. I thought telling my officers to patrol your street would be enough. It wasn't."

"Sure it was," Gates said. "If Dan hadn't shown up, Martha might have caught up to me."

Surprisingly, Carl laughed. Everyone looked at him.

"What's so funny?" Maggie asked sternly.

"I don't see anything funny about this."

"I'm sorry, Mrs. McClure, it's just that Martha wasn't going to chase Gates anywhere." Turning to Gates he said, "I've been dying to ask you this: Just what size truck did you hit her with?"

"I don't understand," Gates said.

"Well," Carl continued, still smiling. "After Officer Wells put you in the car, he called for backup then went charging into the house. He should have waited for another officer, but he didn't. I'll talk to him later about that. Anyway, he charges in, gun drawn and finds Martha Crews face down on the floor unconscious. We had to take her to the hospital too."

"She's here?" Gates asked alarmed.

Carl shook his head. "No, of course not. She's a prisoner. The paramedics said her injuries weren't life threatening so we had her taken down to the county hospital. She's under guard there. Although I don't think she's going anywhere."

"Why?" Gates asked.

"Let's see if I can remember." Carl raised a hand to his chin and struck a thoughtful pose. "Oh yes, I recall. She was being treated for a broken kneecap, a sprained wrist, a mild concussion from a blow to the face and forehead by a hard, blunt object, and a broken cheekbone. We think she got the last one when her face hit your dining-room floor. Officer Wells also tells me that Martha Crews was found draped over a dining-room chair. In short Gates, she's a train wreck and I think you were the train. So what did you hit her with?"

"I'm not very proud of this, but I broke her kneecap with my foot."

"And . . ." Carl prompted.

"Okay, okay. I hit her in the face with a telephone and then a pot, and later, when she was charging me with the knife, I threw a chair at her feet. I think that's when she hit her face on the floor. Like I said, I'm not proud of it."

"That's okay," Carl said with a broad grin, "I'm proud enough for both of us. Just don't get mad at me. I don't think my insurance will cover it."

Gates chortled then stifled it. "This shouldn't be funny."

"Gates, the woman attacked you. You did a good thing defending yourself. That's what you're supposed to do."

"I suppose," Gates answered. "So what happens to her now?"

"She's under arrest for a number of things that range from vandalism to attack with a deadly weapon. I plan to scour the criminal code and see if I can come up with a few more things. We're also investigating the possibility that she might be the killer of Dr. Warren. The detectives will run her prints and compare them to those they took from the room. That's still a long shot since motel rooms have so many people staying in them, but it's worth the effort. I already have people out asking questions and showing her picture around to see if she can be placed at the scene."

"She didn't kill Warren," Gates said flatly. Everyone in the room looked surprised.

"Oh, come on, Doc. You've almost convinced me that Dr. Meade here couldn't be the killer . . ."

"That's good to hear," Norman said.

"I said almost," Carl responded sharply. "Besides, in your case what I think doesn't matter anymore. That's up to the DA." Turning back to Gates he continued: "What makes you think Martha Crews isn't capable of murder?"

"I didn't say she wasn't capable of murder, Carl, only that she didn't kill Warren."

"I don't understand, sweetheart," Maggie said.

"Look," Gates began as she attempted to reposition herself on the bed. A grimace followed each move. "The hotel room in which Warren was killed was left neat, tidy. The murder itself was clearly premeditated. I mean, the murderer had to think far enough ahead to steal Norman's equipment and then set up Warren's body like it was a suicide. Just knowing enough to use succinylcholine to bring about respiratory paralysis shows premeditation. Everything Martha Crews has done to date has been a function of wrath: striking her father, resisting you, vandalizing my car, office, and home. Even her attack on me was nearly mindless with rage. She works in a fashion that is the opposite of Warren's killer. No, Carl, you need to keep looking. Martha Crews is a deeply disturbed woman in need of a great deal of help. But she didn't kill Warren."

"That just leaves Norman here, then."

"No, not true," Gates said. "There's someone else."

"Who?"

"I don't know, Carl. I just don't know." An odd sensation percolated up from her subconscious. Something that she had just said struck a bell in her mind, but she couldn't place it. Shifting in the bed, she winced once again and took hold of the control that would command the top half of the hospital bed to rise so that Gates could sit up. She pressed the proper button and slowly the bed lifted her upper torso. "My arm is killing me." She rubbed the bruised spot.

"Well, you did take quite a beating," her mother said.

"No, this is different. This is where the nurse gave me the Demerol IM."

"IM?" Carl said puzzled.

Norman answered: "Intramuscular. An injection given in the muscle tissue as opposed to intravenously."

Gates continued to rub the spot. "It feels like she took a running start at it. You'd think that a nurse would know how to give a . . ." Gates let her words trail off.

"What is it, Gates?" her mother asked, concerned. "Are you in more pain?"

Gates didn't answer, instead she gazed off in the distance, her brow furrowed.

"Gates?" Maggie said. "Should I call the doctor?"

"No, I'm fine." Suddenly Gates turned to Carl. "I need you to check on something, Carl. I need you to call the detectives investigating Warren's murder and have them gather some information. You may need a court order."

"What are you up to, Gates?" Carl asked suspiciously.

"Do you remember a couple of days ago I asked you to see if the coroner had found evidence of a recent injection? We were on the front porch of my parents' house."

"Yeah, I remember. It was just this last Tuesday. We were talking about the succ . . . succiny . . ."

"Succinylcholine," Gates said. "Did you check with the coroner?"

"I didn't need to, it was in his report. I just hadn't noticed it before," Carl answered. "There was an injection site and bruise located on his right side just above the belt line. Maybe he was diabetic."

Gates shook her head. "Not with a bruise. A diabetic on insulin injects either in the thigh or the abdomen, and they have time to do it right. Bruising from an injection is usually the result of poor work or a difficult patient. I'll bet you that Warren was surprised by his attacker who injected the succinylcholine when Warren's back was turned."

"Who would do that?" Norman asked.

"I have an idea, but I need a little more information." Unconsciously, Gates rubbed the bruise on her arm and smiled.

"Are you sure you're up to this?" Carl asked. "You've had a really rough time of late."

"I'm up to it," Gates said from her spot in the front of Carl's patrol car. "I think it's important that I be there."

Parking the car in the lot in front of the strip mall, Carl exited and walked around to help

Gates out the passenger-side door. Together they walked toward the front door of the real estate office. Before entering, Carl looked back and saw one of his officers drive around to the back of the building. Once inside, Gates led the way, walking slowly, limping slightly. A moment later both she and Carl were standing at the entrance to Bob Lemonick's office.

"Doctor McClure!" Lemonick said with surprise as he quickly stood behind his desk. "What on earth happened to you? Here, sit down."

"I had a run-in with your ex-wife," Gates said evenly. "She had some unresolved issues to share with me."

"I told you she was crazy, Doc. You should never have gone near her."

"She came to me," Gates said.

"I hope your injuries aren't too serious." Lemonick oozed concern. Gates felt the emotion was genuine. "Is that why Chief Berner is here? To talk about Martha, I mean?"

"Carl was good enough to give me a ride." Gates made direct eye contact with Lemonick. "I need your help."

"I'll help any way I can," Lemonick replied.

"When I was last here we were talking about Martha and whether or not she was capable of destroying my office and car. You said that she was. In that conversation you mentioned a couple of things that didn't sink into my brain at the time."

"Such as?"

"I believe you said that you and Martha lived in San Diego for a while," Gates prompted.

"Yes we did. When I was in the navy."

"I'm sorry to bring up painful memories again, but didn't you say you had a son who was ill and tragically died while there?"

Bob Lemonick cut his eyes away. It was clear that this was still a sensitive subject. He nodded. "Yeah, I said that. It ruined Martha's life and almost ruined mine. Everything fell apart: our marriage, my career, everything." He paused, then changed the subject. "Martha really did this to you?"

Gates nodded.

"I'm so sorry," Lemonick said. "I haven't had contact with her in a very long time. I hope you don't hold me responsible for the attack."

"Of course not, Mr. Lemonick," Gates answered. "May I ask who treated your child in San Diego? Your son had aplastic anemia, didn't you say?"

"Yes, but that was a long time ago. I don't think I remember who the doctor was."

Carl spoke up for the first time since they arrived. "We checked, Mr. Lemonick. It was Dr. Ed Warren."

Lemonick said nothing. He sat stone-still, letting only his eyes move from Gates to Carl and back to Gates again. Several silent seconds later he spoke. "Isn't that private information?"

"Normally yes," Carl answered, "but we were able to secure the appropriate legal papers to search for that information. The doctor who treated your son was Dr. Ed Warren, wasn't it?"

Lemonick nodded slowly and then started to speak, but Carl cut him off. "Mr. Lemonick, before you say anything else I need to inform you of your rights." Carl then recited the rights and then asked, "Do you understand the rights I've just read to you?"

"Yes," Lemonick said softly.

"Do you wish to have an attorney present during questioning?"

Lemonick shook his head. "No. Am I under arrest?"

"Not at the moment," Carl said. "But I do suspect that you may be involved in the murder of Ed Warren."

"Why?" Lemonick suddenly snapped. "Because he treated my son? He was a pediatrician and treated hundreds of children."

"True," Gates said. "He also was accused of malpractice several times and ultimately forced to leave active practice. All of that happened about the time you and your wife were in San Diego. Carl made a call to the local newspaper down there and asked if they carried any stories about Warren's troubles. They said that they had. Most likely the electronic media did too. That's easy enough to find out. Even Norman Meade knew of it. After leaving his practice, he continued to teach but also became involved in medical activism. In recent years he became one of the chief opponents to physician-assisted suicide. Was your son one of the cases Warren was accused of botching?"

"No," Lemonick replied firmly. "But he should have been." Lemonick's jaw tightened noticeably. "I don't think he cared about his patients. He was always too busy stirring up some hornet's nest or another. He should have been concentrating on my boy. If he had, my boy would still be alive. Things would have been different."

Gates felt a sadness fill her. "Mr. Lemonick, I can't and won't defend Warren to you. For all I know you might be right about him, but you need to know that aplastic anemia is a serious disease. There's a good chance that your son might have died no matter who cared for him."

"I don't believe that," Lemonick shouted and jumped to his feet. Carl matched him move for move and had interposed himself between Lemonick and Gates. "He was a bad doctor. He let my son die."

"Sit down, sir," Carl commanded firmly. "Sit down now."

Lemonick complied. He sat slump-shouldered. "I'm sorry, Chief. I'm still sensitive about my son. After all these years, you'd think I'd be over it, but I'm not. It hurts as much today as it did then." Tears filled his eyes.

Reluctantly Gates pursued the conversation. "When last we talked you mentioned that you had been a medic in the navy. As a medic you would learn a great deal about emergency treatment. Is that where you learned about succinylcholine?"

Lemonick nodded slowly, reluctantly.

"Why don't you tell us about it," Carl prompted.

Tears began to stream down Lemonick's face. He wiped at them with the back of his hands. "I was at the Halloween party like most everyone else. I read the papers and newsmagazines so I recognized Norman Meade when he came in. I also recognized Dr. Warren. He looked different of course;

we all do as we age, but I knew it was him. I've seen that face a million times in my nightmares. When the argument started between Meade and Warren, Meade called Warren by name. That cinched it in my mind. I don't need to tell you about the argument since you were there. I followed Warren out when he left. I even followed him to his hotel. Just seeing him made me crazy with hate, so I drove home and tried to compose myself, but it didn't work. The more I paced around the house, the more angry I became. I had to do something."

Leaning back in his chair, Lemonick sighed heavily and rubbed his eyes. "Who plans things like this? Not me. But I couldn't get Warren out of my mind. I just kept seeing my little boy lying in a hospital. I kept seeing the small casket we buried him in. It all kept running in my mind like a movie. My wife's crackup, my alcohol problem, all of it, and all I could think of was how it was all the fault of Dr. Ed Warren. So, I decided to do something. It only took a moment to formulate the plan. I mean, I had a scapegoat right in town."

"Norman Meade," Gates said.

"Exactly. He's backed by a big organization and is world famous. I knew he could beat the charges if they were laid on him. It was just a matter of time. It was perfect. All I had to do was get close to Warren."

"Just how did you do that?" Carl asked.

"It was easy. I put on my best suit, bought some fruit from the grocery store and a decorative basket, and threw together a little gift. At first I thought I could poison the fruit, but I had no way of knowing if he would eat it, and whatever poison I used would change the flavor of the fruit. So I knew that wouldn't work. Besides . . . I wanted to see him die."

A revulsion filled Gates, but she said nothing.

Lemonick continued: "Anyway, I knew that I needed to misdirect attention away from me, and since Meade and Warren had just had this big fight, well, again, Meade made a good patsy."

"Where did you get the succinylcholine?" Gates asked. This was the one thing she was uncertain of.

"The town hospital," Lemonick said matter-of-factly. "There's a guy there that I know. We were drinking buddies years ago, and well, he got himself into some trouble down the hill. Got into a fight at some bar and cut a guy up with a broken beer bottle. He had no place to turn, so he called me. I bailed him out and helped him with some legal bills.

Anyway, he owes me and since he worked as an orderly at the hospital, I convinced him to steal some succinylcholine for me."

"But that would be noticed in inventory," Gates objected.

"So what," Lemonick countered. "Drugs get stolen all the time. As long as it couldn't be linked to me or my friend, I didn't care."

"So you now have the basket of fruit and the drug, then what happened?" Carl asked.

"I went to Warren's hotel room and knocked on the door. When he answered I said, 'You won't remember me, but I used to live in San Diego years ago. You treated my son and saved his life. When I saw you at the party I felt the need to say thank you one more time.' Well, he breaks out in this big grin, invites me in, and takes the basket of fruit. When he turned around to put the fruit on the dresser, I stabbed him in the side with the needle and injected the succinylcholine. He spun around but it was too late. He staggered back and fell on the bed. A few minutes later he was dead. All I had to do was reposition the body."

"What about Meade's IV pump?" Gates asked.

"Oh, that. Well, I wanted to point the finger at Dr. Meade, so I stole those things from his car."

"Just like that?" Carl asked. "How did you get into his car?"

"That was easy, actually — he left his car unlocked. When I was on my own and boozing it up, I used to go around the parking lots looking for unlocked cars. Sometimes people put loose change in the ashtray. Finding the car was the difficult part. First, I left Warren's room, being sure I took his room key, and then went back to the party. But Meade was already gone. I didn't know if he was planning on leaving Ridgeline or not, so I drove to the different hotels looking for a rental car. It was a long shot, but it was all I had."

"In the peak season there would be scores of rental cars," Carl said.

"But it's not the peak tourist season," Lemonick replied morosely. "I just drove through parking lots looking for the little rental sticker on the bumper. Of course, even if I found one I wouldn't know if it was his or not, and I certainly wasn't going to ask at the front desk. That would associate me with him."

"So what did you do?" Gates asked.

"As luck would have it, I spotted Meade himself. I was just pulling out of the Ridgeline Bed-and-Breakfast when he pulled in. Apparently he didn't go straight there from the party. I drove around the block and then parked in the lot. I waited for about fifteen minutes but didn't see him again. I guessed he was in for the night. I walked to his car and looked inside. His car was unlocked. It was one of those cars with a trunk release next to the seat. It took only a couple of seconds to pop the trunk."

"How did you know that he had his equipment in the trunk?" Carl asked.

"I didn't. I was just looking for something, anything to place him in Warren's room. I figured that would muddle up the investigation enough to keep me in the clear. When I saw the IV equipment, I knew immediately what I was going to do. All that was left was the taking of the stuff and setting it up in Warren's room, which I did."

There was a protracted silence, then Gates spoke. "So why are you telling us this? Why cooperate now?"

Lemonick shrugged. "I don't know. Deep inside I knew that it would catch up to me. You wouldn't be here if you hadn't figured most of it out." He sighed heavily. "I'm not really a bad guy, Doc. I work hard. I've built a reputation. I've overcome alcoholism and a broken marriage. I guess I just can't get over losing my son. I've paid for his death for years. I just wanted Warren to pay too. I didn't think about the news media, or the crowds in front of the police station. I sure didn't want you to get hurt in all this, but look what happened. That reporter embarrassed you on television and my ex-wife beats you up. Actually, I'm finding it harder and harder to live with myself. This has not been an easy week for me."

"It hasn't been an easy week for any of us," Carl said, standing. "Especially for Ed Warren. You'll need to come with me."

Bob Lemonick stood, stepped from behind the desk and let Carl handcuff him.

"I have another question," Gates said. "Did you contact your ex-wife and let her know about her mother's suicide?"

"Yeah," Lemonick said as Carl patted him down. "I figured she had a right to know. I owed her that much. It seemed the only decent thing to do."

Chapter Twenty-Three

Saturday, November 8
11:45 A.M.

The small gathering of mourners sat on folding metal chairs under a blue-and-white striped canopy. The sun shown high in the sky like a gold medallion and the smell of freshly mowed grass filled the air. A casket of cherry wood sat on thick canvas straps that supported it over the grave. A green plastic cover concealed the open maw in the earth.

Seated in the front row was Eugene Crews. He was bent and frail as he gazed at the shiny coffin that held his wife of fifty-three years. Sadness exuded from him in nearly palpable waves. Despite the half dozen other people present and the fact that Sally Chapman was seated next to him, Gates knew that Eugene was profoundly alone. At the head of the casket stood Pastor Chapman dressed in a dark gray suit, his hair blown by small gusts of wind. He was concluding the graveside service with a reading from the Book of Ecclesiastes:

"To everything there is a season, a time for every purpose under heaven: A time to be born, and a time to die; A time to plant, and a time to pluck what is planted; A time to kill, and a time to heal."

The last words struck a cord in Gates and she immediately thought of Norman. "A time to kill, and a time to heal." Powerful words. Appropriate words. She turned to see him seated at the end of her row and wondered what he thought of the words.

Pastor Chapman led the small group in prayer after which he went directly to Eugene, bent over, and spoke softly. A moment later those gathered rose from their seats. Sally gave Eugene a hug. Carl and Sharee shook his hand and offered words of encouragement. Gates walked over and gave him a gentle hug, being careful of her tender ribs. She wore large sunglasses to hide her blackened eyes, but they could not conceal her swollen nose and cheek.

"Thanks a lot for everything, Doc," Eugene said. "I woulda' been lost without your help."

"I want you to feel free to call me if you need anything," Gates said.

Tears filled Eugene's eyes. "I appreciate that, Doc, especially after what my Martha did to you. I feel so bad."

"It was Martha's doing, not yours."

"But still, I feel responsible, and here you are being so nice to me and I know that you don't approve of what I done." He wiped away a tear with the palm of his rough hand.

"Well, my pastor taught me a thing or two about that," Gates said. "I'm glad to be of some help."

"That preacher of yours is something special. Here he is helping me and I ain't once stepped foot in his church. There's a lot of love in that man."

"That's true, Mr. Crews, and I think that he — we would love to see you in church."

"Thanks, Doc, I may surprise you."

Gates nodded and stepped away and walked toward Norman Meade who stood a few yards away. "I'm rather surprised you're here," she said. "Now that you know that all charges have been dropped against you, I thought you might be headed out of town."

"I am, but I wanted to pay my respects. Darlene was a courageous woman. She could have given up much earlier, but she fought her disease for many years only surrendering when the pain was too great." He paused. "Many people hate me, Gates, but they don't realize that when someone like me aids in a suicide a little piece of me dies too. I'm here to say good-bye to Darlene, to honor her courage, and to say good-bye to a piece of me."

Gates looked down at the emerald-green grass. "I'll never believe that physician-assisted suicide is right. It goes against everything I hold dear."

"I know, Gates, I know."

A tense silence fell between the two. Gates felt great admiration for Norman's drive, intelligence, and dedication. She also abhorred what he did. She was thankful for his rescuing her those long years ago, but wondered how he could risk his own life to save hers, yet be so willing to aid someone in suicide. She knew the logical answers, but she couldn't comprehend the emotional ones.

"Where will you go now?" Gates asked.

"Back to New Mexico. That's where Death with Dignity is located."

"What will you do?"

"Continue my work until it is no longer needed or impossible to do."

"I wish things could have been different," Gates said softly.

"Me too, Gates. I wish that there was a way to overcome this gap between us, but I think it's too wide."

Gates nodded in silence. Slowly Norman leaned forward and kissed Gates on the forehead, turned, and walked away. Gates watched as he strolled to his car, got in, and drove off. Despite herself, some of her drove away with him and she understood what he had meant. She wished that she could abhor him, but she couldn't; she wished that she could love him, but that was not possible. All she could do was remember him.

The truth had been found and it had been painful, but it was the truth and it had set Gates free.

Epilogue

"Well, Mr. Platt," Gates said from her spot at his bedside, "you seem to be breathing much easier than last time I saw you."

"Oh, he is," Colleen enthused. "He's doing much better."

"I thought you might," Gates said to Philip. "You just needed a little fine-tuning from the hospital. Next time you have an attack like that I want you to call an ambulance. There's no need to put up with that kind of discomfort." Gates knew there would be other such episodes, probably several more before his MG became too acute to treat. That, however, could be years away.

"We have other good news, Doctor," Colleen said. "My daughter Cindy is bringing her new baby out here. We've never seen her since they live so far away in Philadelphia. Isn't that great?"

"Wonderful. I bet you both are very excited."

"Oh, we are. But if it hadn't been for you, Philip might not have seen his grandson. I mean, if we followed through with . . . well you know."

"Yes, I know." Gates thought of the event a month previous when she resisted their attempts to convince Norman Meade to conduct a physician-assisted suicide. Fortunately for everyone Norman had refused.

"So we want to invite you to dinner when they get here," Colleen bubbled.

"I'll be glad to join you. Just let me know what I can bring or how I can help."

"Oh, you've done enough," Colleen said.

"Amen," added Philip.

Gates turned to see the corners of Philip's mouth curl up — a majestic smile for one in his condition. A warmth, sudden and welcome, flooded Gates' soul.

The employees of Thorndike Press hope you have enjoyed this Large Print book. All our Large Print titles are designed for easy reading, and all our books are made to last. Other Thorndike Press Large Print books are available at your library, through selected bookstores, or directly from the publishers.

For more information about titles, please call:

(800) 223-1244
(800) 223-6121

To share your comments, please write:

Publisher
Thorndike Press
295 Kennedy Memorial Drive
Waterville, ME 04901

Middlebury Community
Library